That Night on the Bayou

Melissa Woods

Black Rose Writing | Texas

ISBN: 978-1-68433-348-6
PUBLISHED BY BLACK ROSE WRITING
www.blackrosewriting.com

Printed in the United States of America
Suggested Retail Price (SRP) $18.95

That Night on the Bayou is printed in Chaparral Pro

*The final word count for this book may not match your standard expectation versus the final page count. In an effort to reduce paper usage and energy costs, Black Rose Writing, as a planet-friendly publisher, does its best to eliminate unnecessary waste without lessening your reading experience.

**For my husband, Anthony, and our children,
whose unwavering support made this book possible.**

I am so grateful for many people who helped make my dream of publishing a novel a reality. For my early readers and critique partners: Sophia Moskalenko, who read this book very early on and has helped me with subsequent drafts, I thank you dearly. For Sonyo Estavillo, who is so supportive in reading my manuscripts and bouncing ideas off. For my beta readers and their invaluable feedback; Swati Hegde and Jerri Schlenker. Thank you to friends who have helped me work on my craft by reading other manuscripts, including Lindsey Dick and my brilliant, insightful editors, Swati Hegde and Cimone Watson. I thank my publicist, Justin Hargett, for his wonderful ideas. And of course, thank you to my publisher, Black Rose Writing and its creator, Reagan Rothe for this opportunity.

I also appreciate the entire writer's community, both on social media and in person. I am grateful for the members of Debut 19, who have been instrumental in teaching me all about book launches. I thank ARC readers, reviewers, and authors who have written blurbs. The students and staff from the creative writing department at Boise State University have been fabulous. I am forever indebted to them for all I have learned about craft, as well as the art of giving and receiving feedback. My wonderful writing professors include: Ariel Dixon, Natalie Disney, Sam McPhee, Kim Cross, and Dr. Whitney Douglas. Thank you so much for your guidance.

Lastly, I would like to thank my family. Thank you to my parents, Marie and Duane Bokker, and my sister Jacki, as well as our extended family. I have received tremendous support and encouragement from you. Without you to lift me up when I hit a rough patch, I couldn't continue on this path.

My husband, Anthony Woods, has loved and encouraged me all through this process and continues to do so. He is the best partner ever and the love of my life. Forever and always, I appreciate my children for the time they have given me to write. Hunter, Julianna, Harley, Dylan, Piper, and Emmett, I cannot express how proud I am to be your mom.

That Night on the Bayou

Part One

Chapter One

1988

Ruth hiked up her nightgown and heaved her leg over the rusted red Schwinn. She patted her pink curlers, praying they would stay put. Wobbling down the driveway, she shoved the pedals hard, knees banging against the handlebars. She hit the asphalt, picking up momentum. *This bike is far too small! I'll never catch up with her at this speed.* Ruth whizzed by a sea of neighbors who murmured their comments. "Oh, go back in your house!" she shouted. "What is it about this town?" She scoffed and teetered on. Her bare breasts beat against her stomach, sticky with sweat. How girls went untethered these days, especially in this humidity, was beyond her.

Patsy Bundy hurled down the street, her father's Confederate flag under her arm like a football, and Ruth *had* to know where the teenager was going.

·   ·   ·

Patsy was a strawberry-curled high school senior. She had grown weary of living in Cypress, of dealing with her parents. Patsy ran fast, made quick decisions, and had strong opinions. Her sharp tongue struck people, leaving them ten feet behind her in the thick Louisiana air, wondering what had just happened. They said she was exhausting. Maybe this was true. And she despised her father's Confederate flag more than anything. That sweltering evening, a fight ensued between them.

"Daddy, it's just embarrassing. Everyone can see that—"

"It's our heritage. It's the south. I'm not taking down my heritage! And besides, your friends aren't real Southerners. They're all off to hoity-toity Ivy League colleges, because of what I pay their fathers..."

"I am leaving," she said, jaw clenched. She fought the urge to spit.

He pursed his lips, then said, "So, go. I dare you." He puffed his chest out like a bird asserting his territory.

"I'll never come back." Patsy sure as hell never refused a dare. It wasn't in her nature.

She was crazy angry by the time she set foot in the Louisiana heat. She ran from the Grierson-style mansion and headed for the wetlands. Patsy did not know these people who raised her, not at all. Her head spun. Beads of sweat pooled on her brow as she ripped the flag from its pole. She shuddered at the sight of it. The feel of the thick canvas against her hands made her flesh crawl.

Sprinting through the little neighborhood, she passed Cypress Market, and the rows of smaller, pastel-colored houses blurred together. The sickening, acrid scent of death chased her, the vision rolling through her like a rip-tide. Patsy thought she could outrun the feeling, the bizarre intuition that someone, at some time, had died here. That someone wanted to tell her something. Her pace quickened; the galloping began. The roar of the horses' hooves clicking on the pavement intensified. A whistling wind shrilled against their muscled bodies as they passed. The horror sucked her in as she witnessed the otherworldliness of their bright white coats.

The horses hit the dirt. Unfamiliar men clipped their sides, yelling, "Go!" as they broke into a faster canter. Confederate flags flapped in the wind; muskets shot through the air. The stench of the earthy swampland rose into the atmosphere, filling the wetlands with a thick, green haze. Their cream-colored manes resisted the splattering mud. Thousands of them swarmed the wetlands. Patsy held her breath, tried to avert her gaze, but they persisted in her peripheral vision, gauzy against the dropping sun. A man riding by squeezed a woman against him as she screamed. They kicked up dirt, whooshing through Patsy's beloved Bayou. Shaking and numb, she had to get to the tin house, the little cabin that was safe. The men dissipated before she arrived, diffusing like smoke in the trees.

Struggling to take a deep breath in the humidity, she trudged through the spongy grass, feet slurping through the mud. The tin-walled shack hovered on raised beams right over the water. The confines of the metal room burst with trapped heat. There wasn't much to it, a couple of chairs and a gray folding table. It was her childhood hideout, a refuge where she played with her few friends, where she came to read, think or dream about the day she would move away from Cypress, far from the rumors that shot from all directions.

The visions began here in the tin shack. She couldn't have been older than six. "This is what happens, here in Cypress," she told her mother. "There is something evil in this town."

Town legend had it that Patsy was a witch, burning Bibles down at the wetlands. The rumors died out by third grade. But with a population of less than five hundred, everyone knew everything about everyone, leaving an undercurrent of whispers babbling through every layer of the town on the

Bayou.

But Patsy knew the truth. If only because she had *seen* it.

She saw ghosts, at least that's how she described it. They permeated every living creature in Cypress. Only she knew their wickedness. She needed to understand where they came from.

For now, the flag had to go.

•　　•　　•　　•　　•　　•

The cypress trees' delicate leaves laced over mossy rocks, almost tickling the still water, where the gators lived. The summer sun soaked the sky in color; blood-red morphed to fiery orange, spanning across the tip of night like an eagle's wings. Wispy clouds rolled in as they often did before a summer storm. Splotches of gray expanded, blotting out the remnants of day. A light rain sizzled in the warm night, but it did not extinguish Patsy's rage. She lit a cigarette, drew a breath, tried to calm her trembling hands.

She hated him; she hated them all. Her older brother, with his feigned piousness and perpetual parent-pleasing kind of way. Her mother, so tender in that sweet iced tea syrupy kind of way, that slap-you-in-the-face and ask, "Why, whatever is the matter?" kind of way.

At least, she thought, her father did not have a kind of way. He just *was*.

The little tin house was so humid, like inhaling water. You got used to that, living on the Bayou, but it was interminable today—like a steam room. She stumbled out through the sludge and sunk by the water's edge, the only light from the sliver of incandescent moon and the glowing red tip of her cigarette. She blew a stream of smoke out of her line of sight. In her lap was the flag, now dark as night. With her fingers, she felt its stitched edges. A bubble of wrath, a flash of teenaged indignation welled within her.

She flicked the green lighter and touched the edge of the flag with its flame. It did not catch fire quickly. Flick, flick, flick. A little smoke, a tiny ember. Four tries, five. With a roar, it shot ablaze. Her hands went numb with cool panic. For a moment, Patsy stared in disbelief at the edges curling up with fire that lit the shadowy night. It smelled like a mixture of sulfur and campfire smoke. She whipped it sideways, hard, so hot ash could not blow toward her face. And in the water, it floated for a moment, flames licking the water, until they fell quiet and it sunk, leaving nothing but ribbons of smoke.

She did not have a kind of way—she just *was*.

There was a crash, a clatter of metal, followed by a high- pitched scream. It skipped across the water like a stone.

"What the hell?" Patsy yelled into the bushes, smoothing her shirt, now balled up as a tissue.

A disheveled version of Ruth Marks— at least that's who Patsy thought it was— tumbled out onto the dirt, seemingly attached to a red bicycle. Patsy squinted, trying to get a closer look. She waved the cigarette smoke away. It was very dark now. "What the hell?"

She shivered and took a drag from her cigarette, wet with snot and tears. She wept louder still, struggling to form coherent thoughts. *Daddy's gonna kill me. There's really nothing that can be done... it's over.*

Something rustled behind her. She froze, heart thumping.

What is that noise? Could he be here already, with his shotgun....no, no it's just a lizard or—

"Patsy! watch your language. There's no need to talk like that."

"Mrs. Marks? Shit!" She crouched lower to access the situation.

Ruth mumbled a series of swear words of her own, tangled in the Schwinn. The bottom of her nightgown was caught in the chain, ripped clear up to her armpit. Blood ran down her leg, and her head was a mass of pink Velcro scrunched together.

Well, thought Patsy, at least she put on her slippers before she went for her bike ride, otherwise—

"Mrs. Marks," said Patsy. She moved closer to Ruth and helped her untangle the last bits of cotton from the bike. She wiped the grease from her palms onto her jeans, breathless. "What the hell are you doing, riding around on a bike, at night, in your pajamas?"

Ruth raised an eyebrow. "Well, what the hell are you doing here, setting fire to your father's flag? I swear, Patsy, if I hadn't known your mother since kindergarten—"

"It doesn't matter, Mrs. Marks. Even without your intervention, this," she said, waving her hand towards the spot in the water where the flag had been, "will run through town faster than that time Will Thompson spread gonorrhea to half the cheerleading squad." She slumped down, lit another cigarette, and stared glumly at the water, where the reflection of the moon shimmered like shards of melted glass oozing into each other.

"Give me one of those," said Ruth, motioning towards the pack of Marlboro Reds as she plunked to the ground with a thud.

"You smoke?"

"Obviously. I smoked when I was pregnant with Tommy, even. Don't tell anyone," she whispered.

"You did?"

"All right. Not really. I thought you'd feel better if I told you something scandalous about myself." She sighed.

"Scandalous? Oh, my God." Now Patsy was laughing. "Why did you follow me out here, anyway? Just to run back to the old ladies and gossip?"

"Contrary to what you might believe, I care about you," she said. Patsy thought perhaps this was true. "I know you want to change your dad. But this," she said, pointing at the water, "is just gonna get your butt paddled."

"I'm not sorry, you know. He's trying to stop me from going to college in Boston," she said, raising her chin. "But I suppose we should go back. For now."

"Whatever. I can't imagine anyone stopping you from doing exactly what you want," snorted Ruth, heaving the bicycle up the dirt path to the road. They trudged in silence, listening to the crickets chirping and a pungent kind of sorrow hanging in the air. Patsy had the odd feeling something had changed forever, but exactly what was muddled in her brain.

"Well, here we are," said Ruth, as they approached Patsy's large yellow house. Ruth lived next door, her little pink house in the shadows of the street lamps. "Maybe it's best you avoided your father tonight."

"How?" said Patsy.

"Your room is on that side, right?"

"Yes," Patsy said, eyes wide. Was Ruth Marks going to help her sneak into her room?

"I have an idea. You see, my house creates a perfect dark spot where your room is." Patsy knew this was true. She had spent many hot days in the shade provided by Ruth's little house. "They'll never see you. I'll just hoist you up like this—" she laced her fingers together into a little pocket "—and you'll climb in the window."

She cringed, trying to walk on the gravel path that led to the back of the house without making crunching noises. "All right, let's do it!" said Ruth, as Patsy stepped in her interlaced fingers. *Good lord, I can't believe this.* She didn't weigh much, she knew, despite feeling conspicuous at this moment. Hands splayed against the stucco wall, she yelped as she toppled in the open window. "Thanks," she whispered, and tried not to laugh, peering down at Ruth, her hair a mess of half-fallen out curlers, nightgown in tatters. What some people will do, thought Patsy, for a bit of gossip.

She crawled into bed fully-clothed and awaited her fate. The house was dark. And then she heard the creak of the garage door and Daddy's heavy boots thumping up the stairs. He knew she was home; he had been to her hideout. Patsy shivered.

"Patsy!" he yelled, his presence filling her room. Mama stood behind him, smaller, but no less formidable. Her eyes narrowed, and she shook her head. The smell of wet ashes wafted in with them. Patsy's heart stood still. She held her breath and thought the better of speaking.

He threw the flag, muddy with its charred edges, onto the floor, and glared at her. "This," he said, voice composed, "is a disrespect I cannot tolerate in this house." He squared his arms against his chest.

Patsy got out from under the covers and stood across from him.

"This is mortifying," said Mama. "All my friends will find out about this. Hell, they probably already have."

"Heaven forbid I tarnish your reputation," said Patsy, "because you find pride in slavery. And keeping women in their place."

"We have had this discussion. My house, my rules," said her father. "This is more complicated than you understand. But flag burning?"

"Flag burning is perfectly legal. And it's not even a real flag to anyone, but old Southerners stuck in the Civil War. Most of the neighbors have gotten rid of theirs—"

"I am not racist! Oh, my God, you need to go to bed. I'll figure out what to do with you later. I just hope this doesn't affect business." Daddy shook his head.

Patsy thought this was outrageous. Unless everyone in Cypress decided to drive out of town for their seafood, Daddy's shrimping business was perfectly safe. Stanley Bundy was a well-respected man in the town of Cypress. The conversation was ridiculous.

Those days she had spent as a little girl, plowing through the mist on her father's night trawl, hauling in big nets full of crawdads and shrimp, breathing in the drenched air were gone. How she loved running her fingers through the slippery catch, sorting through the nets for what they could sell to the stores.

"You know my 'insubordination' is unlikely to cause anything more than whispers of pity for *you*. For having me as a daughter." She raised her eyebrows and shot him a pointed glance. He sighed, ran his hand through his dirty-blonde hair, and turned away.

Stanley's face was weathered from years of hard work in the sun, and it made him look older. His eyes caught her heart for a flittering moment.

"Just go, Daddy," she said.

"You're grounded. Which means stay away from the shack on the marsh. I can't trust what you're up to down there anymore." He turned toward the door.

"I don't have to listen to you at all," she retorted. "I've been accepted to

Boston University. I was considering staying in Louisiana, but my decision is made, I guess."

"There's always that little obstacle of paying for it," he said.

"GET OUT!" Rage bubbled in her stomach.

"Like I said, you're grounded. College is months away."

"I do not have to stay here at all. My birthday is in less than thirty days. I'll be gone by then." She chewed the inside of her mouth until the taste of blood hit her gums, and added, burying her head in her pillow, "Like *I* said, get out."

Maybe he continued talking, it was hard to say, given how loud anger pulsed through her head. And her mother, so concerned about nothing but her reputation around town, the perfect wife and mother. I'm never getting married, thought Patsy, balling her fists, and cursing into the pillow on the twin bed. Marriage came with unspoken rules and expectations, and Patsy wanted none of it. The house remained silent. She hurled a textbook out the open window. Out, she thought. I am getting out of here.

Chapter Two
STANLEY

Stanley arrived at the dock early the following morning. He'd had a fitful night's sleep, waking up with nightmares. With the rest of the house silent, he took his boredom to the boat. Might as well get something productive done, he reasoned. He started a pot of coffee and dragged the equipment out. This way, they would be ready to go when Stan Jr. and the others arrived. Meanwhile, it was three a.m., and he could work in the silence, except for the sound of owls calling, the morning cicadas' piercing buzz hitting a crescendo, and the gentle swish of the water beneath the boat. The smell of hot coffee emanated from beneath the deck. He tied down each rope by muscle memory, almost in a meditative state.

He had the boat ready by the time he heard Stan Jr.'s pick-up truck roll up, crunching the gravel off the main road. Tommy Marks waved as the two made their way across the dock. Jr. seemed a bit tense to Stanley, but maybe he was imagining it.

"You okay, Pops?" said Jr. as he slid into the bucket seat beside his father. He was a blue-eyed young man with a broad smile and a dimple in just the right place. Stanley often joked that this was a side benefit of marrying the town debutante. People would say, "He's too pretty to be your boy, Stanley!" And then he'd smile and say, "Have you even seen my wife?"

"Just fine," he said, trying not to get sucked into his son's baby-faced sweetness. "Why wouldn't I be? I thought you'd be grateful I'd gotten all the hard stuff out of the way before y'all showed up."

"Well, sure." Jr. gave his father a sideways glance. Stanley pretended not to notice.

Stanley settled into the captain's chair and hit the throttle. He avoided conversation with his son as he pulled the boat from the dock into the salty breeze. Just before dawn, the sun chased the moon into the sea, with the orange hint of color rising in the mist. It was the best time of day for shrimping. Before the intense Louisiana heat beat down, with the quiet satisfaction of being the sole boat in the murky water, he knew today would be a good catch. He let his foot off the gas, in preparation to stop and let the nets down in the shallow coast.

"Y'all come up here," he called. Tommy and Gilmore emerged from below, sipping coffee and preparing for a long day on the boat. "We're ready!" The two men sunk close to the deck, wind whipping against their stocky bodies. Stan tossed the net while his assistant, Gilmore, held the ropes free from the side of the trawl. To get tangled in the ropes could prove deadly.

Stanley hit the gas again, dredging the trawls close to the bottom of the ocean. With a halt, the men turned the heavy crank and rolled the giant nets from the water. The green nets burst with shrimp. "Wooot!" yelled Stanley, and the three men hoisted the nets onto the deck, releasing the catch in a giant swoosh. Shrimp and other sea creatures plopped on the deck, and the men quickly sifted through the pile, working through thousands of them, tossing turtles and other unintended by-catch back to the sea, and the wriggling shrimp into buckets. The men were drenched in salt water and sweat, and the day had just begun. Running his hands through mounds of slippery shrimp still flipping around alive had become a comfortable ritual for Stanley.

"This is quite the catch," he said, partially to himself. He lifted a mound of shrimp to the sky, laughing.

"Wooo-hooo! Sure is!" said Gilmore. "I've got to get more ice from below."

The sun had emerged from the darkness, and more boats joined them. Still, the Bundy family had been in the shrimping business for close to a hundred years. They were known in Cypress for leading the town's shrimp industry. Stanley wiped the sweat from his face, lines indented in his skin from years of squinting at the sun. "Coffee?" he said to Stan Jr., offering him a mug.

"Sure, Pops," he said. He was the oldest Bundy child, and likely to take over the business when his father retired, at least that's what Stanley hoped. Jr. was the compliant child, the one attached to Edna's hip. Shrimping with his boy was refreshing. Jr. didn't argue with everything his father said or did. But Patsy. Well, that girl and her abrasiveness were challenging, and Stanley enjoyed a good debate now and then. But she had begun to push him too far.

The aroma of strong coffee intermingled with swampland felt familiar and comforting. Stanley made comments here and there to his son, teaching him the business with each catch. "Make sure these babies get on ice fast enough. It's hot out," he would say. Or, "Always make sure the ropes are free of the net. You don't want to lose an arm!"

He sighed again, happy with the morning haul. Stan Jr., however, shifted his boots on the deck, creating a clucking sound along the wood that irritated

Stanley. He did this the way some people hummed. "Stop that stomping," he said for the fiftieth time. "That's a bad habit. I don't want to hear your clodhoppers banging around like that."

Jr. continued the feet shifting and pursed his lips. "I heard you and Patsy are at it again."

"At what? You realize she hates me now, right? Screamed and yelled straight to my face and ran down to the Bayou to burn my flag."

His son bit his lip, stroking his dark goatee. "Well, that was wrong of her."

Stanley nodded and returned to his work. "Right. Your mother and I will figure it out, I suppose. The whole damned town will be talking, and you know how your mother gets embarrassed."

Jr. sighed. "If you ask me—"

Stanley had definitely not asked for his son's opinion.

"Please don't tell me you're gonna defend her. It was disrespectful, not just to me, but to your mother."

"Dad," his son said in a loud whisper, "it's 1988. Maybe it's time to stop flying that Confederate flag. Maybe you ought to think about your friends, like Gilmore. Maybe you should trust that Patsy will be just fine at college."

"Gil has worked for me since before you were born, Stan. He's been here since Jeb was alive." Anger flooded his chest, prickling his cheeks with heat. "You know that, Jr. You know that as well as I do." First his daughter, but that was expected. He had a soft spot for his spitfire girl, despite her crazy ideas. Teenage rebellion, he thought. That girl had always been stubborn, but Stan Jr. was soft. He respected his father. Why couldn't one of his children simply agree with him? He was exhausted with the drama.

"Never mind, Dad. Forget I mentioned—"

"It's Amanda, right?"

"What could this possibly have to do with my wife, Dad? She wasn't born and bred in Cypress, so you think she's encouraging Patsy?"

"She's a nice girl, Jr. That isn't what I meant. I'm tired of Yankees and their opinions, is all I'm sayin'."

"No, Amanda did not give me any ideas about Patsy. She loves this town. Don't go blaming this on my wife— It's not just that. Why shouldn't Patsy go out of town to college?"

"Now I know you're getting this from Amanda. I am not saying Patsy should not go to college. But Boston? That's quite the distance for an eighteen-year-old girl. I'm just so frustrated with your sister, Stan." He took a slow breath. "Anyway, we've got to get this boat docked and the fish sold. I don't want to talk this nonsense anymore." He took off his hat, wiping the sweat from his brow. "I've got too much work to do."

"You've never been the same, dad. She's not the only stubborn one. Ever since that night—"

"Don't start. Don't bring this up, Stan." His voice cracked.

"All I'm sayin' is after that night on the Bayou—"

"Shut up, Stan. Just shut up."

He hit the throttle gently and pulled into the spot on the landing. Dread surged through him as he watched the people meandering around the dock with their coolers and buckets. He waved and smiled, trying to read their faces, trying to decipher just how much information had circulated town, and how much about Patsy's visions had resurfaced.

· · · · · ·

Stanley kicked his wet boots off at the front door, and watched his wife chopping vegetables in the sprawling kitchen, her onyx hair back in a hasty braid, and long skirt skimming the floor. She hummed, circling gently from side to side. He knew better than to embrace her before showering. Or come within fifteen feet of her. Edna knew the shrimping business quite well. Her own family had passed the boats down to Stanley as their son-in-law. Still, she found the smell of fish and sweat repulsive. He couldn't blame her.

"Is that you, honey?" she called. "Oh. How long have you been standing there?" She turned around and half-smiled, heart-shaped lips amused.

He shrugged his shoulders. "I'll take my shower."

"Nah. We gotta talk, Stanley. This business around town—"

"You sure? I'm sweating, here."

She folded her arms against her chest, and said, "I know word travels fast 'round here. And well, I'm not sure we should care. Frankly, Patsy pulls some shenanigans every other day." Edna sighed and smoothed her skirt. "But Ruth was here earlier. Acting kinda funny. Why would she have anything to do with this?"

"Tommy was acting strange on the boat this morning, too. Quiet."

"Well, you know how Ruth's been since Jeb died. Granted, she's always been into everybody's business. I guess she needs something to do. It's been a long time."

"Everyone here is into everyone's business. That's just how it goes." Stanley slid down and perched against the flowered kitchen wallpaper. "Our girl is so stubborn. She's got her beliefs and all that, fine. But I can't run a business with this drama running through town," he said, waving his hand through the air. "If I'm not racist, I'm a turtle killer. You know we toss back the turtles that get caught in the nets, right? Make sure they swim away, and everything. Trawling isn't what's making those wetlands disappear."

"I know that, honey. And no one's gonna think anything about her conniption fits except what a brat she is."

"That's probably so, but it's like she has no idea where this all comes from. Perfectly willing to partake in good schooling and food and live on one of the nicest houses on the Gulf, but she puts down everything I do to make it happen." He looked glumly at the hardwood floors he had installed by hand, years ago. Stanley stood, stretching his calves, in front of the kitchen window, waves from the Bayou lapping around the house. "Patsy just doesn't understand what the shrimping business does for this family. Or how important it is to keep a decent reputation. More commercial fisheries in this area all the time," he continued. He drummed his fingers on the counter.

"I didn't want to mention this, Stanley," said Edna. "But maybe you try and see her perspective. Just let things lie. Those visions she claims to have. Do we really want that spreading, again?"

"Why would I do that? She's in the wrong here, Edna. A juvenile delinquent!"

"I've just heard rumors, is all. People taking down Confederate Flags-"

"I'm not racist, Edna. I love Gilmore and his kids and Maggie. It's just the South—"

"Why can't she go to college, Stanley?"

"Of course she can! What's wrong with LSU?" he said, incredulous.

"From Patsy's perspective, you're tryin' to keep her here. I get that you love her, and you'll miss her...but still—"

"But what, Edna? You think I'm wrong because I don't think a young girl is safe traipsing around the city at eighteen?"

"I think you've got issues with Boston, if you want to know the real truth. You know, Yankee liberals. Women's lib." She laughed.

"It's got nothing to do with that."

"Well, consider this— Patsy's always been Patsy. She'd fit right in. But you're right about one thing. Her behavior is out of control. I have been saying this forever. Not that anyone listened."

He rested his face on his palms, thinking of the little girl with the strawberry-blonde curls and the cornflower blue eyes who idolized him. How she had begged for a ride on the boat; she truly loved running her tiny hands through a fresh catch, letting them slide through her fingers screaming, "I got 'em, daddy!"

"What? What are you thinking of now?" said Edna.

"I just don't know why it can't be like it used to be."

"She's just a teenager. And she is a willful child, always has been. You love her so much it's—"

"Edna. I love them both the same. She's just the youngest, the one we didn't plan. She got my heart, that's all."

"Well." She paused and tied the apron around her waist. She turned and said, "Maybe you should care a little more about the one that cares for you."

The sun spread over the water, its reflection shimmering in wavy lines. He avoided his wife's face. "You think she'll really go? To Boston?"

"She will if we pay for it."

"I don't know anymore. If she refuses to go to LSU, she should have an education just in case—"

"I think we should pay for it, let her do what she wants. Otherwise, we're the bad guys. She will never let us live it down."

"Yeah, like I said, just in case."

"In case you can't marry her off? Seriously? I do think a woman can have a career. That's her prerogative. It's the 80s, for God's sake. But we can't condone this behavior. Maybe it will be easier if she goes to Boston."

"Easier?"

"She can sow her wild oats, see how hard life on her own really is. Eventually, she'll see our point."

"Edna," he started, "let's just get through this. I'm gonna go take my shower." She continued chopping without a response. Exhausted, he leaned against the door, eyes drifting towards the nape of her neck. The scent of chili and cornbread permeated the room. But she had to make the vegetable. Every time. A plate of broccoli with chili on the side. A senseless act. He shook his head and headed for the bathroom.

Chapter Three
RUTH

She swept up her grief along with the dead flowers from the funeral arrangements, from the streams of graham cracker crumbs her son sprinkled everywhere. Sweep, toss. Sweep, toss. These two words echoed in her mind, a survival mantra in those early months. Keep moving so the pain can't catch up. Keep moving for your son. She understood she had no choice in the matter. Even now, ten years later, with Tommy seventeen and about to graduate high school, the little pink house was constructed with pieces of Jeb. He breathed through the nails that held family photos to the walls; he was the stucco that kept Ruth together. But it was his goneness that Ruth felt through the neighborhood. In a swirl of couples, Ruth was alone.

That day. The police car rounded up the driveway. The quiet knock on the door. More subdued than you would imagine. That's what struck her the most. No night-piercing police sirens roared to announce that her world was now more broken than those graham crackers, more crumpled than dead flower arrangements. The cops are in no hurry when the emergency has passed. When hope is gone. Sheriff Landon, with his soothing voice, the pattering rain with the scent of summer in the distance, had said, "Mrs. Marks?" holding his hat in his hand. Her eyes had focused on his golden badge, and still it did not occur to her. He wiped his feet on the mat and entered the house. He put his arm around her shoulder, and while she had known Jim forever; they'd gone to high school together, even, this action confused her.

Come with us…. we need identification…seems to have drowned.

What do I do with my son?

"He can stay with Edna," said Stanley, who, Ruth realized, was standing behind the sheriff, tears welling in his eyes.

So, she handed off her little boy and his sock monkey named Farafel to Edna and went to the morgue, where she saw him. Yes, that's him, she murmured.

Gone. The concept of not *being* is one only the brokenhearted get to fathom, and it's a dubious luxury. Knowing a man like she did, how his left toe curved slightly to the right, the cowlick in his deep brown hair, the shape of his fingers and the tiny dimple in his cheek— all of it was unreal. How could that smile exist one moment, and then be …well…gone? Stranger still, was when that dimple appeared in Tommy's cheek. He grew and grew, and that dimple became more pronounced. It stabbed at her heart; she tried to memorize it, to place the rest of Tommy's face into Jeb's, though she understood it wasn't fair, that Tommy was his own human, not a replica of Jeb.

Or the deep-set eyes with flecks of gold and brown that twinkled the same way as his father's. Sometimes she smiled, sometimes she wept, and other times she just marveled at the wonder of genetics. *He even has the same sheepishness to his grin when he's guilty of something, how on earth?* Strange thoughts she never realized possible, until it happened to her. Until she found herself sleeping on the couch with Tommy and Farafel, afraid to go in the bedroom she and Jeb shared.

They slept on the flowered couch for a year. When Tommy was eight, he told her the other boys had beds of their own, often rooms of their own. Ruth remembered the nursery she and Jeb had set up for Tommy. He wanted his room back; he no longer liked the elephant motif she and Jeb had chosen when he was born. This was another loss to Ruth, but she stripped the wallpaper, rolled paint over the walls, taking sharp breaths of noxious fumes as she worked. Ruth was capable of accomplishing hard things. She then went back into her bedroom and slept right in the middle of the queen-sized mattress, alone.

Tommy's new bedroom had plain white walls plastered in baseball posters, with Farafel stuffed in the closet.

Though Jeb was gone, Edna remained.

Even in tenth grade, before Jeb or Stanley, Edna held the title of queen of Jackson High School. Ruth buzzed after her like everyone else. She took comfort in being Edna's favorite, which was laughable twenty years later, but she guessed that was just how high school went. Edna was Miss Louisiana with that dark, lovely hair and striking blue eyes, and being her best friend was an achievement. Sort of. Ruth was the boisterous girl with the frizzy red hair, twenty pounds overweight. She never expected to marry a man like Jeb, to be filled with so much joy. But that's how it goes, she thought.

They had been sitting on the bleachers, watching the football game. He had tapped the metal seat in front of him, and she glared, annoyed by the sound.

"Hey," he said, the flecks of gold in his amber eyes on fire from the afternoon sun, "you're the smart girl, with all the answers in science class. I can't seem to put chemistry together. It's not my thing. I can dissect Shakespeare, no problem. But the periodic table—"

"I'm too busy to tutor this semester," she said curtly. Boys thought she'd tutor them for nothing but the pleasure of their company. Ridiculous, she'd thought. Maybe he would go away.

"I'm not looking for a tutor," he had said with a laugh. "I'm looking for a date." If she had known him better, she'd have understood he was serious.

She held her breath, as his eyes found hers. He was her person, almost from that moment. At least, that's how it marinated in her head, the years they were married. After he died. And the day the morgue gave her the ring from his finger.

•   •   •   •   •

The phone had rung, as she sifted through the otherworldly task of finalizing funeral arrangements.

"We have a bit of good news, Mrs. Marks," said a strange man who'd earlier informed her that her husband was "on refrigeration" (a phrase that stuck in her mind forever).

"What good news could you *possibly* have?"

"We were able to remove your husband's wedding ring...despite the swelling—"

"Just stop. Stop acting like you deserve a goddamn award for that."

"I understand, ma'am. I apologize..."

You understand?

They managed to retrieve the simple gold band with the slight scuff marks without sawing it off her poor dead husband's finger. She was supposed to be grateful. She should have been grateful. Instead, she was angry. Their wedding rings, circles to symbolize past and present and future all melded together for eternity. What a joke! She seethed at this. Thirty years old, she was. With a seven-year-old child. There was no present or future in that ring.

Two days later, she loaded Tommy in the station wagon, gave him a lollipop and Farafel in hopes he would nap and stop asking for his daddy. They drove the windy roads through town, across the bridge and toward the highway. Out of town, and into the city, where no one knew them, she stopped at a pawn shop with cracks running down the stucco walls and a crooked neon sign. The dilapidated building sat empty across from a Dunkin' Donuts. She thought for a moment that it *was* empty, and that perhaps this meant she should not be here. That this was wrong.

But the neon sign flashed the word 'OPEN', though the 'N' had burnt out. She considered leaving Tommy in the car, but gazed around the neighborhood, taking in the nudie bar across the street and the littered gas station next door, and changed her mind. No need to make matters worse with grief-induced stupidity. He had woken up, so she told him they were going inside this shop on a little adventure. He gave her a blank look in return. This wasn't normal, but they were both adjusting to the lack of normal, she supposed. He picked up Farafel and followed, grasping her finger in his sweaty palm.

The shop smelled musty and had a display of guns, used bikes, and even an old motorized scooter for sale. "Why don't you go look around, Tommy?" The boy shrugged and examined the collection of records against one wall.

She carried herself to the counter in a sort of daze. Ruth marveled at the little booth you got in once you got to the front of the line. The clerk, a full-bearded man wearing a baseball cap, said, "That's just for privacy. When we make the offer and hand people their cash."

Ruth slammed both rings on the counter, tears building behind her eyes like a hose spigot about to explode, but she steadied her voice and asked, "How much for these?"

"Um, well...ma'am. I can only authorize fifty myself. I can call my manager."

"Nope. Fifty will do just fine."

"Are you sure, ma'am?"

His sympathy unnerved her. "He didn't leave, you know. He died. He never would have left..." Her voice trailed into oblivion.

"If you're sure, then," he said, gazing at the counter.

She had pursed her lips and shoved the cash in her pocketbook. Nothing would have been just fine.

Her life had been hard, and heartbreaking most of the time, but the one thing—the one thing she had—was this man, this marriage. And then it was taken away. Ruth never got over the unfairness.

When she had Jeb, she was, for once, not different, as far as the neighborhood women were concerned. She grew up poor and never possessed Edna's social graces or conventional beauty. Ruth felt one precarious step behind the other girls for most of her life. The wrong words tended to spill from her mouth at the wrong moments, and she felt teenage judgment radiating through the girls' nervous laughter. But with Jeb on her arm, she had won Edna's approval. My, how she loved fitting in. It was, in retrospect, very silly to care about such matters. But Edna, who was known for her lemon pound cake and penchant for gossip, was her best friend. Their husbands worked the boat together, and she was happy. The ladies met once a week for penny poker, while the children scattered about the spacious yard, rolling in the itchy grass till their clothes were stained. It kept them quiet, and Edna had the secret to grass stains and mud. So, Ruth felt at ease, the smell of fresh baked goods, and laughter between the women, the children sprawled about. All of it was perfect, everything she imagined life should be.

Maybe this was all painted out in her head as so important, this concept of belonging, when really it wasn't so. That consuming desperation repelled people like ants from a can of Raid at a picnic.

Grief, for Ruth, was a solo experience, an exercise in strength she never knew she'd have to muster. Not just because of his death, but because her friends, the women she'd been ensconced within like family, could not handle it. They could not sit in her little pink house down the street, but in their own bubbles they did not want burst.

They dropped off casseroles and had to run to tend to the lives that had not stopped.

Sit with me and stay a while.

I cannot handle it, said her smile. I cannot take what you do.

You could, if you had to. Please, sit with me and stay a while. You like tea, don't you?

Well... I suppose.

Never mind. Thank you for the casserole, darling...

Of course, Ruth did not say this out loud, though she longed to. She was different, a woman whose God had failed her, and yet they said it was his will. Nothing sent her into an uncontainable fury more than those words. God's will? For a child to grow up fatherless? It made her want to spit, the way they said their pretty, pretty, you-know-we're-all-family kind of words. Fuck y'all and your words, she wanted to yell.

Granted, when she was cast her role as an 'other,' after Jeb died, more things gnawed at her soul. Sometimes she thought it gave her perspective. Other times she thought she had just become jaded. Take Edna, with her dark hair swept into a bun, always peeking behind the gingham curtains, suspicious of any 'strange activity' outside the giant house. More than once, a black kid whizzed by on a skateboard or bike, and the ladies would stack up at the edge of the curtains, whispering. Whispering—as if the poor kid could even hear them! Little Patsy Bundy, wise as she was, even at seven or ten, would tug at her mother's pretty blue dress and say, "What's he done, Mama?" in her innocent voice, with those giant blue eyes and strawberry curls.

Edna's reply was always the same. "Oh, Patsy. Just strange boys runnin' through the neighborhood is all." The other women nodded in unison, as if Edna was queen of the world, and therefore always right. Soon after, Ruth faded away into her grief, as it became plain—she did not fit in, as a thirty-year-old widow. She did not fit in anywhere.

Ruth remembered this now. And the more she thought, the stronger her drive to speak with Patsy about her "visions" or witchcraft or whatever it was. Because how could she know, the things that she did, at seven?

Ruth did not belong in Cypress either, which is, she supposed, where her curiosity about the girl came from.

●   ●   ●   ●   ●

Reeling toward the dirt, head first, Patsy felt the surge out of nowhere. Dizzy and unable to hold on to the edge, a giant wave in the choppy sea smashed into the boat, tossing her over. As she plunged into the darkness, the swish of salt water cutting her lungs, she struggled for the surface, taking a breath, only to be knocked under once again.

I'm dying, oh my God, help.

Thrown into the air, she exhaled with relief. Coughing, sputtering, damn it, what happened? She shimmied out of her heavy jeans, treading water. Where was the boat? A ripple of lightning hit the sea, illuminating the mast of *The Patsy Mae*. Something tightened around her neck. Someone yanked it hard, crushing her. Where were they? *The Patsy Mae* splashed in the wrong direction. They left her there. She tried to scream but was silenced by the noose. Hard smacks of water filled her nose. With the next gush, her body loosened and sunk softly. Her eyes went black. *Let go, Patsy. Let go, just let it all go.* She said this to herself, and the feeling returned to her fingers. The blackness receded into a plum-gray, then the usual gauzy haze.

She held her pounding head to her knees and folded her body into the tin shack like an accordion. Her back hit the wall, the hollow bang of metal reverberating through the tiny space like a bass drum. She steadied her breath and fished a cigarette out of the soft pack of Marlboros. Shit, she thought, it's bent. She inspected it further, to make sure it wasn't cracked, and put it to her lips. Her heartbeat slowed as she took the first drag and wiped the beads of sweat that had collected on her forehead with her shirt. Her hands trembled. Not from fear—Patsy was never afraid. But she had not eaten in two days, since the incident with her father. "You wanna put a new flag up?" she had screamed. "Then I'm on a hunger strike!"

Patsy ripped a Twinkie out of her bag, tearing open the plastic wrapper. The crinkling sound made her wonder if Twinkies really could last ten years on a store shelf. Gross, she thought, and shoved the spongy cake in her mouth. She shrugged and turned her boombox on, singing along with The Cure. She swayed about in the sweltering heat, caught in the rapture of Robert Smith's voice. At least the sun can't beat down in here, she thought of her little house. She was so absorbed in her music, she did not hear Tommy slip inside.

"Hey there," he said, laughing.

She twirled his way and felt her cheeks on fire. "What are you doing here? And didn't your mama teach you to knock?" His eyes made her uneasy. Gold-flecked eyes. A shiver ran through her mind. She knew where she had seen them. Patsy had known Tommy Marks since she was an infant, but she had seen those amber eyes somewhere else.

"I did knock. But you were listening to your music—"

"Fine, then. Why'd you come down here anyway?"

"I just heard you were up to witchery again. I figured you might need a wizard or something to help out down here," he said, laughing.

She glared and pushed him toward the door. "I don't have any energy left for gossip. I'm almost out of snarky responses, too. Go away."

"I'm sorry, Patsy. I swear. I'm just kiddin' with you. I came to see if you were okay. That's the truth of it. Let's just hang out. Like when we were kids." He slid into one of the folding chairs, and Patsy sighed.

"You're a good boy. You don't want to hang out with girls like me."

"You're no witch," he said, wiping away a pile of leaves that had collected by the open window.

"Tommy," she said. "What does your mom think about you working on the shrimp boat with Daddy? I don't understand why she lets you—"

"Why?" he said, narrowing his eyes. He furrowed his brow and said flatly, "Because my father drowned on his boat?"

"I'm not trying to upset you. Look, forget I asked." Patsy's stomach turned. She shouldn't have eaten the Twinkie. *Damn it, Patsy! Keep your mouth shut.* The humidity in the room intensified. "I'm going out by the water. Tell your mama I said hello." She traipsed through the brush and down to the red deck that sat above the murky water. Kicking her shoes off, she dipped her toes in, not too far, as there were gators in that swamp. The water shimmered and gently lapped up toward the grassy edges. She focused her attention on the cranes, still on pencil-thin legs, hoping he would just leave.

Instead, he followed, his feet slurping up mud as he trudged to her bridge and flopped onto it. He dangled his legs off the side. "She doesn't like it much." He said this in a matter-of-fact manner. "But everyone here shrimps. My dad was a shrimper, but I don't remember him. Not enough to be scared of the water."

"I saw him," she said, drawing the words in her mind before testing the flavor of them on her tongue. He would probably leave now.

But he only murmured back, "What did he look like?"

Again, she tasted the words, swirled them around her head for a moment, before she answered. She monitored his face as she said, "He was, well—I was—because that's how it works." His eyes locked with hers. "Anyway, I got swooshed off the boat. There was a storm. And a rope pulled me under. Around my neck. Then, I was up, coughing here beside this wall," she pointed, "His body just sunk, with a thick white rope around his neck."

"You sure your dad didn't tell you that story?"

"Never. They never talk about the accident. It's like some tragedy in our house, to them. And it kinda pisses me off, because you and your mama are the ones who lost someone. He just feels guilty." She tossed a stone into the water. Tommy's hands relaxed in his lap.

"That's exactly how it happened," he said, taking a slow breath. "I don't know how you could possibly know about the rope. Only Mama saw the rope marks on his neck, when she identified his body. This is just—we don't talk about the rope." He leaned back and lay across the deck, his arms splayed at his sides. "That's the rule. Never talk about the rope."

She lay back beside him and kept her breath steady. Sinking into the warmth of the scratchy wood, she said nothing. The sun was hot on her skin, yet somehow comforting, with her legs relaxed and hanging over the deck. Blue sky stretched for miles, with the bits of wispy clouds dotted across the horizon.

"You do see things," he said.

She did not reply; there was nothing to say. As she peeled red paint from the deck with her fingernail, they lay there for a while, listening to the water trickling and inhaling the earthen smell of the marshland. Something had happened, but neither of them knew what. Patsy got that feeling, the sense thicker than the Cypress air, that something had changed. It would percolate in her mind for a long time before she put it together. What happened here, so long ago.

Chapter Four
EDNA

Edna loved grocery shopping. Only people with dull lives enjoyed this pastime. If anyone asked her outright, she would be embarrassed to reply, "I peruse Cypress Market for the best fruit." But as they say, it is what it is. So, she spent many afternoons gathering bags of fresh peaches and plums, giving them each a gentle squeeze to test their ripeness, and squinting deep into the souls of the collard greens for signs of limpness. Inspecting the seafood display was a social event for her. Henry packaged her salmon with care and commented on how everyone loved the shrimp Stanley had brought in that day. She swelled with pride and smoothed her pretty blue skirt at the compliment. She feigned surprise, as if she had no idea that she was everyone's darling. "You're a peach, Henry. The crawdads are also quite good this season," she said.

"Oh, yes, Mrs. Bundy," he replied. "We can't keep 'em on the ice!"

She murmured a thank-you, distracted by the forest green Mercedes that pulled into the parking lot. "Well, I need to pay for these and get going. We're having a family dinner tonight."

Yes, she was the wife of Stanley Bundy.

And a fraud at that.

Her hands shook a little as she pushed the basket to the checkout line, focusing on the sound of the wheels of the cart rolling down the waxy linoleum. She piled the groceries on the conveyer belt a little quicker than usual. Susan, the lead checker at the market was fast, but still, Edna tapped her pen on the counter.

"In a hurry, Mrs. Bundy?"

"Oh no, not really," she replied. She gazed out the window towards the Mercedes, then quickly glanced back to her checkbook. Her mind was no longer on groceries. An out-of-towner, an old friend of her parent's, sat in the parking lot, waiting. She would not look his way while loading the groceries in her trunk. But he would follow her out of the parking lot, and up the windy road, to the Bundy's plantation. The trip to the store was her alibi. She had this all arranged in her mind. If her husband asked what she'd done this afternoon, she could say, "I went to the market." So what if she was followed home by a salesman from Shreveport? Salesmen came to the door all the time.

She manipulated the affair so that it did not interfere with her family, with this man her parents had wanted her to marry. But she did not love him. He was conventionally attractive and wore a suit and tie and worked in some big building in the city that Edna was not familiar with. He was a mediocre lover, but a warm body that gave her an additional sense of purpose. She was a mother, the wife of a shrimp boat captain, but she felt her worth as belle of the ball slipping away with each gray hair. Mitch reminded her that this was not so. His presence, from his fancy car to the smell of musk on his neck, was her secret. Stanley had shrimping, Patsy had witchcraft. And she had her afternoons with Mitch.

At first it was a challenge, but now the routine was sketched in her mind like a six-year old's memorization of hopscotch. Shop for a few items, every Tuesday, but not too many, as she went to Cypress Market most other days too, having not much else to do but meet the ladies for bridge or volunteer at the library. With Stan Jr. grown up and Patsy at school, life was tedious as hell.

She gathered her packages, and flashed a smile at Susan, who said, "Goodbye, Mrs. Bundy! Maybe we'll see you tomorrow?" Edna cringed.

"That's probably so. We do have that dinner party, and well, I'm always forgetting little things."

"Understandable, Mrs. Bundy."

Edna sighed, and made her way into the parking lot. She did not acknowledge Mitch's presence. But, at the first stop sign, she checked her rearview mirror. He had waited the prescribed three blocks before following her. As she turned the bend, no one else was on the road or parked at Mile's gas station. Around the curve and up the steep driveway, he lagged behind her. The large pillars, the French windows, the expansive yard; it all loomed over her as she sat in the quiet, waiting. The thinking was the hardest part of the affair.

He appeared at the door with a rose. "Hello, darling." He smelled like aftershave. She now had to get rid of the flower and his smell before Stanley arrived.

"Come upstairs," she whispered with a slight smile.

Mitch kissed her hard, perhaps too hard for her liking, and she lay back on the bed.

The sex itself was quick and furious. Almost immediately after, she'd get up and shower.

"Hurry," she said, suddenly frantic, "someone could be here at any time."

He languished on the bed. "That's kind of sexy."

She laughed, trying to appear coy. No, she murmured to herself. That wasn't it anymore. It wasn't all that sexy. Maybe having an affair had lost its luster. It certainly didn't affect her in the passionate way it did the ladies on Dynasty.

"Here," she said, gathering his underwear and no longer pressed suit. "Get dressed." Mitch wasn't understanding the gravity of the situation. If Patsy came home— oh, God—

He sat on the bed, buttoning his pressed shirt, and started in again, "Why can't you leave? If you're so unhappy?"

The truth was she was not unhappy, necessarily. And if she was, he wasn't fixing it. But, she thought, how do you say that to a person? That she just enjoyed being desired? Except she was wanted, by most everyone. What more did she expect from life? Her head hurt too much to ponder it anymore today. She felt the urge to help him button his shirt. He was moving so goddamned slowly.

"Mitch, you know I can't leave my family. It's not ever gonna happen. Besides, what about Martha? Your girls?"

"I'd get divorced. For you. I think the girls would want me to be happy—"

She laughed. "You clearly do not understand children. Believe me when I say that your happiness means nothing to them, if it means not having you. Don't be selfish." Now she pursed her lips, almost angry. This was not where she ever planned to take this. Still, she helped him with his tie, and ignored his pout. "I need you to go now. Patsy will be home soon. Remember—"

"I know." He sighed. "If anyone sees me, I was here selling insurance policies door to door."

"That's right, love," she said and kissed his nose. "Thanks for this afternoon." Edna shook her head as he padded across the plush carpeting to the staircase, holding his leather shoes in one hand, with his gaze toward the floor. She did not understand why their arrangement had become so complicated.

She needed to shower and put on some clothes before Patsy arrived. The digital clock on the end table flickered. Four p.m. Perhaps she would bake cookies, throw a roast in the oven. It was best to look busy. No, she decided. It was too hot for roast. Even with the air on, the oven would heat up the house something awful, and Stanley would be annoyed. Always hot, that man was, from being out on the boat all day. She would make red beans and rice.

Just then, there was a rapping on the door. Irritated, she yelled, "Oh, come on Patsy! It's open. What, did you forget your key again?" She turned and abruptly stopped, holding a wooden spoon. "Ruth. My God, you nearly scared me to death! And what is going on with your hair?"

"Nothing. I simply saw a strange car in your driveway and thought I ought to check on you. But it seems I've interrupted—"

No, no, no. Ruth Marks cannot be traipsing around town, gossiping.

Edna slowed her breath and patted Ruth's shoulder. "I'm sorry. You just frightened me, is all. The car was just some salesman. Insurance, I think. Stanley handles all that business, so I didn't even know what to say!" she said with a shaky laugh.

"Did you get his card? You never know if these alleged salesmen from out of town are for real. You need to be safe."

"No," she said, "I mean..." She steadied her voice. Damn busy body this woman was! "It is fine. It's all fine. Now, if that's all you came to discuss—"

"Actually," she replied, twirling a stray red hair around her finger, "I came about Patsy."

"I don't want to discuss Patsy. Please. She's a teenager, and we are disciplining our daughter as we see fit." She smoothed her skirt, and began to walk towards the door, but Ruth did not move.

"I'm not here to give you discipline advice, Edna. Come on, after all these years, you ought to know me better than that." She pursed her lips. "I wanted to speak *with Patsy,* not you, dear."

This was getting stranger by the moment. Especially when, not two minutes later, she heard her daughter stomp in the door. "Take your shoes off!" she yelled, like a reflex.

If Edna hadn't been concerned about her own situation, she may not have then turned her attention back to Ruth and said, "Well, okay, then. I've got dinner to prepare." She squinted, watching her childhood best friend guide her daughter to the front yard, to have some apparently private conversation.

This kid was turning out crazier than she'd thought possible. *What the hell was that about? At least Ruth bought the insurance salesman thing...* She shrugged and set off to chop some garlic, considering what greens went best with the seasoning. Vegetables with every meal. That was her rule.

•　　•　　•　　•　　•

Ruth trudged behind Patsy over the massive lawn. She had forgotten how impressive the Bundy house was. She murmured to herself, taking in the large magnolia tree with its expansive, gnarled trunk, and creamy white flowers with centers the color of whipped butter. The cornucopia of smells brought her back to the days Tommy would scamper with Patsy and the other neighborhood children on the grass, rolling about on what seemed to be an endless playground. Tommy would say, as if they weren't over every weekend, "It's like the park, Mommy!"

Like a park. Ruth and Jeb's yard was a patch of grass with a hose to cool off with in the summer.

Patsy led her to another tree, an oak that could have been there a hundred years, judging by the width of its trunk. Hanging from one of the strong branches, with rich scattered soil beneath it, was a wooden swing. Patsy plunked down on it, kicking off flip-flops as she extended her pink-painted toenails.

"What's up, Mrs. Marks?" she asked, pumping her legs into the air, curls flying in the breeze.

"Might as well call me Ruth," she said. "After all that's happened." She sighed, and leaned against the scratchy bark.

"Suit yourself." She shrugged. "Whatcha need, Ruth?"

"Let's get right to it, then. What are you going to do about your father? Rumor has it you're leaving town."

"I am going away to college." Patsy rolled her eyes. "I hardly think that qualifies as skipping town."

"You and I both know his flag and his bullshit version of Southern values have something to do with it," Ruth raised her eyebrows. She wanted to know what was up with this girl. An aura surrounded her. It always had.

"No, it really doesn't," she said. "It's Cypress. I want out of this town... I know what you're thinking, Mrs.—I mean, Ruth. You're thinking, but who on earth would want to leave Cypress! It's so quaint and the people are so friendly."

Ruth laughed. "That is not what I was thinking." The girl did not know her at all. "I was thinking," she chose her words with caution, "that Tommy will miss you."

Patsy kicked the ground, sending dirt flying. "I'll miss him too."

Ruth thought Patsy sounded wistful, but one could never tell with her. "I get it. Wanting to be in the big city. I thought of it myself, for a time. After Jeb died."

"But you stayed."

"Tommy was connected to the people here."

"And you?" Her eyes met Ruth's for a moment, and she turned her head.

"Me? Not so much," she said with a shrug. "So, tell me, why did you do it? With his flag, I mean. You knew that would cause an uproar. You coulda just left for Boston this summer and moved in with a bunch of artists," she laughed, "who would certainly understand your perspective, much better than here."

"Why? Did Tommy mention something?" She would pick this out of Tommy, later, by the way Patsy raised her voice. It was slight, the difference in tone. Humph.

"Why'd you ask that?" Ruth said, with a sideways glance. "What would he know about any of this?"

Patsy took a breath and arranged her hair. "I have no idea why he'd speak about me. Other than the fact he hangs out down at the old fort sometimes." She shrugged and pushed herself off the rope swing. She took a step, as if she was going to saunter off toward the house. A hesitant step.

Ruth could read people better than most folks in Cypress understood the Bible. "Are there really ghosts out there? Tell me."

With narrowed eyes, Patsy retorted, "Mrs. Marks. Ghosts are *everywhere*." She pivoted and ran toward the gravel road instead of the house. Ruth hadn't predicted that one, but she hadn't the energy for another bike ride to the Bayou. As the girl headed off to the wetlands, she just watched, knowing that a story was about to unfold, and it was gonna be good. Or bad, depending on how you looked at it.

Chapter Five
RUMORS

The town legend that had once existed in a whisper now undulated across the Bayou and through the halls of Jackson High in a scream. Teenagers who had known her since birth stood against their lockers in quiet protest, arms squared against their bodies as she walked by. Venomous stares darted from everyone but Tommy. But, being Patsy, she held her head up and met their eyes dead on, until they skittered back into their safe social corners. She had zero intention of apologizing and certainly knew that there was little chance of anyone fucking with her, Stanley Bundy's daughter. And so, she spent most days gritting her teeth, keeping to herself, and waiting to walk across that stage in her cap and gown and right off into the city. The Wham calendar on her wall had only fourteen X marks till it was all over. She lived for the satisfaction of the squeaky black Sharpie against the glossy paper.

It wasn't as if Patsy didn't get along with people at school. She always had. Granted, she could not relate to their plans involving marriage and babies, and it was likely they came over just to hang out in her parents' pool. Their parents were employed by her father, shrimp boater of the greater Louisiana Bayou. And her mother, beauty queen of Cypress, which Patsy was never impressed with, was adored by all the little girls whose grand life aspirations were to win pageants as well.

Oh, you're so lucky! Your mother is beautiful...So pretty she doesn't look like a mother at all...

She doesn't act like one either, not for real...She's pretending, don't you know that? Pretending, just like that wide grin she had on when she accepted her crown.

The big question that echoed through Patsy's mind, hearing the details of her mother's big win, was *who cares*? Patsy's family tree spread in branches through Cypress and came with 'friends'. She rolled her eyes just thinking about how her mother insisted she invite them over. She supposed Tommy and Elodie and Leo were her only real friends; she'd known them since birth. They'd spent many stormy summer days hiding in the tin shack.

Take Susie Baker. She had come to the Bundy house almost every afternoon until the flag incident. Baking cookies with her mother, doing homework (an intellectual, Susie-Mae was not), and applying generous coats of blue mascara until their eyes burned; it was quality time, time well spent. While teasing each other's hair till it matted into permanent feathered glory, Patsy made the mistake of thinking Susie liked her. But now she sunk away from her as if Patsy were contaminated.

Well, Patsy shrugged, witchcraft was not Christian, and Susie's father was the pastor at Hope Church. What a joke. The way they shunned her like a damn evil spirit was not Christian. She sauntered on by, waving at the pathetic group of girls with her copy of *The Feminist Mystique* at her side. If not the flag, she'd have burned her bra like Gloria Steinem. Maybe next week, she seethed, narrowing her eyes at Leigh Jenkins, who fumbled with the books in her locker.

"See you at church on Sunday," she said to Leigh with a smirk. Susie stood behind her, wearing an almost identical dress. She insisted on wearing bright pink (it brought out the color in the acne dotted across her nose, a feature one would not want to accentuate, and Patsy had told her this), but today it was to her benefit. Nearly blending into Leigh like a chameleon, she probably felt safe.

"Uh, you still going?" she said, a platoon of Aqua-net helmeted girls behind her. Leigh, beady eyes set a bit too narrow on her face, and a nose right off a Cabbage Patch Kid, had been the one to spread the rumors about Patsy and her alleged witchcraft in second grade, and it stuck for a solid year. Leigh prided herself on this discovery, and made it known to anyone who'd ask. Granted, people had since lost interest. But now, with the flag-burning incident, Leigh had a new opportunity to bask in the construction of a scandal. It was Cypress, after all. It didn't take much to create a shitstorm that would provide the high schoolers endless hours of entertainment. Most importantly, Leigh's popularity had just increased tenfold.

"Of course. Why wouldn't I be?"

"Well, with all that business at the Bayou, I just figured—"

"That witches were not welcome in God's house?" Patsy said, eyebrows raised. Come on, come and get me, she thought. Do it. Leigh stepped back, banging against the metal locker. Her comrades gazed elsewhere, pretending not to be there.

"What about the rest of y'all? Got questions?" Patsy turned to leave, but a blur of metallic blue nail polish flashed by her face, swirling in her peripheral vision. She ducked, missing the girl's hand, and whipped back around. A pretty blonde girl, whose name Patsy could not recall, stood there. Everyone scattered. She squatted low and punched. Blonde girl's nose sprouted blood like a ripe radish smashed by a pick-up truck. Patsy wiped her brow, straightening her legs, while the girl screamed. She cracked her knuckles and sauntered away, smug.

It was fucking awesome.

As she turned the corner, Tommy rushed right into her. His chemistry book went flying, kicking up dust as it landed on the concrete. He did not stoop to pick it up. "Patsy!" he yelled. "What the hell are you thinking?" He lowered his voice to a shout-whisper. "You are going to be in so much trouble when your dad finds out."

"At this point, I don't give a fuck," she said.

"Come on, let's get out of here," he said, tugging her sleeve.

"Where are we going?"

"Guess."

"All right." She sighed. "Let's go. I'm pretty sure it's not suitable to actually *live* there. But that may be my only option."

As they ran, heading for the football field, Patsy caught the stare of a pale-haired girl curled against one of the lockers. She seemed almost hidden there, as if she'd watched the fight unfold, but stayed behind, back from the other girls. Patsy turned again and tried to place the girl. Torn Levis, stringy, nearly white hair plastered against her face in chunks. The girl lifted her gaze and caught Patsy's eye. She quickly turned her attention back to Tommy. "You've got to stay away from me. You need that job on the boat. I'm not good for you."

"I'm not worried about that right now." They continued through the forested banks, pushing their way into the shade, where the cypress and magnolia trees draped over them. Patsy flicked a mosquito, yelping.

"Hey! Hey!" yelled someone. Patsy kept running.

"It's just Leo," said Tommy, panting.

Leo darted towards them, out of breath. "What the hell are y'all doing?"

"Come on," yelled Tommy. "They're not far off."

"Let's just get to the tin house," she said, "and then you two go home. Your mama needs you to keep that job." They had slowed their pace, jeans splattered with mud. She caught Tommy's gold-flecked eyes in a patch of sunlight, but quickly looked back to the path before her.

"They can find you here," said Leo.

"Of course they can. My father built the place."

"I wasn't referring to your parents," he said.

Patsy had not considered this.

"You think those stupid girls will come out here? I'm not sure they'd risk that."

"I don't know," Tommy said. "Lots of weird shit happens out here." They pulled their boots off before slipping in the little house. Tommy shut the door, and Patsy thought the better of protesting. They melted in the confines of the sweltering metal walls, so she motioned for him to sit beside the window, where a salty breeze wafted in from the water. Regret trampled through her head like a migraine. Except the sound grew louder, into a recognizable gallop. She clenched her jaw. She avoided her friends' faces as a flash of the horse pummeled towards them, its white mane blinding. She closed her eyes.

This will pass, just a moment, it will pass—

"Do you hear that noise?" said Leo.

He interrupted the image in her head, though the sound got closer. Leo had heard it, too.

"Someone's coming," said Tommy.

"Shit, shit, shit," she said, and peered out the window, careful not to raise her head much. It was no vision. It was no ghost. A gaggle of high schoolers trampled toward the tin walls. Leigh and her giant helmet head led the pack, who followed her like a pack of wolves, rushing through the trees.

"Don't look out there," Leo said. "Duck against the wall, where they can't see in the window."

"What if they break the door down?" Very close now, a cacophony of taunting voices could be heard. They chanted, closing in on her.

"Patsy Mae! Patsy Mae!"

"Come out, we know you're in there...witch girl!"

"Where is that bitch, anyway?"

"Casting spells in the woods!" They were gaining on the tin house. If they figured out where they were hidden, it was over. There was no way the three of them could take on half of Jackson High.

"Oh, Christ," said Patsy, "There's no way out."

"Quiet," Tommy whispered. "And they'll leave."

The white, brilliant tail of the horse whipped through Patsy's mind.

They had something, the men.

They held something, and she wanted to see...

The noise quieted, fell into a whisper. She peeked out the window, her body against the metal wall as if she was part of it, hidden so deep she felt like she could disappear within its crevices. Leigh's voice permeated the thick trees. "Let's go, y'all. They're not here. And that party at the Bundy house is tonight."

"Whatcha gonna tell your parents, about your nose?" said a voice she couldn't place.

"I don't know," said the girl with the bloody nose. "Probably something like I banged my face into a locker. Just in case Patsy saw us down here. I almost think we'd be in more trouble than she would."

"Ain't that the truth." The girls' words faded as they got farther away. Tommy looked at her with relief, and she nodded without speaking, just in case.

The woods went quiet, the only sound the beating of her heart against the rolling whirl of the sea; the only smells were swamp and trampled earth, disrupted by the shoes of people that did not belong there. "Tommy," she said, "you ought to go. Really. Being around me is not good for you. I'm serious." She repeated this, knowing it was true.

"C'mon. You know we're in this together. Especially because of what you know about my dad. You *do* see things. Tell me more about this flag."

"Research it. It's racist," she retorted.

"Hell yeah, it's racist. Man, you'd better know that," said Leo. "We can't be friends if you don't understand that."

"I see that," he said. "I mean, why'd you burn the thing? Patsy, you're always stirring shit up."

Leo wiped the sweat off his forehead and sighed. "This is all I've got to say on the matter."

Patsy knew he had more than one thing to say on the matter. Leo always said that when he had many things to say.

"You burned up your daddy's flag. Fine by me," he continued. "I can't stand the thing. You've got no idea what it's like for my father to work on your dad's stupid boat."

She nodded and kicked a rock in the dirt.

"But, if *I* would have done that—hell, if any black kid would've done it— we'd be in a lot more trouble than a few stupid rumors and a girl with a bloody nose. They'd probably kick me out of school, or worse."

"I'm sure that's true," she said. Her face burned with shame. She considered that perhaps she really was impulsive, as people said.

"But whatever. I'm just offering some perspective. You don't have to take it."

"'Course I'll take it!" she said. "Truth is, I know something happened down here. I can feel it. It rattles my bones, and then I've got to live with him—"

"Well, what happened then?" said Leo, folding his hands under his chin.

"I think a woman was killed here. She had blonde hair, but the killer did have a Confederate Flag."

"Holy shit, Patsy. You've got a vivid imagination. You've been sayin' this shit since, what, second grade?" said Leo.

Tommy leaned against the tin wall, sighing.

"What, you believe this crap, Tommy?" Leo laughed.

"I don't know what to believe anymore," he replied.

Leo rolled his eyes. "Come on, let's go. No one's out here now. At least you both have normal lives, aside from a father who's as ignorant as everyone else here, Patsy."

"Not really. I'm different than anyone here, because I don't have a father at all," said Tommy.

"How does that matter? To people, I mean," she asked, confused.

"There's just a way here. My mama feels it too. I can tell. Why do ya think she doesn't hang out with your mama and all her friends? Because she's different. She's said so. Young widows are different here."

Patsy pondered this. "Are you and your mama coming tonight?"

"Yeah, I think so. She likes you." He laughed.

Mrs. Marks's interest in her was something Patsy would never understand.

"How about you, Leo?"

"'Course. My father works for yours." He said this bitterly, and Patsy couldn't blame him. She felt her cheeks color. Night was falling. The sky had faded to the muted blue hue it did just before sunset began. They trudged up to the gravel road quickly, knowing they had to beat the moon if they were to arrive home before dusk. As they walked, Patsy felt a presence, and said, "Wait a minute." She held her finger to her lips, wondering if someone still around. If they should run. They ducked behind a bush on the road. "Wouldn't they have seen us? Wouldn't they have followed, if they knew we were here—"

"Look!" said Tommy in a loud whisper.

A girl sat on a tree stump, staring out at the water. The same girl who hid behind the locker. She flicked a piece of white hair out of her face. Patsy wasn't sure, but she thought she heard her weeping. "Let's go. I don't think she was with them. I'm not sure she knows them at all." Odd that Patsy had not taken notice of this nameless girl at school before today, but something told her not to disturb her. That somehow, she belonged to the Bayou, too.

Chapter Six
PRETTY

Edna rushed from room to room, clucking her high-heeled sandals and swishing her skirt, making sure every detail was perfect. Tables were set with candles on the patio, with colorful lanterns hanging cheerfully above. Freshly boiled crawfish and corn on the cob lined a buffet-style table, along with spicy sausage and, of course, shrimp of every variety. A fountain plumed with rich chocolate, surrounded by fresh strawberries and skewers. Edna was pleased with herself. Who didn't like fondue? Champagne flutes stretched across the bar, along with a cornucopia of bottles of liquor. Daisy and lilac bouquets hung on the rails of the exquisite banister leading to the patio, their sweet perfume intermingling with the scent of smoky sausage. Folding each ivory napkin carefully, she admired her handiwork. She had outdone herself this time. She needed to: a grand affair at the Bundy house would give the neighbors something else to talk about.

Her husband's key turned in the lock, and she fluffed her hair a bit. She wore her favorite off-the-shoulder flowered dress and clunky bracelets up her arms. "Wow," he said, wrapping his arms around her.

"Impressive, isn't it?" she murmured. One of the napkins was off-center. She slipped out of Stanley's arms to rearrange it. He smirked, amused. "What? I just want it to be perfect." She smiled.

"It is nice. But not as lovely as you are, darling," he said.

"Is the dress okay?" She knew it was. It brought out the highlights in her hair. She tapped her foot with frenetic energy.

"What now? Everything looks—"

"Do you think the neighbors will mention Patsy? I feel odd about the whole thing."

"Oh, Edna. Come on."

"I wish that child didn't have to ruin everything."

Stanley rubbed his head, and she went back to absentmindedly folding napkins.

"Well, your clothes are on the bed. You'd best get dressed," she said. "And make sure Patsy looks decent, too."

The air in Cypress felt foreign to her, even in her own home. In fact, she almost canceled the whole annual party, but decided that would appear even worse. Best to be casual about the situation. If anyone asked—she hoped to God they wouldn't—she would laugh and say something about how crazy teenagers could be. She smoothed her dress and checked her hair in the mirror by the foyer, exhausted already. At least she'd chosen a lighting scheme to soften her eyes.

•　　•　　•　　•　　•

Ruth considered staying home. Parties at Edna's were so over-the-top they'd become laughable. The woman planned a wedding reception for every get-together, something most of Cypress looked forward to. Ruth felt like she spent the whole night pretending. It was just depressing. Like the last time, Edna had gone on about how lovely Ruth's dress was, knowing damn well it had come from the Sears catalog.

A woman in yellow asked where she'd gotten the dress. "Did you go to the new boutique on Main Street?"

"No, actually. I got it from the Sears catalog, and dressed it up a bit, that's all." Her face burned. She had not felt ashamed of the dress until Edna had brought it up, and the woman in yellow said, "Oh, well, it's very pretty, anyway."

"Well," Ruth had said, "we can't all afford to shop at fancy boutiques."

"Ruth!" hissed Edna, which only pissed Ruth off more.

"Some of us are widowed and make it by with Social Security."

The women's mouths gaped in horror, but Ruth continued. "I know y'all voted to get rid of that. Sorry it didn't work out."

Ruth skipped a few parties after that exchange.

She sighed and clipped on large, turquoise earrings. They weren't pearls, but they'd have to do. "C'mon, Tommy!" she yelled. "I don't want to go to this thing, but we at least have to make an appearance."

Tommy stepped in the kitchen and leaned on the Formica countertop, smiling. "I don't mind. I want to see Patsy," he said.

"Why, Tommy!" she said. "You look like a grown man." Her son wore a dark suit and tie that she had bought him the year before, for a baptism at church. He had gel or something in his hair. She squinted for a better look. Given that he'd made such a fuss about wearing the suit to church, she raised her eyebrows and gave him a sideways grin.

"So, is there something going on with you and Patsy I should be aware of?"

"No, ma'am," he said. "She is just going through a lot. You should know that."

"I have no idea what that means," she said, changing the subject. "Well, we had best get on with it then. You're a good boy, Tommy." Jeb would have been proud. She patted her son's sticky head and waved at her eyelashes. No tears, or her mascara would run.

Next door, Ruth marveled at how a short jaunt could lead to another world. People trickled about, filling their glasses and plates, and chatting in a low hum. Ruth considered the champagne, but instead, filled a tumbler with scotch. She balanced it in one hand, and a heaping plate of crawfish and sausage in the other. The liquor warmed her stomach. The women strode her way, smiling and offering conversation. She murmured hellos and how are yous and why, whatever have you been up tos…thinking she may as well soak up some neighborhood gossip. Ruth thought perhaps she had drunk too much whiskey, by the stiff and cordial feeling that emanated from the grand surroundings.

Still, a thought burned inside her, from another party, from a different time.

It was 1965, when life was simpler. Edna had embraced her inner hippie, at least behind her mother's back. She ditched her Wranglers and shit-kickers in favor of tube tops and bell bottoms and platform shoes. And Ruth followed Edna like an unrequited dream, not knowing it was nothing but plume of smoke from a bong at a keg party. Her body fit into tight jeans and midriff baring shirts all wrong; she felt like a sausage stuffed in a world that did not belong to her. And Edna, with her straight-as-silk black hair that was impervious to humidity, made Ruth wish she could sink under her frizzy red curls. Edna and her cornflower blue eyes; Ruth with her thick, horn-rimmed glasses. Edna dazzled Jackson High with her row of trophies from the beauty pageants she'd won, while Ruth won a math contest that one time…

But she knew one thing to her soul— Ruth had Jeb, and Edna and Stanley did not have that kind of passion. Edna knew this, too. She felt a stab of pity, watching her old best friend saunter amongst her guests, almost twenty years later. Yes, she thought, you are everyone's darling, but really, how much does it matter?

As if her internal thoughts had slipped aloud, Edna appeared at her table, flute of champagne in hand. She hadn't said that aloud, right? Ruth knew her tendency to do this. Her tongue loosened with each sip of her drink.

"Enjoying the party?" said Edna, with watery eyes.

"I was thinking of heading out—"

"Please," she said, placing a cold hand on Ruth's, "sit with me and stay awhile."

Sit with me and stay awhile.

Ruth dropped her purse with a clunk and sighed. She slid her empty glass across the table. "I guess we're both gonna need a drink, in that case."

Edna motioned for a member of the evening staff and requested a bottle of Wild Turkey. Ruth pretended not to notice that the young man was black, not wanting to get into it with Edna. Oh, she knew they would be getting into it all right, but at least she hoped it would be civil. This family was draining her limited emotional resources as it was.

"It's just this issue with Patsy," Edna began.

"What about her?" said Ruth, looking directly at her old friend. And Edna, with the red-rimmed eyes, who had at least the wherewithal to apply waterproof mascara that evening, appeared shocked in a way that Ruth just could not handle. Like rumors spread by children were such a big deal.

Her chest went heavy with grief and her stomach roiled from the sausage.

"Well. You know about the neighbors and the high schoolers all talkin' about witchcraft and terrible things."

"So, you're worried about her?" said Ruth, who suddenly felt drunk.

"Patsy has brought this on herself," she said. "And business could be affected by the rumors, Ruth. You can't possibly understand how this works."

"Business seems just fine to me," Ruth snorted, and waved around at the decadent party. Her head spun a bit, she thought she ought to keep her mouth shut, knowing that Southern decorum was not her strongest quality. But she couldn't stifle a laugh. Because she tried so hard, thought she'd let Edna confide in her, let her feelings sink below her surface. Hell, she had thought, for the briefest of moments, that Edna was lonely.

"Ruth, that is not what I meant. I care about what she is doing to my husband."

"No, you really don't," she murmured, almost to herself. "Stanley loves Patsy. He does. And you know what I think?"

Edna didn't care at all what Ruth thought, but Ruth continued anyway, "You are so jealous of that. So damn jealous that it *kills* you."

"Oh, fuck you, old bat. You're just drunk."

"That's probably so. Because under ordinary circumstances I'd sit here and listen to you, and maybe even feel for you. But I am not one of your little women anymore." Ruth stood up, staggering a little, and hissed, "I know you. Too well."

With that, she headed for the door, and considered finding Tommy, but thought the better of it. She still felt heady from the whiskey. And besides, she longed to walk in the fresh air alone, where she did not have to hide her tears. "This issue with Patsy," she said, mocking Edna's voice. The woman didn't know a damn thing about real problems. Only ones created by selfishness and foolish pride. She slipped past the guests and into the night, kicking a rock across the Bundy's front yard.

•   •   •   •   •

Patsy slumped in the corner of the back yard, relieved that evening had fallen. The sky was dotted with the brightest of stars. The moon danced above, alive. Cajun music infiltrated every inch of the night. She tried to hide within the music, hum its gentle rhythm in her brain, and forget she was here. Hell, she could, if she tried hard enough, slip through the slats of the wooden deck, a molecule at a time, until she sunk right into the water, where she'd languish in the quiet. Her body tensed with the scent of her mother's flowers and candles and the sweet nothings, oh, and they truly were about nothing, that spun 'round the group of guests. She considered sneaking a glass of wine, but knew she'd get caught, which would make life even worse. The guests got drunker, their whispers grew louder, and she began to hear it all. She groaned to herself, tapped her feet, and counted days on her fingers.

Her thoughts were interrupted as Tommy placed his hand on her shoulder. "Hey. You okay?" he said.

"I'm fine. Why wouldn't I be ok?" she said, jumping. "You surprised me, is all. Don't go sneaking up on people like that." He had certainly dressed up for the occasion. She looked down at her own clothing. A stupid blue dress her mother had insisted on. Patsy knew she was pretty in a girlish way, but she'd never been beautiful like her mother, or Jr. He was all Mama, while she was a sort of mishmash of her parents.

"You look handsome," she said.

"What, are ya surprised?" He laughed.

"Nah, I've never seen you dressed up, though. Which is common with shrimpers, I suppose."

Tommy opened his mouth to speak, but Patsy shushed him. "Did you hear that?" she whispered. "C'mere."

She grabbed his hand, and they made their way through the guests, where they stood against the wall. "Look casual," she said. He seemed confused, for a moment. The unmistakable voice of Stan Jr. echoed in the night. Her brother was soft-spoken, with a light southern drawl, but now there was an unmistakable snark in his pitch.

"Is he drunk?" said Tommy.

"I dunno. Shhh."

Stan Jr. stood beside his wife Amanda, arguing with Daddy. Patsy froze. "Pops, I just don't agree. That's all. Sorry, but it's how I feel," he said. Amanda wore a forest green pantsuit that fit smartly across her round belly.

"Don't talk back to me, son. If you want to run my boat someday."

"Pops! You cannot tell me what to think. You just can't. I am a grown man."

"Like hell I can. You can have your opinions, but not here in my house."

"Look. You have had a few too many, Pops. I don't believe you should be fighting with a seventeen-year-old, no. Patsy is just like you."

"Just leave, son. You're embarrassing yourself."

"Patsy," he said, raising his voice, "is just like you. She ain't ever going to change. You'd best accept that. You're the parent."

"Good lord," said Daddy, laughing. "Just wait till your child is actually born before passing advice out, boy." He swirled the liquor in his glass.

Where was Mama, anyway? The way Daddy stood, arms squared against his body like that, made Patsy wonder if they'd get into an actual fist fight.

"Let's go, Amanda. He won't even remember this tomorrow." Stan whispered something into Amanda's ear, and they disappeared through the mass of people. Mama had made a mistake, having all these guests over, and Patsy felt a little guilty to be the cause of her embarrassment. Just a little.

"Not long now, Tommy. Just a few weeks till graduation." She led him to the door and said goodnight. "I'll see you at school, then."

He paused for a beat. "All right, then."

People could suck the life out of you, she thought. It was exhausting.

The boat swished gently, bumping into the dock now and then, which Stanley felt so comforting, it could lull him to sleep at times. But not today. Each jolt made his head hurt worse, and he lay on the cabin bunk, wincing with shame. Without opening his eyes, he fumbled through the drawer beside him for a bottle of Tylenol and swallowed a few pills in hopes of relief. They stuck to the back of his throat going down, making him gag. A wave of nausea swept over him. Stanley did not drink often, which he figured was why he was suffering from such a hangover. Or maybe he rarely drank because he was a lightweight. Zero tolerance, he thought, groaning and covering his face with a pillow.

He had left the house early, as he always did when shrimping, except today he had more than work on his mind. Luckily, Edna was used to him slipping out of bed at 3 a.m., because he didn't want to face her. Little had been said the night before, after the argument between him and Stan, with the whispering that grew louder as the guests drank more. Still, her stony eyes spoke for themselves. *How could you embarrass me?* That's what she said, in her mind. You knew what a person's eyes said after years of marriage.

Stanley tried to ignore his queasiness as the boat shifted under his feet. He would splash his face with water and get on with it as soon as Tommy arrived, whether Stan showed up or not, because that's how he operated his business. He took a deep, measured breath and slipped on a light t-shirt, glancing at his biceps. He was still in shape, thanks to a life of physical labor.

Just then, Tommy poked his head around the corner. "Oh, there you are! Sorry, I didn't hear ya coming up the dock."

Tommy shrugged, smiling. Good, thought Stanley. The boy must not have noticed the argument the night before. He was aware that Tommy had been hanging around his daughter, but that had been forever. Since Patsy was born. Had Tommy been around more than usual? The thought flickered through Stanley's head, but he dismissed it. "Well, let's get going then, son."

Tommy didn't ask about Jr. Stanley sighed and prayed Tommy hadn't gotten an earful of gossip about the party. He gulped his coffee and began the arduous process of setting up the nets. Working in silence, he passed one rope to Tommy, which they tied in its place, moving to the next in a methodical motion. The cool water lapping over his hands and the salty breeze was familiar; the tension in his head relaxed by the time he was ready to start the trawl. "How's your ma, Tommy?" he asked, breaking the silence.

"She's all right, I guess." He cracked his knuckles. Stanley cringed. He ignored it, though, and hit the gas, shifting gears as they moved away from the deck. He got a lump in his throat sometimes, being around Jeb's boy, with his sheepish grin and gold-flecked eyes. It was haunting, the two of them shrimping together.

Tommy would always be the little boy with the sock monkey and sleepy eyes. The confused child who, half-asleep, he had packed in his pick-up truck. "Edna will watch him," he had said to Ruth. He still woke from nightmares with hot tears in his eyes. He could never talk to Edna about it, not really. She had not been there, and her friendship with Ruth became tense since the accident, which confounded him even now.

That night on the Bayou, the sky shimmered with the electric full moon and a sudden dip in temperature that shrimpers in the area lived for. A full moon meant a big catch. He remembered the excited banter between him, Jeb, and Gilmore. They had laughed, as they pulled on their London Fog raincoats and heavy rubber boots, that they may as well be trawling for giant octopus, the way their wives geared them up. "Right?" Jeb had snorted, taking a sip of hot coffee from his Thermos. "Do our wives know just how grimy we're gonna be after this haul? London Fog!"

Stanley could see dark clouds ahead, but he'd never feared taking the trawler out in stormy weather before. In fact, the choppy water was a good sign, because the momentum from the waves shook the shrimp about, resulting in more of them landing in the nets. The sky splintered with lightning rods, the thunder rolled in, and it occurred to Stanley that they should move away from the dock carefully. The wind whistled around them, the boat unstable from the top-heavy outriggers. "Drop 'em!" he yelled, an uneasy feeling settling in his chest. The boat swayed from side to side, the arms of the outriggers stretched out like it was balancing on one leg. They secured the wooden otter boards and released the nets, sinking their bodies low on the deck of the boat. Gilmore continued to drive, the trawls lightly scraping the bottom of the sea.

"Feels a lot more stable," said Jeb.

"Hell yeah, it does," Stanley agreed. Rain shot at them from all directions. The wind blew so hard, saltwater sprayed in sideways sheets. The sky shattered with whips of lightning, as thunder growled back to it. "Still," he yelled, "sit tight a minute."

"Right. I don't wanna try and lift those nets yet," said Jeb.

Stanley wished he had listened. Every time his thoughts slipped to that night, he would wonder: *Was there hesitation in his voice? As if he knew? No, that couldn't be…it was so stormy we were yelling just to hear each other.*

A person could drive themselves crazy, wondering like that.

"Let's just do it," he had said. "Pull up the nets and get the hell back."

He pulled one side up, the net so heavy with shrimp the mesh chafed his hands even with thick gloves coating them. "Keep going!" he yelled. An ominous vibe roared through the blackness. The full moon was hidden behind dark clouds. Even with the fog light pointed down at the netting as they yanked it upward, they couldn't see much in the dense fog. Except, Stanley caught a glimpse of Jeb's boot, so close to the slippery edge. "Watch your footing, Jeb! Jeb, man!"

In one gust of wind, Jeb's foot caught on the edge of the boat, and he slid backwards right under the water. Stanley jumped in after him, as he was wearing a life jacket. All three of them were wearing vests, but they did little good with the waves hard and breathtaking. The salt water cut into his lungs and he coughed and spat, looking for his friend. The boat surged about again, knocking the light towards the turbid water, and he saw him. Jeb, with the white rope tight around his neck. His eyes fixed open, face contorted in an expression of terror, gazing straight ahead. Right through him. The boat had pulled the rope as it moved, tightening around Jeb's neck like a noose. They kept swimming, trying to reach him in the darkness.

But they could not get to Jeb. His best friend drowned that night, right there on his boat. And he had strangled him, dragging that rope through the water.

The night that would never, ever leave him, not for the rest of his life. It was carved into his brain with a pocketknife so sharp you could gut a fish in a single swipe. Just as surreal was Tommy standing across from him, with his father's eyes. It was like being transported to that night on the Bayou ten years before. Sometimes in Stanley's mind, it was like Jeb had never died. He could almost convince himself that the boy with Jeb's eyes and wry sense of humor was the man he had shrimped beside for years, had known since kindergarten. Sometimes, he thought about it in a more existential sense, when he was tired and had pulled in several loads of shrimp in the Bayou heat. He thought that by having Tommy with him, on the boat, he had a piece of Jeb there too, because in a sense he did. He liked the boy. Tommy's laidback manner comforted him, made him easy to work beside. Except a new fear came upon him; he imagined standing at Ruth's door again, this time with the news that he'd lost her only son. He did not allow Tommy to go night trawling. He didn't take the boat out in stormy weather at all.

He ran his shrimping business the way he wanted to, just as Henry Betterman owned Cypress Market, and Pat Reed was the town barber. Since the accident, he wasn't going to take that trawler out in a storm. The hell with the money. Edna had a new insecurity, that they were judged by the damn neighbors for Jeb's death. He had always known that on some level, Edna was afraid of everything. He wanted to scream, "Edna, he died out here! He died, right on my boat, and now his wife and child are alone! Who cares if people judge us?"

The little boy with the monkey named Farafel—Stanley never forgot that—was almost a man. He supposed Edna could never relate, because she did not see it. She was not the one on the boat that night, when Tommy's father slipped into the dark water, his body tangled in the rope they had tied together so many times. She did not feel the pain that built in his chest every time he saw Tommy, how it brought back that crushing velvet night.

• • •

The beauty parlor was nestled amid the neat row of pastel-colored buildings that lined Main Street. They were stacked beside each other, some higher than others, all different shades of pink and yellow and blue, all owned by someone Edna had probably had over for a meal or gone to school with. The pungent smell of seawater wafted through every corner, although Cypress residents were impervious to it. The slight lacquering of salt felt like home, and the sound of the waves lapping up gave them a particular solace. It would seem off if it wasn't there, like a baby trying to sleep without a lullaby or whirling ceiling fan they were used to.

Edna was about as hot with fury as the dryer that helmeted her head at Sally's Salon. Stewing under the roaring heat, she had not begun to recover from the evening before. She gazed at the black and white checkered floor and tried to relax her neck into the white pleather barber's chair. Her back was dotted with a splattering of knots.

"We're just covering some gray?" said Sally with a smile. Her cheeks were round and fleshy, like the rest of her. She had a chin-length bob streaked with silver, and Edna often wondered why she didn't cover her own gray, given her desire to fix everyone else's.

She smiled, and replied, "Yes, ma'am. And perhaps a slight trim off the ends." Sally nodded, but she cut her hair too short, and Edna hated this. "Just this much," Edna indicated, holding her thumb and forefinger close together. "No more than that."

"You got it, Mrs. Bundy," she replied. Edna detected a slight sarcasm in her voice. Sally thought it was about time she switched to a shorter, more 'mature' style, as she put it. Or perhaps Edna was imagining the tone in her voice.

She wasn't in the mood for chatter, as her brain kept replaying the previous evening. Where had she gone wrong? She expected Pasty to be defiant, and for her husband to act somehow shocked by it. As if he didn't know that she was every bit as stubborn as he was. Well, she supposed he did, but he just loved Patsy so, identified with her, even. It hit him in the gut.

She had to admit, Stan Jr. was talking utter nonsense, and he wasn't even drunk. Fighting with his father, right in public like that! He and Amanda could have their views. Edna did not have this attitude her husband did about the Confederate flag. She understood Patsy's position, though burning the damn thing was another story. But the two of them, fighting like that, right at her party, the one she waited all year to host. Well, that was just not tolerable.

Edna wanted to have her hair done in silence. But it was a beauty parlor, after all, where talk is an additional charge or included in the hairstyle, depending on your perspective. Or in Edna's case, what type of day she was having. Currently, Edna was in no mood for gossip. All she could do was dig her nails into the fake leather chair and wait for it to be over.

"We need the place painted again. And the wood out back is damaged. Can you believe it?" said Sally, running a fine-toothed comb through Edna's hair.

Edna could believe it, because that's what happened to all these buildings. The price of the ocean view included extra maintenance from the salt water and sand. It was a rhetorical question, given that Sally mentioned this every other month. "Really?" Edna murmured. "That's just awful."

"Don't I know it. It's gonna cost an arm and a leg," she said, swirling the chair around, continuing to clip. If there was such a thing as déjà vu, this would be it.

"I think that's about as short as I want to go there, Sally."

"You sure? I could do just a few layers on the sides. That would be so pretty on you," she said, pushing her glasses into place.

"No, no, don't cut anymore, that's just fine, thank you," she said firmly, as always.

She paid and fished through her pocketbook for a phone number. She never called him, as a rule. They had their weekly plan at the market. But today, she needed a distraction. The bells hanging from the beauty parlor door rang a bit harder than usual on her way out, and the screen screeched closed slowly. Edna's voice shook as she said, "Goodbye, I'll see you next week, ladies." She ensconced herself in the pay phone out front. Of course, the moment she lifted the receiver, Sally was knocking on the glass. Damn it, what did the woman want?

"You can use the salon phone, ma'am—"

"That's all right, hon," she said, and gritted her teeth, "I've already put my change in." Sally looked as if she might say something else. Good God, what now? She waved and put her finger to her pursed lips.

"Mitch," she whispered, "I'm taking a drive into the city today." He was delighted when she agreed to meet him at a hotel in Shreveport. He would probably assume she had reconsidered her plans, which of course, she had not. Still, she got in the truck and took the dirt road out onto the main highway for the first time in, gosh, years. The wind undulating from the open window and through her freshly-colored hair eased her anger. And the further away from Cypress she got, the more she realized she could not meet Mitch in some hotel in the city. She could not see Mitch ever again. Because she was seeing him, sleeping with him, out of spite. It was a way of telling Stanley, "Fine. We're even now." It was a terrible way to live, a terrible way to be. Edna was not a perfect wife, far from it, and probably an even worse mother. She had the sense of this, that maybe family life was not the right choice for her.

But it was the one that she had made.

She would be back that afternoon, guilt extinguishing enough of her anger that she could breathe again. Stanley would come up behind her, and wrap his arms around waist as he whispered, "I'm sorry." She'd have a pie ready, and nod, leaning into him with a smile. That was how they'd made up, for the past twenty-five years. A light kiss, a gaze into his eyes, and the soot in her lungs was washed away. There was something about being together for so long that made the fiery passion she'd thought she needed seem childish. Life was not a beauty pageant. She knew this, but it was a bitter truth.

Chapter Eight
GOODBYES

Patsy ran from the mailbox in tropical print flip-flops, kicking up dust from the gravel, little rocks sticking to the rubber bottoms. "Mama! Mama!" she yelled, barreling in the front door, with a stack of bills and circulars and other mail under one arm, and a letter she held between her fingers, beaming.

Daddy and Mama sat at the kitchen table, drinking mugs of steaming coffee.

"What, Patsy?" Mama said, rushing towards her. Probably because Patsy had spoken about four words between the two of her parents since that night, and now she stood screaming, her voice choked with excitement. Daddy sat back, arms squared against his body, without speaking.

"I'm going to Boston!"

"Not this again. Daddy and I have discussed this—"

"No, Mama. You don't understand," she said, and tried to steady her voice, although it still shook. "I got a scholarship. Full ride."

The crumpled look of surprise on her mother's face was so precious she wished she had a camera to capture the moment. Instead she smiled and said in her mother's syrupy-sweet tone—she had learned from the best—"Well, I guess that settles the matter. I'll be off to see if Tommy and Mrs. Marks are home. I'm sure they'll be just thrilled with my news." Her smile was wide and true and angry all at once.

Patsy started toward the door. Her mother stood, clenching the red linen napkin in her hand. But her father did not move. She caught his eye, for just a moment. His face softened, just a little. The wrinkles carved into his tan skin seemed to relax. "It's your choice, Patsy." He sighed. Then he turned to Patsy's mother and said, "What can we do about it, anyway?"

"That's true. Might as well get on with it. See y'all later!" said Patsy. She darted back down the gravel road, stopping once or twice to dig a rock out of her shoes and down the dirt road to the Marks's little house. Taking a leap across the walkway, she tiptoed along the sidewalk, almost like a melody. Two steps to the left, three steps round the bend, a quick hop over the crack in the middle, and there she stood, banging on the door, maybe a bit too hard. The heavy door creaked open, and Tommy gave her an amused smile. "What the heck is goin' on?" He laughed.

"I'm going to Boston! Full scholarship. Doesn't matter what they say. I'm going anyway!" She stopped, as Tommy's lips pursed and he gazed toward the ground. "What, you aren't happy for me?"

"It's not that. No, of course I am! I'll just miss you, that's all." He smiled, running his hand through his hair.

"Oh, you don't have to worry about that. We'll visit. I'll be here every other weekend, I'm sure." In her heart, she knew this was not true. And, she thought, so did he. Still, he widened the door and waved her inside.

"Mama will be excited for you too."

Ruth rounded the corner to the front room, hearing her name. Pictures hung from the walls in the dark hallway. "Come on in, Patsy." Her hair in ringlets, she was fully dressed in a lime-colored suit and tan pumps. Mrs. Marks had a sadness about her that mixed with her effervescent personality in a way Patsy had always found pleasant. She was boisterous and every bit as gossipy as the other women in town, but she told you what she thought right to your face. Patsy admired this. "What's the hollering about?"

"I got a scholarship to Boston University. I'll be leaving in August."

"Oh, sweet Jesus! That's amazing news! Tommy, did you hear that?" He nodded, and Ruth continued, "Oh, honey. I know y'all will miss each other, but you've got to be happy for her!" She turned Patsy's direction and said, "Take this opportunity and go. You must not let anyone convince you otherwise."

"Oh, I won't, Mrs. Marks," she said. "Are you on your way out? I'll be going."

"Well," she said, wide-eyed, "I've got news of my own." Ruth leaned toward Patsy as if to reveal a very big secret, and Tommy rolled his eyes. She paused for effect and said, "I have a job."

"What? I can't believe it!"

Tommy sunk in a chair at the kitchen table and tore into a biscuit.

"You are looking at the brand-new assistant librarian at Cypress Library," she said, twirling around to show off her suit.

"Congratulations, Mrs. Marks! I didn't know you took interest in books so much," said Patsy. Ruth offered her a biscuit and some jam. Patsy sat next to Tommy.

"I've always loved books. Especially now that Tommy's good as grown, I need something to occupy my time." She shifted her gaze. "I need to tell you, Patsy, it was you that inspired me."

Patsy sighed. "Oh, Mrs. Marks. Do we really have to talk about this?"

Tommy gazed pointedly at Patsy, as if to say, "Here we go."

"Just listen. Please. Truth be told, you are right, about that flag. I spent hours researching it, at the library, of course. That's when Mrs. Sherman offered me the position."

"Because you were researching the Confederate flag and women's rights?"

"Of course not. Because I was spending so much time at the library! So, you see, you are the reason I got the job. Well, inadvertently, I guess." Ruth opened a pocket mirror and applied a coat of lipstick, smiling.

"Proud of you, Ma. But Patsy and I've gotta go," said Tommy, grabbing her hand and shoving her towards the door. "Let's get out of here. She'll talk your ear off for another hour, if ya let her."

•　　•　　•　　•　　•

They saw it from the dirt path, well before their feet even hit the wetlands. It was quiet and desolate out there, at this shack Patsy felt both uneasy and enamored with. Frogs croaked and blue herons clapped, as they'd done forever. She thought that coming here with Tommy, perhaps for one of the last times, was a nice idea. But then they saw the red tin wall, and she knew that she was wrong. She had never belonged, there was nothing left here but the darkness from her visions, and worse, the people.

The rust-colored house, so charming with its walls made of slats of metal on wooden lifts her father had made, sat on the water all wrong. The water she'd been told never to swim in, there might be alligators, he'd told her. Snakes too. Just don't swim, okay, honey? No swimming in the water.

She felt like her chest had been gutted by a gnarled alligator in the swamp, seeing her precious house that day, with the word 'WITCH' spray painted on it in black. Tommy held his arm out to her, tried to go with her, but she swallowed hard, the tears in her throat. God dammit, you don't cry. She told herself this, again and again. Because she would not let them make her cry, but the pain in her chest was physical, as if those white horses trampled over her, leaving nothing left but a body.

"Stay here," she said.

He did not follow.

Sweat leaked from her pores, and maybe she cried too. It was hard to tell because of the heat. All she could think of, trudging back that evening, with Tommy a few feet behind, was getting out of this place. There was no other way, no other choice. She looked back at Tommy, then turned away, eyes fixed straight ahead.

"Patsy..." he would call, now and then.

"Don't," she whispered, no breath left inside.

He could not hear her, she knew. There wasn't much to say, anyway. If she had a shred of doubt about leaving town, it was gone.

·   ·   ·   ·   ·

The evening sounds echoed through the silence, with the sun setting over the marsh. Stanley's eyes watered, taking in the ugliness of the spray-painted tin shack. He had built this for her, just before she was born, finishing the last coat of brick red the very evening Edna went into labor. He told his son, "This is for the both of you to play in." And he had believed it to be more of a boy's hangout, but it didn't work out that way. Patsy was drawn to it the way other little girls grew attached to baby dolls. Now, it was desecrated much like his flag, much like his family. At this moment, a heaviness in his chest came from nowhere, and he remembered that evening, nearly eighteen years ago, when Edna's water broke. Patsy's birth had been an emergency, and they both nearly died. The rush to the hospital, the way it traumatized his wife, it would never leave him.

In 1970s Cypress, men were rarely present at births, although they often took place at home. The boy was born at home, and onto Edna's chest, where they both wept freely, despite his fear of the process, and how strange and magical it was all at once. At that point, they laughed through their tears. When she gave birth, he felt a closeness to his wife that he did not know at other times through their marriage. It was deeper than falling in love. It was like falling inside a person, becoming part of them, taking up all the space in their chest and sharing the rise and fall of their breath. This was what childbirth was for Stanley, though he'd never say out loud, or admit a sort of envy towards his wife, and all women, really, because he could never experience it fully.

With Patsy, it was different. After the surgery, the doctor handed him the sweet child, still smeared with bits of creamy vernix. She would not meet her mother till later that day.

Edna had refused to get out of bed for months after Patsy was born, did not shower, only cried. Patsy always had this fire about her, and he felt a tenderness for her that he did not have for his son. Oh yes, he loved Stan Jr. But since she was not being cuddled or nursed like her brother, Stanley had this sense in his heart that she needed to be nurtured. He handled much of the diaper changes and feedings, out of necessity, but he also rocked her gently when she cried. He came to revel in, the way mothers do by instinct, the smell of an infant's head and how delicious it is.

Edna barely spoke, much less acknowledged the palpable sadness that hung in the air, the way it intermingled with the joy of birth, of the sweet little girl. At first, he resented Edna. Then he felt sorry for her, and all she was missing—especially later, when he learned about postpartum depression and how it could be treated. Patsy's dimpled smile and chubby feet and indignant scream (this never changed) made their way into his heart and sewed themselves there. There was a place for Patsy on his lap, the sweetness of strawberries in her curls.

Her defiance troubled him. He wouldn't admit it to his friends, but he was one to spare the rod. Perhaps he had spoiled his children, but he couldn't bring himself to do it, or even see the point in it. Patsy had taken his values and burned them to the ground. Yes, it made him angry. Furious. But he still went back to scraping off the damaged side of the tin wall, and then coating it with fresh paint.

Patsy was leaving, and there was nothing he could do. He was livid, a fire inside him he thought would never fade. Except, he knew he'd load her suitcases in the pickup truck and drive her to the airport and hug her goodbye. It was one of those things, he sighed, that a father did, no matter what.

Part Two

Chapter Nine

1996
BOSTON

Several inches of snow piled on the sidewalk, with more promised over the next few days. Patsy admired it from her window, the way the fluffy flakes fluttered softly to the ground, the sky clear enough that bits of orange and rose peeked through the clouds at sunrise. She had dressed in warm jeans and boots with a hat, gloves and a scarf because that's what you did in Boston in December. The pristine pine trees and the little shops outside her brownstone apartment were lovely, as if they had been arranged on a miniature train set, but when she stepped out into the bitter cold, the white powder turned wet and soggy. Nothing ended up exactly as it appeared, she thought, from a window or in a photograph.

The boxy apartment, with its overstuffed red couches in the living room, and crisp white sheets in the bedroom, suited Patsy's tastes all right, but she wasn't one to care about that sort of thing. Pierre tinkered with the apartment's decor regularly; Patsy hardly noticed. A rectangular glass table with clean beveled edges served as a place she stacked mail and circulars, which annoyed her boyfriend. Rolls of film and manila envelopes could be found about the apartment, where she'd set them down before moving to another set. "Can't you file these somewhere?" he would say. She tried.

Patsy took photos for a living. Well, she had wanted to be a writer, but she had a good eye for the camera, and sales from her pictures paid the bills. She took nature photos, mostly, and some still life. She did not enjoy photographing people. The lack of control bothered her. A tree or a mountain was just that, and if she chose the right lighting and captured the best angle, the picture would turn out all right. People were unpredictable. People moved at the wrong moment.

"Pierre!" she called. "You're going to be late for work. Are you ready?"

He stumbled out of the bedroom, still wearing plaid flannel pajamas and leather slippers, probably Gucci. "Seriously? You're going to be late."

"I quit," he said. "Last week."

"Why?" Patsy tried to keep her voice even. Pierre did not, as a rule, keep jobs for long.

"I know you don't understand this, but having a 9 to 5 job just kills me. I feel trapped, every day in that cubicle," he said, sighing. His face was perfect and angular, and she found it difficult to hate him most of the time. But the casual way he yawned and poured himself a cup of coffee irritated her. He ran a hand through his black hair, which fell back across his cheek in a peculiar manner that had attracted her to him. But now, it just seemed pretentious.

"So, you're stifled, as a poet? We've discussed this—"

"You don't know what it's like—"

"What the hell?" said Patsy, anger bubbling in her chest. "You write poetry that no one wants to publish. And you never think to improve it. Just that your work is too good for anyone, 'too controversial'." She mimicked him, knowing it was spiteful.

"People pay for your photographs because you sold the fuck out."

"I'd rather people buy a damn calendar and pay the rent with it, than live off my parents," she said, glancing pointedly toward the slippers. A thousand bucks for those, she thought. At least. His father was a podiatrist, his mother, a lawyer. She had, at one time, admired how they believed in nurturing his soul so he had the time to find himself, to create. She thought they'd create together. She rolled her eyes at her eighteen-year-old self.

"I have to hit the gym before work. I guess we'll talk about this later," she said, a gush of icy wind pouring in the door as she opened it to leave.

"Eat something!" he yelled.

She pursed her lips and wondered what she ever saw in him. "Bye, Pierre." She had a headache and it wasn't even eight a.m. Eat something, she grimaced. Easy for him to say. She had a job to do, and limited time for a gourmet breakfast. She sighed and slammed the door behind her.

• • • • •

She gripped the steering wheel, gradually letting her foot off the gas, rather than hitting the brake at the stop sign. She'd grown accustomed to slick roads and black ice, but her first instinct still screamed brake, resulting in a crunchy slide into traffic. She inched along behind a row of cars, heading through the brownstones like ants, tall and slim packed against each other, with steps marking where each one began, and winding through the Commonwealth. Colorful lightbulbs adorned the skeletal trees, and mounds of snow had been plowed away from the street and piled along the sidewalk. The sunrise, in purple and orangey tones, still spread across the sky. Good, she thought, these photos will sell.

She removed her gloves and shoved them in her pocket, pointing the 35 mm camera at the Christmas light-dotted sunrise. Perfect. She flipped through a few rolls of film before she was satisfied with the results. She slid her gloves on, waiting for the numbness to dissipate from her fingers, and headed to The Roast for a cup of coffee. The old coffee shop had attracted her in college, and she liked the familiarity of the wooden booths and shaky tables. She loved Boston because it was huge and packed with people, and no one cared to engrave your every secret on the steps of Town Hall. It wasn't that the city was judgment-free, but rather that people had their own problems, and Patsy preferred that sort of anonymity. Still, there was a certain joy in having one place to make the exact same coffee every time, and where the baristas knew her regular order. She slid in a chair and inhaled the warmth. She lifted her eyes and searched for the barista. Instead, Pierre greeted her, holding two lattes, hers with no sugar, an inch of milk. He set them on the unstable wood table and smiled. "Do-over?" he said, taking off his camel-colored wool coat and arranging it on the back of the chair.

Patsy groaned. "I guess."

"I don't want to fight. I'm sorry."

"You quit your job again," she said, unfolding a napkin. She stared at the table and stirred her coffee.

"I know. I'll find another. My parents pay for everything, whether I work or not. Why does it matter?"

"Still, you're a grown-up. When you win the Nobel Poet Laureate you'll have that freedom. Till then—"

"Oh, come on. You've got rich Southern parents. You can't go there."

"You know that my rich Southern parents are racist, misogynistic, vote red?"

"Everyone's racist. And everyone's sexist, too. Even you and I," he said.

"I know that. All I'm saying is that I wouldn't take a dime from them." Patsy raised her eyebrows. "They would hate you."

"Oh, come on. There's got to be something interesting about this place."

"It's complicated." Patsy gazed out the window. There was something majestic about Christmas up north. She imagined her family down in Cypress, which had a different kind of loveliness. She yearned to see Tommy and Ruth, but the price of dealing with her parents was steep. She had lost sleep ruminating on the topic. "There is something about little towns you can't understand unless you've lived in one. Good and bad."

"Like what? I think it's fascinating."

"Well, everyone meddles in each other's business. Your neighbor likely knows what nights of the week you have sex. And if they don't, they simply make it up," said Patsy.

"Oh, come on. That's not so horrible." He laughed.

"That's true. Pierre, it's the witch thing that gets me."

"You were a kid."

"Yeah, I know. But my own parents were more concerned about their damn reputation than their own daughter. And I was six."

"I get it." Pierre shook his head, sipping his coffee.

"Yeah, well. It doesn't make you feel exactly welcome."

"I guess not," said Pierre.

Patsy slid her seat back and gathered her purse. "It's better now, that I'm away from there. Southern hospitality, my ass. Maybe for other people." The coffee shop bustled with noise this morning, and Patsy found it irritating to listen to Pierre and the Patriots game at the same time. She turned to leave, when something made her whip back toward the TV.

"Convicted murderer...Cypress, Louisiana...release date approaches."

And then, those pictures. The Bayou was ravaged by flames, but she could still trace the exact area the photos were taken in her mind. Because she'd seen it happen.

"Isn't that where you grew up?" said Pierre, incredulous. "Look at those charred trees...right over the water," he murmured.

Patsy slid back in her chair, wide-eyed, a million thoughts spinning in her mind. She drummed her fingers on the table.

"Did you know about that? It says it happened in 1970," he said.

"Sort of," she said.

"What does that mean?" he asked, with narrowed eyes.

"Nothing. It means nothing, Pierre." She turned to the television, dazed at this news. Archibald Parson. Now that, she admitted, was not a name she'd heard before.

•　•　•　•　•　•

She was six years old, and she wasn't supposed to be at her tin house. She was grounded. Patsy did not remember why, as she was relegated to her bedroom often. This hot afternoon, she was livid and indignant at the unfairness of being there. Restless, she snuck out her bedroom window.

In a glum mood, she slopped down to the tin house, watching the sun plunge into the water. It had been raining on and off and another storm was predicted. But for now, it was peaceful, the sky layered with pink and orange and light gray clouds. Angry tears gathered in her eyes, because the whole world hated her for some unfathomable reason. She slumped against the wall and wished she could live alone in her hideout.

It was hot, encased in metal like this. And getting hotter. She was used to that swimming through steam feeling. But she imagined the heat so intense the tin was melting, folding in on her, except her fingertips grew cold. Dewy sweat clung to her clothing.

I must be gettin' sick…Maybe I should go home to Mama…

Patsy plunged her head out the window for a moment, to see if the breeze would cool her face. Her hands shook. She wasn't sure she'd make it home, much less up the fire ladder to her bedroom. The thought of lifting her body with chafed hands and weak arms was overwhelming. It wasn't even dark yet. Except the sudden smell of smoke, like a campfire, wafted through the air in wisps of gray. Her eyes flew open. The sky was dark and scary. Panic rose in her throat, so dry she could hardly swallow. Big puffs of blackness made the whole world go dark, like someone had painted over the sun with a can of black paint. She slid against the wall as the room turned thick, and she coughed, choking on soot. Tumbling out of the tin house, she gasped for air.

She fell to the ground, her cheek resting against the mossy earth. *What is happening? Fire! What did Daddy say to do for fire?* Her mind was a mess of ideas, of all the emergency information she remembered. Then it hit her: stay here. Smoke rises. So, she pressed her face to the ground, under the haze, and waited for firefighters to come. Yes, that's what you did. Fear sizzled in her brain like eggs in a hot skillet. The fire rolled in like a giant wave from the sea, threatening to swallow her alive. Orange flames lit the Bayou, roaring through, and licked the surface of the water.

I am dreaming. I am dreaming.

Then came the horses, galloping right by her, kicking up mud, their white coats spotless despite the raining ash. She got up and scurried behind a nearby tree, watching, as the horses disappeared, filtered away in a gauzy haze. It was a vision. Just one of those visions. Soon the sky would be swept clean of soot, and the clomp of the horse hooves would ride away.

The blackness remained, with one man left riding a single horse. Maybe this was not a vision, not a dream. This was real. The horse's color was indistinguishable, but the Confederate flag hanging from his back was unmistakable. Patsy scrunched her face at the sight of a big tub of something that he tossed into the water. Boom! The explosion echoed through all of

Louisiana, as far as Patsy was concerned.

She felt she was watching this all happen, like a movie. Like she was on the other side of the screen. Her fear dissipated.

A woman screamed a desperate kind of scream that Patsy had not heard before.

"Shut up now, you hear?" said the man. His voice hit her in the chest like a baseball bat.

"Let me go!" she screamed.

"This town don't need no sluts like you."

Next, Patsy hid her face in her hands, but she could not turn off the sound of him kicking her, the guttural sound of her voice, the quiet followed by her screams. The voices softened to a whisper just above the roaring fire, and Patsy opened her eyes. She thought he must have let her go, although she did not hear his horse leave, until her eyes adjusted to the smoke, and she saw him close to the swamp. The woman's head bobbed up and down at his shoulders, her arms draped down his back like a sack of horse feed. He slung her into the swamp, head first, where she floated for a moment, before sinking under with the gators.

Patsy got up, running. Her eyes burned from smoke and tears. If she didn't get to the open road, he would kill her too. Her feet hit the wetlands with a slurp, each footstep like pulling her leg out of deep slime. She felt her legs giving out, but kept running, breathless. She reached the dirt road, the darkness lifting with each stomp. She stooped down, coughing.

With that, it was sunset again, with the pink and orange colors drifting into one another as they did before night fell. As they did every evening. There was not a hint of smoke. Not on the horizon, not on the Bayou, and her clothes were as clean as they ever had been after a day at the hideout.

The Bayou was untouched, and so was Patsy. She brushed off her clothes and headed home, climbed the ladder with ease, and flopped in her bedroom window. She sat for a while, steadying her breath. Just a dream, she thought. A crazy vision, they'd convinced her. Just her wild imagination.

•   •   •   •   •

If Patsy saw a picture of the woman, she would remember her. She knew it on a molecular level, down to her soul. Imagination. She considered this for a moment, let the possibility swirl in her mind…that she knew something of this man on the television.

"Pierre," she said bluntly, "do you want to visit my parents for Christmas?"

Pierre raised his eyebrows suspiciously.

"I just think it's about time to let bygones be bygones," she said, steadying her voice.

"This has something to do with that murder on TV, doesn't it?"

"I'm curious, of course. But I figured you'd want to meet them, and Louisiana holidays sure are unique."

"Really? What's it all about?"

"Jesus, Cajun food, and Mama one-upping the neighbors."

"Oooh, I can't wait. Cajun food," he said. "For the record, I think you're full of it. But if this is the only way I get to meet your parents—"

"Fair enough," she said, smiling.

"You're going to cause some kind of drama, aren't you?"

"I swear I'm not. I'm going to say hello to Ruth and my family. And maybe check things out if the occasion should arise."

"All right," he said, sighing. "Please don't start something—"

"Why would you think I'd do that?"

"Oh, come on. You're good at it. You know it's true." He slid out of the wooden chair and retrieved his jacket from behind him. "You ready?"

"Nah, I've got another set of photos to take. Meet you at home?"

"All right," he said.

She buttoned up her jacket. She needed to get out of here to call Ruth. And her parents. Best not to indicate she knew anything about Parson.

•　　•　　•　　•　　•

Patsy was wary of the change that swept over Pierre the week before they left to visit her family. Still, it gave her hope. She met her poet laureate at the gym while studying for finals in college. It surprised her, the ideas and revelations she had while running. Patsy wrote most of her college papers and deconstructed calculus during those jaunts around the track. Ideas bounced through her head and gave her that feeling of winning. Patsy lived to win.

Anyway. He'd run up beside her, and she thought, Who the hell do you think you are?

People did not, as a rule, whizz past Patsy on the track. And if they tried, she'd blow by them with the most satisfied smirk she could muster.

"Hey," he said, panting. "You're fast."

She ignored him and his green short shorts and white Nikes that hadn't seen a Boston winter. She envisioned him packing them in a large gym bag, along with a hefty load of self-care items like aftershave, an electric toothbrush, and pressed clothing.

Patsy ran faster, ponytail bouncing off her neck. "Who do you think you are, Prefontaine?"

"I like the accent," he said. Patsy glared.

"That's original," she said, and hit the ground with long, smooth strides. She beat her fastest time that day. And the next. He was determined; she had to give him that. Eventually, she agreed to have sushi with him…and a lot of sake.

It must have been the poetry, she thought with a sigh.

And the sake.

But one night, she trudged into the apartment, wet with melted snow. Patsy had spent the holiday season photographing quaint Boston suburbs that reminded her of Cypress, except frozen. The kitchen reeked of burnt garlic and Pierre was chopping vegetables so fast he could chop a finger off. She watched as he swore and tossed sausage and Creole seasonings into a sizzling pan.

"What are you doing?" said Patsy.

"I am making seafood jambalaya," he said with a proud smile.

"What is the celebration for?" she asked. "Do you need help with that rice?"

"I have news! Great news. Except this damn shrimp is burning. I can't move fast enough. This is stressful!"

"First, you have to have everything ready to go before you start. Sausage casings removed, shrimp cleaned, rice ready to go."

"Okay, I think I get it."

"Also, shrimp turns to rubber if you overcook it. As soon as it's opaque and pink, it's done."

He scraped charred sausage off the pan and tossed it in the sink. "Gross," he said, opening a window. A cold gush of air wafted through the apartment and the smoke dissipated before the smoke detector could go off. "Anyway, you are looking at the new copy editor for *Slice of Life* magazine, which is a small cooking magazine out of New York."

"Yay! My baby is employed!" she said, laughing. "But I think you need to practice first."

She pointed to the charred mess in the sink, where wisps of smoke lingered.

"Editing, I can do. In all genres."

Genres? Patsy didn't know cooking was a specific genre.

"I realized you were right. You've been right, all along." He kissed her on the nose. "My stupid pride has stopped me from getting a job. I can still write. Besides, who gets into writing for the money, anyway? Especially poetry."

"Good point," said Patsy. "What has inspired this change?" She pulled her boots off and set them by the door.

"It just hit me. Writing is my soul. But stupid rejection letters killed my pride." He shook his head. "I'm sorry. Real do-over?"

She laughed. "Well, as you so aptly put it, I support myself taking pictures for calendars."

"I didn't mean it, babe. I was just upset." He kissed her on the lips and dashed to the refrigerator. He produced a bottle of champagne and said, "Despite the failed dinner, the guy at the liquor store assured me this fine beverage will not disappoint."

He had a job. She felt her standards dropping like an elevator with a broken shaft. Maybe this trip to Louisiana would be romantic, and not just about the fiery murder, but rekindled love. One could hope.

Chapter Ten
TOMMY

Tommy gazed around the little house, stunned. It looked as if it had been gutted. Linda had cleared out her stuff, and a good deal of his. A deep indentation matted the carpet where the floral loveseat and couch had been. He considered who had purchased it and decided it didn't matter much. It was theirs, and she was gone. Nothing adorned the walls except a yellowed picture of his parents from the 70s, his mother all smiles and wearing a loose flowery shirt, his father with a long beard.

He had met Linda in college. A colossal-sized dude had crushed him while playing football for LSU. He had to have been seven-foot tall, just as wide, and made of pure muscle. Tommy was running down the field (speed was his talent) and this giant of a man swept into him from the side. A red and gold helmet and outstretched arms built like something from a science fiction movie pummeled him. He lay there, crunched into the grass, as he imagined the weight of the player's body pushing him straight through the earth. But when he came to, his eyes so bleary and spinning he thought he had met his maker, there was Linda, a kinesiology major doing an internship in sports medicine. Once he healed from his concussion and promised his mother that his football days were over, they began dating.

He found her capable nature appealing. He liked that she parted her dirty blonde hair right down the middle after she showered, that she didn't fuss around with makeup or spend time blow-drying and curling her hair like other college girls. Tommy found smart and sensible women attractive. Yet, even before they moved in together (a sin, Tommy's pastor had told him) he had this inkling in his consciousness that something was off. He ignored it.

Linda was not one to wait around for a man, and he didn't want to let her go, either. "Tommy," she had said after graduation, "We need to take this to the next level, I think. Decide if we want to continue this."

"Can't we wait a little?" he replied.

"Why? Are you having doubts about us?"

"No! We're just young, is all."

"What do you mean by that?" she said, scrunching her face. "I don't do anything I'm not certain of. It's not fair to string me along if you aren't sure about us."

"That's not it, exactly—"

"Well, what is it then? 'Cause if so, we should just be done with it now. We aren't college kids anymore."

He felt uncomfortable with the concept of moving in together to avoid 'being done with it' but he thought he loved her. The swiftness of her thinking amazed him. He had a soft way of making decisions, just flowing with what seemed right. Looking back, he realized that it was his age that made him so malleable. In any case, they moved into a little place not far from his mother, another thing Linda was not fond of. His brain became more muddled at every turn.

"It's not purposeful," he had said. "The house is available. And it's near work." Tommy had begun to feel that Linda thought everything he did was a personal affront to her.

"Are you planning on working the shrimp boat your whole life, Tommy?" she said, a hint of condensation in her voice.

"Well, it's not the worst job in the world, Linda," he said. This felt like an insult to his father. His heart swam in his belly.

"No, but we're losing so much land here by the Bayou. It's not exactly a sustainable career like it used to be."

He had to admit she had a valid point about the shrimping life. But in his heart, he felt something was missing in his relationship with her. It was an intangible feeling that whirled in his mind at times, late at night. But, being young and wanting it all to work out, he blotted these thoughts from his mind. Now and then, he felt the essence of Patsy Bundy in his dreams, though he knew those feelings were from a different time, a different age.

He wanted to teach literature at the high school and thought she would find this more ridiculous than shrimping. He could hear her say, "They don't pay lit teachers shit. It's not a hard science."

Patsy would not say this. He missed that, missed her. So much, that occasionally he visited their tin shack, and took in the familiar heat and earthen swamp odor as if it smelled like dozens of roses. The brick-red metal, the paint now peeling and faded, was a security blanket of sorts. The tin shack stood on its thin stilts as a memento between the two of them. Silly, he knew.

But Linda did not find it silly when she followed him there one afternoon. "Why would you come here? This place is dirty and gross."

"Just an old hangout as a kid. I come here to think."

"You know this place is possessed, don't you? Patsy Bundy and her witchery."

He laughed at this. "I never envisioned you as a believer in that stuff."

"I'm not sayin' she's a *real* witch, Tommy. That's silly. I'm saying the woman is crazy."

Tommy's chest burned. "Why did you follow me here, Linda?"

"I don't know. I just thought I'd visit you after work, and you came here instead of home. Why does that matter?"

"Patsy is not a witch," he said. "She was put through all kinds of shit in high school, just for her beliefs."

"Wow. It sounds like someone has a crush for the girl who left years ago. Unrequited love, maybe?" she said. He had not seen this side of her. It made him ill. So much for level-headed.

Linda vanished a few weeks later. He couldn't say he was all that broken up about it. Still, four years of his short life were wasted. He rearranged the furniture that was left and assured his mother that he would survive.

It took all he had to keep his fingers from the telephone, from dialing her number in Boston. He knew his mother called her every week, complicating his situation further. He didn't understand this relationship between his mama and Patsy—he figured it had something to do with her boyfriend, Pierre.

However, today would be different. He would move on and enjoy the holidays. The town of Cypress looked forward to Christmas, as they did every year. But something unsettling touched Tommy to the bone. This feeling shot through him for a week, thick as molasses running through his blood. He couldn't quite attribute it to the breakup, either. He hoped he wasn't going mad.

Two weeks before Christmas, he sat in his armchair and flipped through the channels on TV, searching for the college game scheduled for the evening, when he stopped on a national news channel.

The newscaster said, "In the little town of Cypress, Louisiana..."

What? This Cypress?

"Convicted murderer Archibald Parson's release date approaches..."

Murderer?

"In 1971, Parson was convicted of murdering a prostitute and setting her body on fire in Cypress, as well as the surrounding marshland in the Louisiana Bayou. He pled not guilty by reason of insanity. Parson reportedly believed the murder was justifiable because the woman sold sex."

Black and white photos flashed across the TV screen, pictures of the Bayou lit with fire. He identified that area, knew it by heart, even engulfed in flames.

Tommy paced the empty apartment, nausea building in his chest. He dialed Gilmore's number, shaking. "Hey, Gil. Tommy here. Did Leo arrive yet?"

"Yeah, he just landed in town earlier today. Something wrong?"

"No, I just wanted to meet up for drinks. It's been so long," he said, keeping his voice even.

"I'm so proud of my boy, Tommy. He doesn't want anything to do with shrimping, but law school will have to do, I guess," he said, laughing. "Y'all goin' to Charlie's? I'll send him that way."

"Thanks, Gil. See you at work tomorrow."

Tommy tried to breathe evenly, concentrating on the rumble of his pick-up truck as he drove. He tapped the steering wheel impatiently as he winded down the hill, to Main Street where there was street parking. The warm winter breeze was a respite from the sticky heat that bore down on Cypress most of the year, but sweat still leaked from his pores. People who worked the fishing industry met at Charlie's after they docked their boats on Friday afternoons, before the rest of the Friday crowd bustled in. As Tommy flew through the mahogany saloon doors, the pungent smack of fish, sweat and alcohol assured him that it was indeed happy hour for the boating crews. The familiarity of it wafted through his consciousness easily. He scanned the room for Leo.

Leo, however, was no longer familiar with the smell of dead fish after a semester at Yale. He sat at the counter on a red vinyl swivel chair. His dark brown skin was tinted green. Tommy waved and strode toward the bar. "Hey man, it's been so long. How's law school?"

Leo, in gray slacks and a Polo shirt, hugged him warmly. "What's the matter, dude?" he said, narrowing his eyes.

"I don't know. You tell me," he said, with an earnest look. "Who's Parson?"

"The one who's up for parole?"

"Yes! That's the only one I know of, as of an hour ago, anyway. There was a murder in Cypress that this guy's been doing time for our whole lives?"

Leo rolled his eyes and called the bartender over. "Hey, Bob! Two beers. On tap, ok?" The bartender indicated he had heard and went back to sliding shot glasses across the table and yelling for the waiter to fetch another order of hot wings.

"Alright," he said. "I may be in law school, but I know nothin' more about it than you do. Nothing about this story till last night."

Tommy lowered his voice. "We played there, Leo. When we were just kids! I saw the footage—"

"I know. It was within feet of the tin house. Strange world we live in," he said, stroking his chin. "What's weirder is that everyone knew about it. My dad remembers it clearly. He was out on the boat with Stanley when the fire started."

"I don't understand the secretiveness. This town lives for gossip. Little Patsy and her witchcraft...shit like that."

"I'll tell you why that is," said Leo. "She was a hooker. They wanted to sweep that shit into the neighbor's yard."

Tommy held his head in his hands. "I guess it's best not to ruminate on it. It just shocked me, is all."

"It's the real world, dude. If you're black, you gotta worry about this shit all the time." Leo waved toward the bar. "Hey, Bob, another round here?"

Bob slid two mugs their way and smiled. His round fleshy cheeks grew pink when he grinned. "Howdy, Leo! You just get home?" He leaned against the bar on his elbows, folding his thick, ruddy fingers against his chin.

"Yup," said Leo, and gulped his beer.

"Bet y'all are excited that Patsy's coming to town for Christmas."

Tommy's eyes widened, and he exchanged a confused look with Leo. "I didn't know anything about it."

"Ah, sorry. I thought you were buddies with her. Damn it, I'll be back. I've gotta get a refill for a customer." Bob wiped his hands on his apron and poured a shot of tequila for the man. The hum of conversation inched up a few decibels as the patrons got drunk. Bob disappeared into the crowd. Tommy and Leo had to yell to hear each other speak. Tommy's ears buzzed. He said, "I bet everyone else is off work about now. I oughta get going."

"Mmm hmm. I'll bet this whole Parson thing's why she's coming," said Leo. "But that don't mean you can't use this situation to your advantage, man."

"That sounded awful, Leo," said Tommy. "Use a dead woman to my advantage." He shook his head. "Anyway, she's got a boyfriend. She and my mama are best friends or something. I get all the gossip." He rolled his eyes.

"That doesn't mean a damn thing. You love that girl, you've always loved that girl. You gotta stop being such a coward."

Tommy sighed, and said, "Really, Leo. I've gotta go. Are you coming to Edna's Christmas Eve party?"

"I am now." He laughed. "Someone's gotta help you out."

"What does that mean?" Tommy ran a hand through his hair.

Leo said, "You tend to make a fool of yourself where Patsy's concerned," and laughed heartily. "What is it about that girl? I mean, she's cute and all."

Tommy considered this. He wondered if she was just an old crush, the one who'd been there when his father died. The one who could be strong, even at six or seven years old. "We were kids, Leo. That's all." He laughed and caught Leo's eye. The beer warmed his stomach and loosened his mouth. "Remember when we'd all sit out in that shack of hers, and you'd be yelling at Elodie for wearing those fancy lavender shoes down to the swamp?"

Leo laughed too, his breath catching in fits and starts before he could respond. "Yeah. Remember, fraternal twins are just like regular siblings genetically."

"Oh, come on, it was cute. Anyway, I'd be sitting there reading my books. Daddy had just died." His eyes wetted, though he willed them not to. Dammit. "You all would be making fun of me, for reading Jane Austen or something."

"I had to read a lot of those books in college, and I must admit, man, you were right. *Pride and Prejudice* is some good shit."

"Shut up." He threw his hands in the air.

"I'm not fucking with you, man. I'm serious."

Tommy laughed. "The point is, Patsy stared y'all down and said, 'You don't know what you're talkin' 'bout. Tommy reads books that have so much soul you can't help but get lost in 'em.'"

Leo's lips curled upward, and he squeezed Tommy's shoulder.

"Just like that. Saved my life," said Tommy.

"Patsy loves you, man. 'Cause knowing her, she was lying. About the book, I mean."

Tommy hugged his friend. "I shoulda gone to law school. I wasted too much time playing football and majoring in English. Now here I am, stuck on a shrimp boat."

"My dad loves that damn boat," said Leo, swirling around the last bit of foam in his mug.

"I know it. I'd quit if not for Stanley and your dad. For some people it's a spiritual experience the rest of us don't get, I suppose." Tommy said this thoughtfully. He understood that many people found him altogether mystifying too. Especially Linda.

"My mama doesn't like him working with Stanley. That damn Confederate flag he flies —"

"Why does he, then? I never got that."

"Can you keep a secret?" said Leo.

"Of course!"

"Well," said Leo, drumming his fingers on the bar. "It's because of me."

"That makes no sense, Leo. Gilmore is delusional about Stanley. That's the truth of it. My dad died on that boat with them, and—"

"I know that's part of it. But he'd quit that for Mama. Thing is, Stanley pays him well. All the other fisheries in town are tiny. They don't hire outside of family, and my dad is right about one thing- they're racist fucks too. Worse. I think Mama would rather have him make less doing some other job, for the principle of it."

"But that's got nothing to do with you." Tommy was confused.

"No. It does. Mama doesn't understand how much Daddy pays in student loans for my tuition." Leo sighed, and gazed at the floor. "Dad doesn't want me to have a huge debt to pay off just starting out after I graduate, so he pays 'em."

"That's amazing, Leo. And you deserve it. You got part in scholarships, make good grades. Gil knows that as soon as you graduate and get a job up there, you'll pay them back double."

"That's my plan. Doesn't stop the guilt, though. Especially when my mama gets talking."

Tommy thought for a moment, the bar now pulsing with conversation and Loretta Lynn's husky voice on the jukebox, the football game on TV. "Let's get going," he said. "My head's pounding. And mother guilt is the worst."

Leo nodded and tossed some cash on the table to settle the bill. They stepped over to the saloon doors, into the cool night. The sun had set long ago, and Tommy realized they had been sitting (and drinking) at the bar for many hours. "Did you drive?" said Tommy.

"Nah, Elodie dropped me off. She knew we'd drink too much. Wanna ride?"

"I think I'm going to walk," said Tommy. "But I'll see you at the Bundy's, okay?" Leo waved goodbye as Tommy trudged toward the empty apartment. At least living alone gave a man time to think...

Stanley sank in his orange chair, flipping through the channels on TV. The house buzzed with chatter and the grandchildren were begging his wife to get out the Christmas decorations. He sighed and pulled up the wooden lever on the side to raise the footrest.

Little Norene padded in the study, though the only studying he did was that of football games, but he liked the sound of it. "Grandpa! Gonna come decorate the tree with us?"

"In a minute, sweetheart. Your old gramps is exhausted from working all morning," he said.

She approached him for a hug, cute little thing she was. Another mini-Edna from Stan Jr. and Amanda's brood, she was four years old and curious about everything. "Wanna see something really, really neat?" she said. An ornament, shaped like a Christmas tree, hung on red yarn from between her fingers. It was hand-painted with acrylics and splotched with dots for lights. She continued, "Where did this come from?"

Stanley turned over the homemade ornament to read the toothpick scratched name engraved on the back. "Why, I guess Aunt Patsy made this when she was a girl. Probably around your age." The sound of her name pinched his heart.

"Where is Aunt Patsy? Why do we never see her?"

"It's a long story." He thought a moment. What was there to say? That Patsy left because of his foolishness? That Patsy would never come back because he was too anxious to call? That he might admit to Patsy he was wrong, but she would know he was lying for her benefit? Deep in his heart, he knew he was childish. You can be right, or you can be a father.

He had chosen to be right. Stanley's cheeks burned.

"I'm sure Grandma can help you make an ornament just like this one. All you need is flour and salt, I think. Why don't you ask her after y'all are done decorating the tree?"

The little girl ran off, looking for her grandma. Stanley didn't remember Edna having so much Christmas spirit with their own children. He knew that people changed with age—he just had not known his wife to be one of them.

He meandered into the kitchen to a gigantic mess of decorations and baked goods. He helped himself to a sad-looking gingerbread man, ugly as sin, thinking no one would mind.

"Grandpa! That's my cookie!" said six-year-old Jonah.

"Well, I apologize," said Stanley. "I swear I didn't know."

Jonah put his hands on his hips and said, with serious eyes, "You shouldn't swear, Grandpa."

"You got me, boy. I'm sorry."

Edna took a lump of cookie dough and dusted it with a bit of powdered sugar. "This is how you keep your cookies nice and tender," she told Jonah. "If you use too much flour to keep 'em from sticking, they don't turn out as well."

"Wow, Grandma. You're the smartest person I know!"

"They taste sweeter too," she said, patting his head as he scurried off.

Stanley came up behind her and kissed her cheek. "You really enjoy this, don't you?"

"I guess I do," she replied. "Sit down and decorate with us. The good news is, we clean them up, Amanda comes to fetch them, and then we relax."

He laughed. "Yeah, I'm not going out on the boat tomorrow morning."

"That's great. I'm happy you've decided to spend some time with family."

He nodded. "That, and we haven't been bringing in enough. It almost feels pointless."

"What do you mean?"

Stanley thought a minute, stroking his chin. "It seems like we just don't get what we used to. This morning we barely hauled anything. Louisiana's shrinking. The Bayou is kinda a mess. I'm not sure what to do, honey."

"Have you thought about retiring? I dunno. How many years can you keep it up, anyway?"

"What about Stan Jr.? What about Gilbert?" he said, picking up a piece of raw cookie dough and popping in in his mouth. "I planned on passing the business down to Stan. Then of course, Gil has worked with me for over twenty-five years."

"I don't know, honey. But we're fine for money."

"Edna. I do not want to live off your father's money. I've always supported us. Maybe he got us started. But I've kept this business in Cypress—"

"Stanley," she said. "The man is dead. He cannot emasculate you at this point."

"Just forget it," he said under his breath. "I'm sure the business will pick up, anyway. Have you heard from Patsy?"

"Oh, you know how it is. Patsy never visits. She calls for a two- minute conversation."

"I wish she'd visit. We haven't seen our daughter in years," he said, gazing at the floor.

Edna clasped her hands and returned to her cookies. She was done with the subject. "You know what? Let's not worry about it. They're grown-ups. They can sort their own shit out now."

She smiled wide. Marriage was a funny thing to Stanley. Full of ups and downs and sideways twists, but if you made it through to the middle, the rest of the ride mellowed out like a reward for staying around for the wild times. He loved her more than when they married. More than before gray had streaked her hair and tiny lines etched her skin. She was still Edna, though. Still went to the beauty parlor to cover that gray, still bought the tonics and lotions and wrinkle cures. He had just accepted her insecurities and tried not to trample over them, tried to avoid the tender parts of her heart that he used to be oblivious to. It wasn't so important to be right all the time. He considered his daughter. Tears threatened to betray his eyes.

"What did Patsy have to say?" he said.

"She's well. I guess Tommy called her, too. Did you know that Ruth talks with her every week?" she said.

"No, I didn't" he said. "I guess I'm not surprised."

"Well, you know how Ruth is. She's in everyone's business, so she keeps up with the gossip."

"I don't think it's that, exactly," he said.

Edna went back to rolling cookies and put a couple of sheets in the oven. It must be nice not to care so much, he thought. He wished he could just move along like his wife. He watched as she set about her business, humming *Oh Come All Ye Faithful*...and then he wondered how Edna would feel if Stan and Amanda moved away. If they took the grandchildren. He suspected it would be different. "Do you love her, Edna?" he asked.

"What on earth? Why would you even ask that?" Edna spoke in the whisper-yell tone she took on when he'd crossed a line, but the question now lay thick in the air. He could not unsay it.

"It's just," he said, and cleared his throat, "you don't seem to mind her not coming home."

"It's not that at all, Stanley. I simply refuse to get upset about stuff that never changes. Not at my age." Edna drew her lips into a pencil-thin line.

"I suppose you're right. I just miss her, is all. We haven't seen her since college graduation, but she talks to Ruth every week."

"Please don't take offense to this, but that's kinda on you," she said. She rested her forearms on his shoulders and said, "Ruth has a weird kinship with Patsy. I don't get it, but I'll be honest when I say I don't understand either one of them."

"Oh, come on, Edna." He stifled a groan.

"Well, you don't leave town for a bunch of beatniks because you've got differences from your parents. And if you do, your father takes it in stride, being the grown man and all. Hell, I know I disagreed with my father on a lot."

"Like what?" he said.

"First of all, he wasn't too fond of you when we met," she said, pointing at his chest.

"Why? 'Cause I wasn't some rich dude like y'all are accustomed to?"

"Pretty much!" She laughed. "But I did what I wanted, and he accepted it," she paused, "eventually. My point is, neither of you is very accepting."

"Oh, whatever," he snorted. "I'm going to watch football. You might want to figure out where the kids ran off to before something happens."

"I'm just sayin'…" she called after him.

"And by the way," he said, walking away, "there's no such thing as beatniks anymore."

He slumped back in his chair and clicked on the TV, sulking. He'd always known her father hadn't liked him. He hit the remote, looking for the LSU game, but stopped at a national channel, and focused on the screen. For a moment, he felt the breath sucked out of him, could hardly speak. He cleared his throat, and yelled, "Dear Lord! Edna! Did you *know* about this?"

Edna appeared in the study and groaned. "What now?"

"Honey! Look at this. They're releasing him."

"Who? What the hell are you talking about?"

"The murderer. Remember that night before Patsy was born? The fire?"

"You mean the murder on the Bayou?" His wife's eyes flooded with blankness.

"Yeah, he's being released." He focused on Edna, trying to discern her mental state.

"How the hell is that possible? Why? He committed murder and arson and he gets what, twenty-five years?"

"Crazy," he murmured. It was one of Cypress's worst moments.

His wife covered her hands and paced back to the kitchen. He sat back in the chair and changed the channel. Depressing shit right at Christmas. He hoped the psychopath wasn't considering living in Cypress. He shuddered at the thought. That poor woman, dumped in the swamp like an animal. It had affected Edna for years.

"It's awful, Stanley. He killed her, set the town on fire, and they're letting him out, just like that?"

"Edna, I know it. But it's Christmas. Can't we just have a decent Christmas?"

"I doubt her family's concentrating on the holidays, Stanley." She glared. His attempt to assuage her concerns had failed, as it had years before. The phone rang in the kitchen. "I'll be back."

He remembered that night, long ago. He wished he could erase it.

"Hey, Stanley! Guess who that was?"

Stanley groaned. "Let me guess...one of the neighbors called to report that an unidentified dog shit on their lawn and now we're hopping in the car to go to a meeting somewhere about it?"

"Why would that be exciting?" She wrinkled her nose. "Anyway. That was Patsy," she said.

"What, did something happen? Why are you acting all casual, Edna? Our daughter calls like every six months and—"

"Nope, it's good news." Edna smiled and clasped her hands like an excited little girl.

"Stop enjoying teasing me, honey. What news?" He felt like one of the ladies after some gossip. Hell, he guessed by now he was just like them, thanks to being married to Edna for nearly thirty years.

"Your daughter is coming to visit. Flying in Christmas Eve," she said, wide-eyed.

"Oh, my Lord. Wow. I can't believe it...I just can't. Everything's okay, right? Do you think it's got something to do with Parson's release?"

"Nah. I don't even think she knows about that. It was before she was born."

"Well, she's gonna find out, I guess." He frowned.

"I don't think it's anything to do with him." Edna paused dramatically and raised her palms. "She's bringing a *boy*."

"A boy?" Stanley was confused for a moment. "You don't think they're getting married, do you?"

Edna's eyes were huge. "Well, she didn't say as much, except the man wanted to meet us. My guess is he wants to get your blessing."

"That's not really Patsy's style." He laughed. "But still, I'll take it."

"I'll take any good news just about now, Stanley," she said, sighing. Her eyes trailed out the window. Stanley did not speak. He knew his wife's thoughts had drifted to the swamp Parson had thrown that poor girl into.

Edna did not have a logical reason to believe that Patsy's visit had anything to do with Parson's release, yet a coldness rushed through her. Just nerves, she told herself. That's all it is... still, she feared that her daughter had heard of the release and would stomp through town unearthing things she knew nothing of. That unfathomable night. How Edna had come undone.

That evening lived deep in her belly, where her daughter kicked and turned in that alien twisting sensation that borders on painful during those final weeks. Oh, she wanted that baby out! She had experienced this with Stan too, so it did not surprise her, but the sharp level of irritation she felt was still disturbing. If everyone would just go away. She wanted everyone to disappear and leave her in peace.

It started one afternoon in early May. Stanley, Jeb, and Gilmore were out on the boat when a light haze formed over the house. Edna stepped into the front yard and smelled smoke. A mild wildfire, maybe. Except within minutes, plumes of thick smoke dripped across the Bayou like molasses. The air grew so dense and dark that she feared for her husband, out on the Gulf, and Stan Jr., who ran about the house playing. She could do nothing but peek out the window, praying her husband would come home. Hours before the evacuation notice blared on television, she knew she should pack quickly, tossing every item they could need in a suitcase. They would go to her parents in Shreveport. But she didn't want to leave without Stanley! And what about Ruth? What about Tommy? Her mind swirled with this anxiety, this culmination of thoughts and worries that drove her to anger and tears.

She flipped on the TV. Walter Cronkite spoke with authority, and behind him was a mess of broken branches and charred land, visible in the dark to those who knew the bloom of magnolia trees and wide-based oaks and their stately presence in the area. She'd neither seen or heard of Cypress on national news.

"In the small town of Cypress, Louisiana, the unthinkable has happened," he said, with a dramatic pause. "A woman, whose name we cannot release, was kidnapped from a hotel in a neighboring town and raped and murdered. An arrest has not been made, but witnesses say suspicious activity occurred in the Bayou..."

"Mommy!" said Stan, "Why is the whole town on fire?" He had said this with wide blue eyes, just a simple question unlaced with fear, as sheltered children do. Meanwhile, Edna worried that Stanley was dead at sea and the house would burn down.

"It's not, sweetie," she'd said, biting her cheek to keep from crying. "Everything's fine. We're just gonna get in the truck and go for a little adventure to Grandma's where it's not so smoky."

Just then, Stanley's truck rolled up. The unmistakable sound of its big engine crunching up the gravel slowed her quick heartbeat.

"Edna! Edna!" he yelled, rushing through the front door, and quickly slamming it shut, as smoky air swished inside with him. He smelled like burnt toast and sweat. "Get in the car. Are you listening to the news?"

"They're saying to evacuate, Stanley. Where've you been?"

"I had to pull the boat up to the dock with zero visibility. Couldn't see two feet in front of my face. Now, it's bad out there. Let's cover our faces and get in the truck. Don't breathe this stuff, honey." He tore through the drawer by the oven and threw several dish towels to her.

They ran for the truck, coughing despite the towels. Chunks of ash rained from the sky and the ground was dusted with light gray powder. Like dark snow. They drove down the hill to Ruth's house, tires squealing as Stanley pulled into the driveway.

"Come on, Jeb! Dude, get Ruth and the baby and get in the truck!"

"All right man, I'm coming," said Jeb, through the gray curtain. "I gotta cover Tommy's head or something...I'm not sure how to do this..."

"Just run! We gotta get out of town."

Ruth held baby Tommy against her as they made their way through the gauzy night. The road ahead of them grew clearer as they left town and drove onto the highway. A somber quiet filled the air till Edna couldn't bear the pain of it and turned on the radio.

A body was found beside the swamp. It appears the killer panicked and set the trees by the wetlands ablaze...We will report later with further details...

Edna had put her head in her hands, weeping. Not here, she thought. Not in my town. She never got over that. That she should have a baby when a woman somewhere had lost her daughter that night in the flames. It didn't seem right. In her mind, it would never be right.

How, she thought now, a chasm formed between her and the daughter in her belly because of that man. She gritted her teeth, feeling guilty. She had a daughter. Another woman did not.

Chapter Twelve
EDNA AND RUTH

Ruth pushed the heavy door of the Bundy's house open. She poked her head around the foyer, and up the stairs. "Edna!" she yelled. Her eyes grew wide at the sight of the house. Edna had really outdone herself this time. Banquet-style tables were arranged in the spacious dining area, lined with heated metal serving dishes. A fountain bubbled with champagne and an array of liquors and wines sat behind the bar. The Christmas tree, decorated with little ceramic doves and white shimmering lights, was so tall it grazed the ceiling. The scent of pine needles intermingled with savory sausage. Ruth stood back, taking it in. "Edna? Y'all right, honey?"

Edna sauntered down the circular staircase, wearing a black velvet dress and dark stockings. Her hair lay in smooth sheets down her back. She must've had it done today, surmised Ruth. No one of her age has hair the color of a twenty-year-old. Humph.

"The place looks stunning." Ruth helped herself to a deviled egg. "I like how you've got the little flames underneath all the warm dishes. Salmonella sure ain't fun," she murmured. "What are you gonna do about the little kids? You don't want them to get burned."

"They know better at their age, Ruth. Why do you have to find something to be negative about all the time?"

"Oh, I'm not. Anyway, it's beautiful. Patsy and Pierre will be impressed, I'm sure," she said.

"I bet this has something to do with Parson's release. I'll bet you anything," said Edna, shaking her head. "I know it."

"I'm sure she is just coming to introduce her boyfriend to y'all," said Ruth. "Why do you always think the worst of her, anyway? If you ask me—"

"I did not ask you, Ruth. I'm just venting, is all. Is that allowed?"

Ruth flopped into the Bundy's cushy couch, glowering. "Of course. Now where's that tea you invited me over for?"

"I'll get it from the kitchen. Make yourself comfortable," she said, as Ruth put her stocking feet up a pillow. She had no intention of providing Edna with the details she wanted. She had to admit to gloating a tiny bit. Patsy entrusted

Ruth with more information than her own mother. Ruth rolled her eyes at this jealousy Edna had for her friendship with Patsy. It was exhausting. Over the years, how hard had Edna really tried to mend the relationship with her daughter? And why was Edna so damn immature?

Edna arrived back in the living room and set a tray of tea and cake on the coffee table. Ruth casually plunked a piece of pound cake on her plate and took a sip of her tea. "You've never given me this recipe. It's always been just delectable."

"You never asked," said Edna. "'Cause then you'd have to bake it yourself now and then."

"Oh, come on. I was being polite, and you're getting all snarky with me. It's not a nice way to behave when you have guests, you know."

"Ruth," said Edna, "please stop." Upon closer inspection, Ruth noticed her tired eyes.

"I know you're nervous. You haven't seen her in years and all that—"

"What are you saying?" Edna rubbed her temples.

"I'm saying you tend to be nasty when you're upset. I understand this about you, so I let it go. Patsy is not so good at this." She cleared her throat. "Obviously. So just play nice. That's my advice."

"What if she's come to stir shit up about this murder on the Bayou? You know how she is. You know it as well as I do, and you refuse to give me so much as a warning."

"Edna," said Ruth firmly, "like I said, *play nice.*" She stood and arranged a stray red curl. She patted her friend's back. "I cannot break Patsy's confidence. Not that I know a thing. However, you should be glad 'cause I wouldn't go telling your secrets either."

The murder had been a shock to every person in the town of Cypress, but it had nearly consumed Edna. Maybe it was because she'd been nine months pregnant. Maybe it was Patsy's emergency birth. As much as Edna could irritate Ruth, she'd never forget those days just after she came home from the hospital with Patsy.

•　　•　　•　　•　　•

Ruth had banged the on the door, balancing the hot macaroni casserole on one knee and the pan of brownies with her free hand. Exasperated, she set both on the porch and tried the doorbell. Tommy remained asleep in his stroller. The ding resounded into the house, but no one answered. Stan Jr. clamored about behind the door as well. Ruth attempted to peek through the frosted glass windows that surrounded the door, but they were too opaque. She muttered her annoyance under her breath and tried the door. It was unlocked. She kneeled down to pick up the food and shoved it open, yelling, "Edna! I've brought food!"

Ruth's voice caught in her throat upon entering the house. Her mouth fell agape. Toys streamed everywhere, something Edna never allowed. Laundry, unsorted and potentially not even clean, poured over the couch like a pile of deflated balloons. Ruth set the food in the kitchen, amid stacks of dirty dishes, when she heard the baby howling. Poor thing sounded like she'd been crying a long time, the way she'd stop, hiccup and start again with newfound zest. Now, she knew something was off. Edna would not let a newborn cry like that. Not ever.

Ruth climbed over more junk littering the hall, and up the circular staircase. She swallowed hard, throwing the door open to the master bedroom. "Edna!" she cried. Her friend lay there in bed, curled on her side. Baby Patsy was in the bassinet beside her, screaming.

"On my Lord, Edna! What is wrong, honey?" Ruth picked up the baby, and shushed her gently, till she calmed and conformed to Ruth's body. "What the— Why are you not picking this child up? She's hungry, Edna!"

"She just ate an hour ago," said Edna, rubbing her eyes. Her voice was hoarse.

"Well, she's a newborn baby! She needs to eat when she's hungry! Why are you just lying there?"

Edna sighed. "I'm still in pain, Ruth. It's hard to get up, lift her out, and feed her. I'm just not myself yet, that's all."

"Well, you should have called. I'm here. I'll help you, till you get settled and the incision heals," she said. Still, looking around the bedroom, Ruth could not conceal how flabbergasted she was. It wasn't that the house was dilapidated, or unfit for human habitation. It was that she'd seen Edna polish imaginary dirt. The woman refused to hire help because no one did it right! And now dishes and toys and laundry—well, it was just not like her. Ruth took a steady breath. She needed to get to the bottom of this situation.

"Maybe we ought to move the cradle closer to the bed?" said Ruth, thinking. She'd heard of women going crazy after childbirth. God, she hoped that wasn't what was happening to Edna. "Stanley's working now?"

"Yes," she sighed, clutching the pillow beside her. "To be honest, he's been doing most of her care. On account of the surgery. Ruth, you have no idea just how dangerous childbirth can be." Her eyes flooded with tears. "I coulda died. Just like in the old days, women can still die."

Patsy could have died too, Ruth knew. Yet Edna didn't seem to care much about the baby. Ruth had read about this somewhere, and it scared her. "Still, you've gotta care for her when Stanley isn't home. Maybe I should be here, during the day. Just till you're back to yourself."

Edna shrugged and lay back on the pillow. "Did they find out what happened? To that woman?" she said.

Ruth pursed her lips, hesitating. "Well...sort of..."

"What does that mean? Sort of?" Dark circles hung from Edna's eyes.

"Okay," she replied, sighing. "A woman over the hill...you know, in Fuller." She waved her arm with raised eyebrows. Fuller was a high-crime neighboring community. The people of Cypress spoke of it only in hushed tones. "A lady of the night, you know what I mean?"

Edna's eyes widened and she slid back on her elbows, lifting her head up and close to Ruth. "What happened?"

"She was with a man— a John. That's what they call it."

Edna nodded, eyes wider still. "My Lord."

"In the hotel over there. I can't remember the name of it, but that really scummy one," said Ruth, lowering her voice. She peeked around the door to make sure Stan couldn't hear.

"Oh, come on, tell me!" said Edna. "He's all the way downstairs."

"All right. Apparently, he strangled her, dumped the body in the swamp, and set fire to the bald Cypress trees." She inhaled slowly, hoping Edna wouldn't go even more insane than she already had. But, she decided, might as well get it all out in the open. It would be worse for Edna to catch the story on the evening news.

"How the—"

"I know. But apparently one can set fire, even down there, with copious amounts of *gasoline*."

"Sweet Jesus," Edna murmured, "I can't believe it. Still, I can't say I'm not a bit relieved."

"What? Why?" Ruth narrowed her eyes. The woman had certainly lost her mind. Ruth was sure of it, now.

"Well, a hooker and all. In a bad part of town. I'm not saying it's her fault. Risky choices, is all," she said, and shook her head.

"Edna, I know you're in a bad way," she said, raising her voice and gazing at little Patsy. "But it's easy enough for us to say she made bad choices. Maybe she didn't have a choice. She coulda had a kid to feed. We just can't judge."

"Of course," said Edna, her cheeks flushing.

Ruth patted her friend's arm and continued, "Can't judge anyone but the monster who killed her."

Edna curled back in bed, staring at the wall. Ruth sighed, noticing the mounds of greasy hair on the pillow. "Honey, you're dirty. I think you'd feel just a tiny bit better if we got your hair clean."

"I can't get the incision wet. Stanley's been sponge bathing me. I'll be fine for a few days, Ruth." She pursed her lips tight, tears welling in her eyes.

"C'mon, sweetie," said Ruth firmly. She slid her arm under her friend, who still felt hollow-boned, despite having just given birth. Edna winced, pressing her hand to her lower belly. "I feel like an elephant. It's going to take forever to get rid of this weight."

"It's okay, we're just taking about ten steps to the bathroom," she said, embarrassed by the thickness of her own waist and thighs. She sucked in her stomach and focused on guiding Edna to the large, crisp bathroom. As she drew open the curtains, the afternoon sun poured in. The Bundy's lawn stretched out like a football field. A lavender painted wood bench was surrounded by ivory daffodils with their bright orange centers. Funny how alive it was out there.

A memory of the two of them, with a gaggle of other teenaged girls piled in this very bathroom, when Edna's parents still lived in the house, floated through Ruth's mind. They were grooming for a football game at Jackson High, puckering their lips in the mirror and powdering their faces, when Edna decided that it was "time to do something with this hair, Ruth!" The girls nodded in agreement, and Ruth sat down, feeling ashamed of her red frizzy curls. The humidity did not help, and no blowout or smoothing iron could beat the thickness of the air in Cypress, could compete with the texture of Ruth's hair. The second she stepped outside, whatever shape she had cajoled her hair to take reverted back to frizz. And oh, she'd been made fun of! When they hit sixteen, Edna decided that taming Ruth's hair was a personal project. Ruth sat in the chair while they murmured and tugged, her face collecting fat beads of sweat from the heat of the roaring blow dryer. And, as her wet hair dried, it puffed up yet again, except this time all crinkly and hard from the copious amounts of cold gel Edna had run through it. The disapproving shake of her head, the feeling that welled in her chest, that adolescent pain; Ruth thought it had gone as the years went by. But there in the bathroom, with the sight of her own flabby stomach in the mirror and the maternity stretch pants she'd struggled to pull over her hips that morning, well, it rose inside her again...

But today, Edna wobbled to the bathroom, where Ruth had set out a wooden chair from the kitchen and spread white, fluffy towels on the floor. "You know," said Ruth, "I understand you're recovering and all, but my aunt is a labor and delivery nurse. You should be taking light walks around the house." She spoke with authority.

"The doctor said that too," Edna murmured under her breath. "Easy for him to say."

"Well, clean hair never hurt anybody," said Ruth, peering back toward the bedroom. Patsy was asleep in her cradle. Tommy's chest rose up and down, with his head cocked to the side and full, pink lips puckered like rosebuds. Ruth smiled and turned her attention back to Edna, who leaned her head back and shut her eyes. With a basin of warm water and soap, and a pitcher with fresh water for rinsing, Ruth went to work. "Now, just pretend you're at a beauty parlor," she said, covering Edna's forehead with a washcloth to protect her eyes from soap, like she did when she bathed Tommy. She massaged a thick dollop of shampoo at her scalp, letting the suds run down the length of her hair. She poured the warm water over Edna's dense black hair, running her fingers through it, till it lay in sheets of velvet over the sink.

"Doesn't that feel better?" she said. Edna smiled weakly and touched her hair with her fingers. Ruth squeezed out the excess water in a clean towel, combing gently through the knots, first with her fingers, then a comb. She worked wordlessly, and wrapped a towel around her friend's head, pretending not to notice the tears that streaked Edna's sallow cheeks and the choking noise she made as she began to cry.

"Well, I'm going to change these sheets," she said, heading toward the bedroom. Edna's eyes fluttered in acknowledgment. Ruth took Patsy, still satisfied with a belly full of milk, in one arm and pushed the stroller with the other hand. Trying to push the stroller in a straight line while cradling the infant was arduous, and Ruth felt a tinge of sorrow for Edna. It couldn't be easy, she thought.

Stan Jr. had quieted—never a good sign, Ruth knew. "Stan!" she yelled towards the playroom. "Whatcha doing?"

"Playing!" said Stan, as she arrived down the hall. Piles of toys blocked the entrance. Talk about a fire hazard, she thought with a groan. This room was her first order of business. Ruth's eyes met the little boy's, who radiated excitement and held back peals of laughter.

"Hey, Mrs. Marks," he said.

Why was this boy so happy, being left to play alone all day?

Then she saw it. The boy had emptied a bottle of talcum powder and the dust from it formed a hazy cloud. "You can't be breathing that, Stan!" She pushed the stroller back, set Patsy on the floor, who woke up screaming, and rushed in to retrieve him from sure lung damage. "Goddammit, Stan! You're gonna suffocate! Why on earth would you empty that out?"

"Big cloud," said Stan, and pointed to the sky, showing off his burgeoning language development. "It's a *really* big cloud."

Ruth knelt to Stan's level, and said, "How do you like having a baby sister?"

He banged a toy pan with a wooden spoon and shrugged. "She's all right, but she doesn't play games."

"She will when she gets bigger. How's your mama been?"

He pointed to the bedroom. "Tired and sad. She doesn't play anymore. Daddy says she'll be better soon."

"I'm sure that's true, honey. Aunt Ruth's gonna be around to help for a while. Does that sound fun?"

Stan smiled and said, "Oooh, that will be so fun! Do you know how to make stuff with Play-Doh?"

"I suppose I'll figure it out. Can you teach me?"

"Yes, I can! I'm bestest at making stuff."

Ruth patted his head, as his blue eyes grew wide with excitement. "All right, Stan. But you've got to promise to be a good boy for your mama. Everyone's still adjusting, but it will be back to normal soon."

"That's what Daddy said. We've just got to wait it out. Right?"

"You're a very smart boy, Stan. No more getting into stuff, though." Ruth shook her index finger sternly. The boy nodded and ran off to his next adventure. "And maybe we can play outside. You need to run off that energy."

•　　•　　•　　•　　•

With this memory, Ruth understood that there were limits to what Edna could handle. "Are you okay?" she said.

"I'm fine. Why wouldn't I be fine? Geez, Ruth." She pursed her lips.

"I'm just making sure, honey," said Ruth. "I know this murder business affected you. Maybe because you were so pregnant."

"Ruth, it was a horrible thing. Just awful. It affected everyone." She meandered into the kitchen.

"All right...if you say so." Ruth twisted her face in concern.

"I don't want to discuss it anymore," Edna replied, smoothing her skirt. She arranged a stray hair behind her ear. "I've got work to do."

Ruth trudged across the living room and to the door. "You could be nicer when a person shows concern for you, Edna."

"I'm plenty nice."

"Yeah, yeah. Tommy and I will be back over later." Ruth snorted and went home.

Daisy finished up the last few jobs before her shift was over. Shoved the rough bristled broom in short strokes against the warehouse floors, kicking up clouds of dust as she worked. Wiped down the public restroom counters and rusty sinks that would never come clean, scrubbed the stained toilet bowls till her fingers bled. It didn't help that her swollen wrists ached from arthritis. She peeled off the yellow rubber gloves and washed her hands, though the smell of bleach still stung her nose. Sitting on the bench in the break room, she took a breath or two before gathering her things from the locker and changing out of her shiny black shoes. She found comfort in this routine.

She unpinned her name tag, stuffed it in her pocket, and approached the manager. "Off already?" said Mr. Johnson, glancing at his wristwatch. Daisy had worked at this Walmart for twenty years. Mr. Johnson had a kindness about him, as long as you got the job done. And Daisy never failed at this.

"Yes, sir. I was wondering if you had my check?"

"'Course," he said, flipping through a stack of envelopes. "Thanks for working overtime this week. We needed it."

"Any time, Mr. Johnson. I sure could use the extra money, too." She folded the envelope and put it in her bag.

He returned to his paperwork. Daisy headed from the darkened warehouse to her car, praying the engine would turn over on the first try. The Pontiac coughed a few times, exhaling a sputter of exhaust. She hit the gas, hoping to coax the engine to life.

Whew. It started.

Daisy's heart pattered. She headed down the road and out of town a ways. The brakes crunched as she pulled into the parking lot of the payday loan store, where she cashed her checks and made a small payment on the loan she'd taken out the last time the Pontiac broke down. Old cars were expensive. Poverty was expensive.

A new girl stood behind the counter, wearing thick glasses with red frames and brown hair pulled back in a ponytail. "Hi, ma'am," she said. "I need to cash a check and make a payment." Daisy slid the check and her ID under the thick glass window.

"I'm sorry, Mrs. Greene, but we can't cash this. ID's expired."

Daisy sighed. "John cashes my checks all the time. I plan to renew my ID, but I've gotta wait till I get a day off. You know how it is?" She said this with pleading eyes. The rent was due today. Hell, it was due last week. She'd had to beg the landlord for the extra few days.

"This is the last time, and then you're out," he had said, with a snap of his fingers.

"All right," said the girl. "Just this once, okay?" She counted the cash out and passed the stack of bills to Daisy, minus twenty-five dollars toward the loan. Daisy sighed. She had grown weary of asking people to make exceptions for her. *Just this once.*

Daisy murmured a thanks and rushed to the safety of her car. She worked out of town, took out her loan out of town, and shopped out of town. She could not risk people talking. They kept the curtains drawn in the little house, and with the exception of work, she and Rosie rarely left the house.

Except today was payday. They needed groceries, and with the overtime, Daisy could treat herself to a coffee. She tried to frequent different stores, large ones, not like the little stores in Cypress where everyone knew everybody. People who came to small towns to hide had it backwards, she thought. You gotta be where you can blend in. No one would notice a grandmother in a Walmart uniform with gray hair and deep wrinkles at a supermarket. She could fade into the aisles as people bustled by to buy their groceries and get home to make dinner.

•　　•　　•　　•　　•

"Oh, Mamaw, what are we gonna do?" she said, pacing the tiny dark house. "Why can't we move? Get out of this place." She pointed to the overgrown yard, where a ribbon of sunlight cut through the half-drawn curtain.

"Too expensive, Rosie," said Daisy, holding her face in her palms. "We've known this was coming. He's no danger to us." She said this less convincingly than she intended. She moved away from the window, as if the worn velour curtains had created shelter for the two of them all these years. Really, all they had was a tiny dilapidated house ensconced in weeds dense enough to rip a foot open and Parson's imprisonment keeping them safe. Daisy understood that everything depended upon Archibald Parson remaining behind bars. Hiding only kept the town quiet, and hell, the need for that had passed. The town had forgotten her daughter long ago.

Matilda's ghost wasn't floating around the Bayou, she thought, indignant at this notion. The only ghosts hidden in the thickly-wooded swamp were her and Rosie. "I wish we could, though... boy, I wish we could just up and move. Start afresh."

"Again, the problem is money," said Rosie, smashing a clenched fist into her palm. "Always money. Lucky it's payday. We've got toilet paper, at least."

Daisy felt her cheeks color. God, the guilt that burned inside her when Rosie said these things! "I've done my best...I think your mama would know I have tried."

"I know, Mamaw, I know. I'm just scared. What if this man—"

"Nothing's gonna happen," Daisy said firmly. "And you know what? You're gonna quit that crap job of yours at the Piggly Wiggly and go to the junior college. There's one good thing about the whole town knowin' everything..." She smiled, shaking her index finger.

"What?" said Rosie.

"We've got nothing left to hide." Her voice cracked into a peculiar laugh. Rosie joined her in this maniacal laughter, till they both had tears running down their faces. Daisy plopped on the thin carpet, and said, "I'm too old for this shit. I really am."

"Let's go out," said Rosie. She smiled, tentatively at first, and then wider. Daisy had not seen her granddaughter smile like that since she was a child. "Alright. If that's what you want."

"I think I do," she replied. "Can we go to Charlie's? Everyone in town goes there. I've always wanted to see what it's all about."

Daisy's stomach twisted. She rifled through her purse and opened the wallet. God, they could not afford this. Christmas would be bad enough. She inhaled slowly, and finally said, "Let's go then. And honey, brush your hair. You've got your mama's beautiful hair, but you just let it hang there—" She stopped herself; it was the first time Rosie had anything but a scowl on her face and she didn't want to spoil the moment.

But Rosie had already wandered into the bathroom, fumbling around for a brush. "Get the keys. I hear the place is crowded Fridays. For all we know we'll blend right in. Like you said, it's been a long time."

Daisy doubted this. Matilda's picture was plastered all over national television. The whispers had already begun, but she was more concerned about Parson, about to spring loose like an alligator crawling out of the swamp.

They chose a dimly-lit booth at Charlie's. Daisy found the noise of the patrons grating. She'd spent years cloaked in silence, a side benefit of relative isolation. But the way Rosie chattered made her heart swell, and when she had asked if they could afford hot wings, Daisy said yes. She added up the bill in her head, the rent and how much they had left till payday...oh, every bone ached with exhaustion! She couldn't stand the idea of breaking the girl's spirit further. As her stomach swirled with a warm buzz from the six-dollar beer, she decided to deal with the consequences later.

"Mamaw, I think I'm going to put a song on the jukebox," she said. Daisy watched Rosie step tentatively through the crowd with a quarter for the machine. Her granddaughter was a twenty-five-year-old little girl. She laid her head on her arms, now dotted with brown splotches and spider veins. She closed her eyes, immersed in the music, ignoring the up and down rhythm of conversation around her.

Entranced by the candle that illuminated the wall in an exaggerated shadow, Daisy watched Rosie dance with a group of people. A couple of boys racked pool balls on the felt table; the music permeated the small bar. Rosie looked so much like her mother from this distance that Daisy felt a surge of fear. She was now older than her mother had been when she died, and far less carefree.

Daisy motioned for the bartender and ordered a bourbon, ignoring her light wallet. A couple sat on her left, holding hands and talking in hushed tones. On her right, a crowd of young women shared a pitcher of beer. She took in the world slowly, inebriated enough that she could put herself back in her old life.

"So'd y'all hear Patsy Bundy's coming to town?"

"Yeah, for Edna Bundy's annual Christmas party, I suppose."

"Nah. She hasn't been back for years. I highly doubt Edna's little shindig means much to her. She's a city girl, now. A Yankee."

Daisy flew out of her hazy state and listened close.

"How much you want to bet it's got something to do with Parson?"

"I heard she's bringing her boyfriend to town..."

"Yeah, right. It's got something to do with her visions. She isn't the type to bring a boyfriend home for daddy's approval."

The group chortled.

Christ. Daisy gathered her purse and got up, leaving her drink half-finished. She walked across the bar, breathing steadily, and grasped her granddaughter's arm. "Let's go," she said. Rosie stood straight and followed. They stepped into the night, arm in arm. They would not be seen in Cypress again.

"Work and home, alright? Till this mess is sorted."

"Got it," said Rosie. She squared her arms against her body and twisted her lips into their usual scowl.

Chapter Fourteen
THE POET

Patsy stood in the parking lot of the rental car place as Pierre arranged their luggage in the trunk. She shut her eyes tight and took a slow, deep breath. The heavy, salt-infused air lay on her shoulders, and she felt the wetlands hiding somewhere in the distance. She envisioned running through the wet mud on rainy days and choosing the tallest galoshes that made the biggest, cloppiest sound possible. It was a balmy winter day, something Pierre kept repeating. "Can you believe it's so sunny?" he would say, as they drove through the city and into Cypress.

"Indeed, I can," she would say with a laugh.

"This is amazing! Pull over and sit on the moss-covered rock over there so I can get a picture. It's so pretty with the shade from the tree."

"You know how to work a 35mm?" she said, with raised eyebrows.

"I'm sure I can figure it out. Pass it over."

She watched him fumble with the settings. "It's not a Polaroid, Pierre," she said, "and I'm not setting up a tripod here. Let's go."

For someone who didn't respect nature photos, he sure made good use of her photography skills. She gloated and leaned back in her seat. "Enjoying the view?" They passed through the smooth city streets and hit the dirt roads and gravel of town, kicking up dust. She coughed and rolled up the window. "I guess I'm not used to it anymore."

"It's like something on TV."

"That's how I felt the first time I saw snow. Then I discovered it was cold and wet."

Pierre rummaged through his bag, clinking his electric toothbrush against a can of deodorant. "Crap," he said.

"What now?" she said.

"I need the foil thing that goes under my shaver. Is there a store around here?"

"Pierre, for shit's sake. We're in Cypress. Why didn't you tell me this back at the airport?"

"Well, there's gotta be a store around here," he said with a shrug.

"Yeah, there's a general store with batteries and stuff. But not a Nordstrom's with the accessories needed for that," she said, pointing at the polished electric shaver. "I guess we can stop and get you something to use temporarily...Humph," she said, examining the razor. "That thing could be a vacuum cleaner with all those attachments."

"Like what?"

"Like Bic."

He sighed and slumped in his seat, glowering at her.

"Seriously. You asked me what small towns are like. I gave you a rather extensive list of what we *don't* have."

"Whatever," he said. "I can rough it a couple of days, I guess."

Patsy smirked and pulled into the General Store. It seemed tiny with cracks running down the beige stucco walls and a sign hung haphazardly in the window. Patsy felt unsettled walking into the place. The door swung open a little too loud. The bells rang throughout the claustrophobic space, announcing their arrival. Shampoos and feminine products and batteries lined metal shelves. "It's kind of like a dollar store," said Pierre.

"Exactly. If you want groceries, there's Cypress Market. If you want a goddamn electric shaver, you get it in the city, *where we just were.*"

She peered around the aisle for Mr. Betterman. As she turned the corner, a little boy ran into her, screaming. His mother followed, yelling, "No, dammit. Peter. I said NO!" The little boy had three bags of candy clutched in his hands. "All you need is more sugar."

"I'm sorry, ma'am," said the mother. "This one's a bit out of sorts..." her voice trailed off as she met Patsy's eyes. "Wow, Patsy, I haven't seen you in years."

Leigh stood before her, clearly pregnant and chasing after a wild toddler. Patsy found it difficult to hate her in this moment. She gave Patsy a half-hug and a conciliatory smile. She wore a flowing dress and flip-flops. Her round belly prevented her from fetching the boy. He ran back to the candy aisle. Leigh wiped the layer of sweat from her face. She held the small of her back with her hand, swaying back and forth.

"Yeah, I'm here to visit my parents for Christmas," said Patsy.

"Have you heard what's going on around here?" said Leigh in a low voice.

"You mean Parson?"

"Yes, that's what I mean. Isn't it just terrifying?" Her eyes widened.

"It is," she said casually, not wanting to get dragged into Leigh's gossip. "When's the baby due?"

"Any time now," said Leigh, staring at the floor. "It's a girl."

"That's amazing! Now you'll have one of each."

Leigh bit her lower lip, and said, "I can't wait."

"Why do you look so glum?" Patsy was confused by Leigh's demeanor. Every friend of hers who had children hoped to have a daughter someday. "I thought y'all love doing girl stuff like pedicures and dolls." Patsy had never enjoyed such things. Her mother was confounded by her penchant for playing with mud.

"It's this murderer being released, is all. It scares me. I was so happy to find out she was a girl. But then—"

"Then what?" Patsy was very confused.

"It's still a dangerous world for us, Patsy. You know that. And as much as I teach *my* boy about respecting women, well, there are men out there that don't know a thing about it. I'm scared. With this man about to be freed."

Patsy understood that this was true. The two women's eyes met. "I guess I don't know how I'd feel, expecting a baby girl in this world."

"I'm so angry at this man. Did you know a thing about it when we were kids?"

"Nope. They tended to keep murder and prostitution a secret, I guess." Patsy grimaced.

"Little girls playin' witch was another story," said Leigh. "I'm sorry. We were awful."

"Well," Patsy started, but Pierre popped up behind her.

"Hey, found a razor," he said, holding up a package of disposable razors. "They'll be okay for a few days." He flashed a wry grin, and added, "Is this a friend of yours?"

"Yeah, Leigh, this is Pierre. I guess we'll see you at my parent's party?"

"Oh, yes. And this one will be at home." She laughed. "Talk more then, okay?"

Patsy nodded and they headed to the car. "That kid was crazy," said Pierre.

"I think they're all like that," she replied, barely listening.

"You remembered your birth control pills, right?" he said, with a smirk.

"Hilarious." She laughed. "Why, you aren't ready for a child climbing all over the place just yet?" She fell back into her mind, and Pierre gazed out the window. He stopped commenting on the foliage. Uneasiness coursed through her blood, thickening with each mile. Parson had served his time. That's what they said. She gripped the steering wheel. She wanted to flip that car around and head back to Boston. But Patsy didn't operate that way.

"Pretty sexist of that woman to not want a baby girl though. Besides, I thought all women wanted girls. I think my mother was disappointed when I turned out to be another boy."

"I'm sure she was not," said Patsy.

"Then why did she force me to hang out with her all the time like the daughter she never had?"

"I don't think that's what Leigh meant," Patsy said. "She's not unhappy the baby's a little girl. She's scared...Parson's getting out of prison. The world is full of men like him, men who commit these awful crimes and don't get nearly enough time. You think if it was some rich girl uptown he would have gotten off so easily?"

"You mean like you?"

"Yes. That's what I mean."

Pierre turned toward the window, gazing into the sunshine. "We've got murderers and police brutality and rape in Boston, too. I think you've romanticized the city," he said.

"We do," she agreed.

But was impossible for Pierre to understand the catcalls, the fear of being followed to a vehicle at night, the endless warnings of how to avoid date rape. What to wear to avoid rape. What not to wear. To use caution in being too enticing to the vulnerable eyes of a man.

None of this had fully changed. Not in Cypress. Not in Boston. Not anywhere.

They drove the last stretch of the journey, a light wind picking up rust-colored leaves from the oak trees, scattering them about as they rushed by. The red and gold leaves were the only indication that winter had arrived. This year it didn't appear to Patsy that the trees would even go bare. Certainly nothing like the dainty, skeletal trees in Boston. The car grew even quieter the closer they got to the Bundy plantation. She felt the soul of the Bayou undulating through the air. Funny how there are certain places like that, she thought. Towns that feel alive.

Someone wanted to tell her something here. She felt that electric surge to the very tips of her fingers. As they drove up the winding path to her parent's home, she wiped these thoughts away. The yellow house stood tall as ever, the wide-based oaks still rooted deep in the soil, and Mama's garden was manicured and neat, with the same freshly unfurled flowers poking up from the ground. Patsy took a piece of gum from the pack on the dash, and chewed it till her jaw was sore. "You ready?" she said.

"Hell, yes, I am," said Pierre. "This place is amazing."

"Good lord, Pierre, stop. Your parents' place is a mansion."

"I know, but this is, like, historical."

"Shut the fuck up," she snorted. "We aren't tourists."

"I know, I know. We're playing detective under the guise of visiting your parents." He tossed a bag over his shoulder. "Lead on."

They started the walk up the drive when Mama and Daddy appeared, waving. Both her parents rushed to meet them, and Edna threw her arms around her daughter. "You look beautiful, honey. Just beautiful."

"This is Pierre."

Stanley shook his hand, and Edna led him into the house, gushing about the food. Pierre's parents frequented country clubs and attended charity dinners. He moved with an easy confidence. He could handle one Southern belle for the evening. "So, did Mama plan a massive Christmas celebration to relax her nerves?"

"Pretty much," said Daddy, with his smile emphasizing the new wrinkles around his eyes. They crinkled as he took her hand warmly. "Do-over?"

"Of course," she said, "as long as you behave yourself."

"You got it." He slung one of her bags over his shoulder, and they headed up the walkway to the house. "Ruth'll be over soon."

She could not hold back her happiness at this. "Tommy?"

"Him too."

"I suppose Mama's invited half the town," she said.

Stanley rolled his eyes. "Probably all of them."

Chapter Fifteen
PAST LIVES

She caught his eye from across the room. His lovely, upturned lips and thumbs hooked to the belt loops of his faded Levis, sent her back in time. Tommy's presence reminded her that you could make hard stuff seem easy. That was what she'd liked about him. And Ruth too. They had been through hell and it sure as shit could have killed them, but it did not. In the glimmer of his eyes, she felt a sorrow that bubbled over him, oozed down the back of his neck. Not everybody could see the calmness about him. How he set people at ease. He did not like fiery confrontations. Patsy was already embarrassed for him. She would not fight with her father. She promised herself this, twice.

He was nothing like the Bundys. Her cheeks grew hot.

She smiled and waved, leading Pierre over to the oysters chilling on ice. Ruth stood beside her son and sucked down a raw oyster slathered in hot sauce. "Patsy!" she exclaimed, tossing the shell in the trash and wiping her hands on a cloth napkin. She threw the crumpled ivory linen on the table, and briskly crossed the room, the aroma of her perfume wafting along with her. She drew Patsy into a crushing embrace. Ruth hugged hard. Mama gave graceful half-hugs. Patsy was uncomfortable with both.

She writhed out of Ruth's grip and noticed Pierre looking forlorn several steps back. "Pierre, come meet Ruth and Tommy," she said.

Ruth's loquaciousness relieved a bit of the palpable tension that flowed between Tommy and Pierre. "Didn't your mother do such a lovely job on the place?" she said. "Why, these oysters are delicious. Try one, Pierre. I've heard so much about you."

"Shouldn't you introduce me to your friend?" said Pierre.

"Oh, why, Tommy and Patsy have played together since they were in diapers! Didn't you tell Pierre all about that? It really was cute how they'd run around naked in the sprinklers together," said Ruth.

Patsy groaned. She was not easily embarrassed, but Pierre's cheeks colored, and he gazed at the ground. "Well, why don't you guys...catch up? I think I'll try this amazing Creole food Mrs. Bundy has prepared."

He disappeared and could be heard profusely thanking her mother. He asked just how her delicacies were prepared. And did she order them in? She did not! Edna had spent hours on every dish! This, of course, flattered her mother immensely, and the knots in Patsy's neck relaxed.

"How's it going, Tommy?" she asked, lips turning up slightly.

"It's going." He leaned against the buffet table and tapped his foot.

"Tommy is doing wonderful, Patsy. I'm not sure why he's always so shy about his accomplishments. He's looking at grad schools, aren't you, honey?"

"Well…I have…but I'm not sure…" His cheeks turned the color of a ripe tomato, maybe from the heat emanating from the buffet table, she thought. Except they stood by the oysters and crabs nestled on mounds of ice. It must have been strange for him, seeing her after all this time.

"I guess you heard about that murderer up for parole, right?"

"Oh yes, it's shocking." He appeared relieved to change the topic.

Ruth agreed. "Twenty-five years for murder and arson…it's not right," she murmured. "I need to help your mother, Patsy. You two all right?"

"Yes, we are, mother," said Tommy. "We ran around naked together as children," he added, glowering.

"Oh, shut it. I was just making conversation. Everything embarrasses this one, Patsy. I tell you, it's exhausting." She stepped away and called for Edna, frizzy curls bobbing as she sailed through the crowd.

Patsy laughed. "She tries, Tommy. You gotta give her that."

Their eyes met again, and Tommy raised his eyebrows. "She's a good mother."

"C'mon, let's get a drink," she said. "You'll like Pierre, I promise."

Tommy groaned. "I know why you're here. It's got nothing to do with Christmas or your boyfriend."

"What makes you say that?" she said, trying to appear surprised.

"It's about Parson. It's about your visions. Don't lie to me, Patsy Mae. You're not capable of it." He raised his eyebrows, smirking.

"Oh, whatever," she said. "Don't you get *bored* here, eventually?"

"It's not the city, that's for sure. What do y'all do up north?"

"I take pictures," she said lamely. "And go to museums and concerts—"

"What about your friends? Are they marrying off yet?" He laughed. "That's the problem here. All my friends have deserted me for relationships."

"Friends?" Patsy considered this. "I guess it's me and Pierre now."

"Uh huh," said Tommy. "Truth is, you've got trust issues."

"Shut up! That is not—"

"Yep. That's it. Trust issues," he said, shaking his head. "Your brain has been like the unconquerable Rubix cube in my life forever…"

"Good lord, you're drunk."

"And now I've figured it out."

"You haven't figured a damn thing out. How much whiskey have you had? I need a drink, too. Coming?"

Tommy grumbled and followed her into the decadent table only Mama could set up, and all on her own. She plucked a mini-cheesecake off the dessert bar and filled her glass with champagne. Following the back of Tommy's neck, she watched the casual way he leaned against her mother's linen table. He didn't give a shit how much that set up cost or how long it took. Her breath caught in her throat, and she averted her gaze. Where had Pierre gone?

Guests trickled in like ants raiding a picnic. The Ladies' Club acquainted her with their usual smiles and how do you dos...

Isn't it snowing in Boston now...a real white Christmas...why, I'm so jealous, dear.

Parties in Boston involved kegs of beer, stacks of pizza boxes, and real Chinese food. But people were just people. Unless they were family, thought Patsy. That's what fucked up a place. Familiarity. She felt naked here; she knew her arrival was second only to Parson's release, as far as rumors went. They imagined her to be self-confident, and she had thought she was, until they exited the plane and her mind began to spin.

This vulnerability did not sit well with Patsy, but fortunately it did not last long. Elodie and Leo appeared at her side, offering warm embraces. With this, Patsy reminded herself that she did have friends. Real friends, not the ones her mother conjured up for her from the Ladies' Club.

"Patsy!" cried Elodie. "Where have you been all these years? I get one phone call every six months and a promise for a visit that never happens." Elodie wore a black velvet dress and neat cornrows in her hair. Patsy smiled, remembering how Elodie used to complain when her mama put her hair up with those elastic ponytail holders with the plastic balls that smacked against her head. It was every 80s child's nightmare.

"You blame it all on me. I know you've got children but none of y'all come up to Boston."

"That's true." Patsy had suspected Elodie would settle down first, of the four of them. Leo thought he knew everything, and sure, he was smart. His arrogance pissed Patsy off at times. The two of them could argue. But Elodie kept everyone straight, managed every disagreement. Patsy now understood how tiresome of a child she must have been; now she exhausted herself. She wanted to go home.

She would make it through this evening, snoop around for a bit of information, and get out of here.

"Oh, Elodie. Here's Pierre. Come and meet Pierre," she said, and the two women crossed the room, calling his name. She watched him stroke his chin, making small talk with her father. Her anxiety skyrocketed. She could have sworn her blood pressure plummeted to her feet.

Seven years was not so long, at Stanley's age, especially when his youngest child stood before him in the living room, the same except perhaps, Edna had said, she had done something with her hair. In his mind, she was still the baby in his lap, and then the little girl catching lightning bugs in the backyard on summer nights. Even at this party, the sound of the screen door clanged somewhere in his heart, his wife yelling at all the neighborhood children, "In or out! In or out! You're getting your wet feet all over my clean floors."

The moment he caught her eyes in his heart, the anger that had knocked around in his chest since she'd left disappeared. She was sophisticated as Edna, mingling with a man on her arm, who filled her flute with champagne, and all the niceties he expected from a suitor of his daughter's. Yet, she was still Patsy, and he should not have gotten caught up in such reverie with a head full of liquor and the weakness he'd always had for his daughter. Her blood ran blue. This would always be the case, yet he'd hoped she'd see his side of things; he always had that hope. He would try to convince her, though by his age he knew people don't decide that they're wrong just because you say so. Even your own children. Hell, with your children, these disagreements almost never end well.

This time, it had been seven whole years. He yearned for her to stay home for good. He promised himself, no matter what nonsense she said, to keep his mouth shut. He loved her, and she loved him, and there would be no talk about Confederate flags, women in business or politics. She had matured, as it was. What was the worst that could happen? He doubted she would run down to the Bayou just to set a flag on fire. They had gotten past that, he thought.

It started with France.

Everything was fine; Edna glowed from the compliments she received on the food and the tree, and the children were so excited that she'd put up their decorations, right toward the window where Santa could see them better, while the guests could not. Patsy had her arm around his waist, beaming, and Pierre seemed to be a nice enough fellow. Stanley relaxed on the couch with his beer, relief pouring into the muscles in his neck that had been knotted for days.

Christmas music wafted through the new surround sound speaker system Edna had made him install. He admitted it did give the party a lovely atmosphere, as his wife would put it. People buzzed about in conversation and general cheer, when he asked Patsy's boyfriend, "What part of France are you from?"

The boy appeared confused, searching Patsy for answers, and said, "I'm not French, Mr. Bundy."

"Well, why did your parents give you a name like Pierre, then?"

He had intended this as an honest question, but the guests laughed, as if he was indeed making fun of the boy.

"Daddy! Why would you ask such a thing?" Patsy had said, and whispered, "Pierre, I'm sorry." This embarrassed Stanley, that she was embarrassed of him, as it was. His ears grew warm with shame and the liquor that coursed through his blood.

"I mean no offense, of course," Stanley said. People continued to suppress laughter.

"It's fine, Mr. Bundy. Really, it is. People assume I'm French all the time. My mother just liked the language," he said.

Patsy sighed and took a sip of her drink. Stanley gulped his. "C'mon, dad, let's go sit and eat. You need food in your stomach."

Stanley was grateful his faux pas seemed forgiven. Still, his face burned as they sat on the couch. "Edna," he called, "come talk with your daughter and her suitor a while."

Patsy and Pierre exchanged glances. He was having trouble articulating anything right, it seemed. Edna touched his shoulder lightly and smiled. "Why, hello there. Are we all finally getting a drink together? You know you're my guests of honor. Did you try the crème brûlée? I hear you're French. Our town is known for the French Creoles."

"Oh, my God, don't start that shit again. The boy's not French. His mother liked the name, is all," said Stanley.

Patsy shrugged. "That's my parents, sweetheart," she said.

"Well, any man who my daughter loves is just perfect to me," said Edna. The woman had grace that he had not been blessed with, that was for damn sure.

"Anyway, your daddy and I were talking about what plans you two had," she winked and arranged a loose strand of hair back to its place. "I mean—"

"Oh, Mama. It's not a problem. We can stay here for a couple of days, but we're heading back to Boston Monday morning. I have a photo shoot and

Pierre has to work." Patsy seemed excited about this. Stanley wondered if he'd ever been that happy to work, ever, but she finished. "Pierre just got a new job."

"Well, isn't that lovely!" said Edna. "I'm actually talking about future plans." His wife folded her hands on the table, smiling expectantly. Patsy and Pierre glanced at one another, before Patsy gazed back towards her mother with partly raised eyebrows.

"What do you mean?"

"Well, marriage, of course," said Edna. Stanley had to admit his wife was speaking as if this were the only natural reason the couple could be sitting in front of them. He winced inside.

"Edna, I'm sure we don't need to pry into their personal business right here at dinner." He smiled nervously.

"Why on earth not? Stanley! I'm simply asking what their intentions are. I hear y'all are livin' together," she said, and lowered her voice, "And you know the old adage..."

"No, Mother, but I'm sure you're going to tell us."

"Well, you know. Why buy the cow if you can get the milk for free?" She laughed, but Patsy was clearly not amused. Stanley knew his daughter. It may have been a while since they had seen each other, but he felt like sinking into his chair and under the table when Edna said this. This is a turn of events, he thought. Edna embarrassing *him*. And herself, really. He decided to keep his mouth shut.

"Are you comparing me to a farm animal that should be sold off as such, mother?" said Patsy, furrowing her brow. "Because this is wholly inappropriate. And not part of my—our—belief system *at all*."

Ruth Marks, who'd been standing nearby, intercepted before anyone could respond. She put her arm around Edna, and guided her to the kitchen, whispering something about the food, infuriating Stanley. Patsy and (not French) Pierre played with her niece and nephew, whom she had never met, irritating Stanley further.

Edna slipped into the kitchen, anger collecting in her eyes, and Ruth tried to reason with her friend, as usual, to salvage the evening. Stanley lowered his head. He couldn't seem to mend this relationship, no matter how he tried. Edna was off in the kitchen like she had been sucked into a vortex of teenage drama at a school dance.

Stanley sighed, and made his way to the fireplace. "Patsy, please, why don't we just have another glass of champagne?" he said, moving close to the couple. "It's been a long time. Pierre, what'll you have?"

"Wild Turkey would be great," said Pierre.

"I knew my daughter would choose a sensible man," he said.

Pierre smiled, and Patsy mumbled an apology. "Let's just have a nice Christmas, okay?" said Pierre. He gazed directly at Patsy.

"The kids are great," she said.

"They're beautiful, aren't they? I keep thinking Jonah looks just like you."

Stan Jr. walked over to fetch his children, or at least pretend like he planned to do so, when he noticed Patsy. "Little sister. Look how you've grown. You're a beautiful woman."

Stan had changed quite a bit since Patsy boarded the plane to college seven years before. He was still Edna's boy, and Stanley wondered about him taking over the business. He understood his son didn't possess this passion he and his crew had; he didn't have that infernal desire to be on the boat. Without that, he didn't think the hard labor was worth it.

"Stan," she replied. "It's wonderful to see you."

"Life is good. It's such a joy to watch the kids grow and learn. Amanda has them in Montessori school. It's supposed to nurture the growing brain," said Stan.

While Stanley found this amusing, he loved how much his boy cared for his children. Jonah smashed one of his new trains into his sister, who screamed. Stanley smiled and said, "Jonah has a similar personality to his Aunt Patsy, as well. Right Stan?"

"Damn straight," said Stan. He took a swig of beer and said, "Can you play with them a bit? I gotta check on Amanda. She's involved herself in a conversation about politics."

"Yeah, yeah. Don't let them talk too much," said Stanley.

He turned to Patsy and Pierre. "Amanda is also a Yankee," said Stanley. "Alcohol and politics don't mix."

"Dad," said Patsy. "Stop while you're ahead. Please." Her eyebrows shot up.

"See what I mean, Pierre?" he said. "Be careful with my daughter. I don't worry about *her*, it's her boyfriends that have a challenge."

"Oh, Daddy," said Patsy. "I've missed you."

One crisis averted, thought Stanley. He was going to be drunk by the end of it.

•　•　•　•　•　•

Edna perched on her toes against the kitchen wall, sobbing till she thought there was nothing left of her. Just as her eyes swelled so she could hardly see, it occurred to her that she would, at some point—Good God, she hoped soon—lead her guests out into the night, where they would go home and celebrate their own little Christmases. She splashed her face with water, and thought she'd blame the puffiness of her eyes on allergies if anyone mentioned it.

Now that she'd stopped wailing, her husband's voice boomed from the living room. Not about to partake in another dramatic incident, she slid against the wall, towards the swinging door, always a sliver open, which she was grateful for now. She blew her nose and hoped to God the conversation revolved around sports.

Patsy and Tommy were discussing the murder, she knew that much. How they had been just babies when it happened, and all that. Edna dabbed her eyes, thinking that kind of information interested her, too. But the murmur of gentle party conversation drifted up a few decibels, and Edna strained to hear. She slid closer to the door, inching it further ajar.

"That was such an awful night," Ruth said. "Just terrifying."

Edna nodded to herself.

"Well, if you ask me—"

Edna groaned.

Nobody asked you, whoever you are.

"If that woman hadn't been turnin' tricks in the first place..."

Edna's fists balled up in her lap.

"Now, now. That may be so, but it still wasn't the woman's fault," said Stanley.

Exactly, thought Edna. Her husband had done one thing right that evening.

"I'm not sayin' it was her fault. I'm sayin' prostitution is a sin, too."

"Are you serious?" said Patsy.

Edna's head was about to explode.

Everyone just shut the fuck up and go home.

"Yeah, I'm serious. You take a risk like that, what do ya expect?"

Edna couldn't even identify the voice, only that this man had ruined her party. Snot ran down her face.

"That's disgusting. Daddy, did you hear that? Your friends think murdering women is justifiable!"

"Patsy, I swear. Stanley, you never did get control of this one, did ya? The one who burned your flag to a crisp."

Silence spread across the room for too, too long.

"This isn't about the damn flag, Richard."

Oh, right…Richard from down the hill…

"Y'all need to stop this," said Ruth.

Please.

"Damn straight I hate that flag and all it stands for," said Patsy.

Oh shit, here it comes.

"Patsy, we've discussed this. My flag is my prerogative."

Edna stood to run up the stairs. Then she caught a peek of Gilmore and Maggie gathering their coats and stomping out the front door. Her cheeks flamed in abject shame, and she sobbed in her hands.

Her parties were cursed.

Chapter Sixteen
CHRISTMAS

Daisy stared at the ceiling, unable to take her eyes off the thick layer of mold that sprouted from it and snaked down the wall. She had tried to ignore the leaky roof, knew it could affect Rosie's asthma, and now that the cola-colored blob had turned fuzzy and olive green, something needed to be done. Daisy hated the thought of calling the landlord, who had a gruff and dismissive demeanor. But mold was too dangerous to let go.

Her heart pattered in her chest. She dialed his number. Maybe he wouldn't pick up. It was Christmas Eve, after all. She would leave a message and wait for him to send someone over Monday.

He answered on the first ring.

"Mr. Walker. Merry Christmas! It's Daisy Greene."

"Merry Christmas to you, too, hon." He paused a moment. "What can I do for you?"

"Well, it seems we have a situation with mold—"

"Mold?" He sighed into the receiver. "That's a situation, all right."

Relief spread through Daisy's chest. "Yeah, sure is. The roof has a leak. When can you get someone out here?"

"Well, that's the thing, hon. You owe five hundred bucks in back rent. The mold situation has got to be cleared up. A water leak could gut the place. But I can't fix it unless you give me the five hundred in back rent."

"What are you saying, Mr. Walker?" Daisy twirled the phone cord around her finger and sucked in a breath. What could he possibly mean? She didn't have five hundred dollars. "I wouldn't be calling if I had the back rent."

"I'm saying, take care of the leak on your own, or I'll need to evict you for the back rent and handle it myself. Plus, you know I can get more a month for the place. I'm givin' you a deal and you're still late all the time."

Mr. Walker was not, in fact, giving them a deal. The place had rats and roaches, water leaks and lead, paint that hadn't been touched up in decades. No, he was not giving her a break at all. Daisy was infuriated.

"All right, then. I'll get the five hundred." The back rent was bound to be less than the leaky roof. Her voice wavered. She hung up the phone and began to cry. Calling Mr. Walker had made everything worse.

What a Christmas. What a life. She raked her hands through her hair and pulled at the thin gray strands. How much more could she take? How many more years could she stand? And where would she get five hundred dollars?

The answer was indefinite. She would do what she had to do, fall down and sob, then get up and do it all again until the breath was sucked out of her and she was buried in a pine box next to her daughter. She had made a promise to Matilda: I will take care of Rosie. I will do what needs to be done.

She paced the living room. The floorboards under the shag carpet creaked under her feet. She drew open the curtains. There was nothing to fear, not really. The sky was inky and swirled with looming clouds. She hoped there would be no more rain, but her expectations were low. For all she knew, the roof could cave in. Her stomach pinched with anxiety. She was not one to give up. She would not give up. This was a problem. All she needed was to come up with a solution. Daisy had become quite good at finding creative solutions to issues typically resolved with a checkbook. They had picked through dumpsters for aluminum cans and exchanged them for coins on those days she needed a few dollars to stretch her gas out or buy milk. She was friends with all the loan sharks in town. They could only be called loan sharks. Daisy recognized that she'd been making payments on the same three hundred dollars loan for years. Problem was, Daisy knew a roof repair would be more than that. And besides, she was tapped at every local place. Did she have the gas to drive out of town? Maybe, but she had an expired driver's license. Her breath caught in her throat.

Don't panic, she thought. Nothing good ever came out of an emotional meltdown. Won't fix a thing. It's five hundred dollars.

Still, her neck spasmed. The night fell heavily on her shoulders. Rosie was working at The Piggly Wiggly in Fuller, which was good because Daisy preferred to worry on her own. She couldn't puzzle a thing out with Rosie's drama. Instead, she inhaled the stench of the moldy room and remembered that Rosie had coughed more than usual that morning. Or maybe that was her imagination. God, she hoped so.

Christmas. Daisy had always managed to get a few gifts for Rosie under the tree. She sighed and flicked on the little flickering lights strung on the tree. The tree was a little skeletal in the back, a bit dry, but it wasn't so bad. She got a discount and picked through the barren trees and faced the brownest part toward the wall. People wasted money over the silliest of issues. Why spend extra when half the tree is hidden against a wall of some sort, anyway? It's going in the trash in a few weeks, anyway. Daisy supposed it was part of the festivities for some folks, but for Daisy and Rosie, Christmas and all its rituals were a source of stress.

She picked up each gift, painstakingly wrapped, and played with the ribbon. Daisy had a call to make, and the thought of it sent bile up her throat. But what else could she do?

Daisy punched the number into the phone, absentmindedly twirling the long phone cord in her fingers. She squeezed her eyes shut. Her chest thumped in her throat.

Don't be silly, she thought. Worst he can do is say no.

But no matter the outcome, Daisy would feel small, less than. Like she always did when forced to beg someone for money.

"Hullo?"

"Mr. Johnson!" She spoke brightly. "Merry Christmas! It's Daisy Greene."

"Why, hullo, Daisy. What can I do for you?" He chuckled.

"I hate to bother you Christmas Eve—"

"Nah, nah. It's not a bother. Is it something about the schedule?"

She inhaled sharply. "No, it's nothing like that. I was wondering," she said, stammering, "I was wondering if I could have a small advance on my pay—"

"You know we don't do Christmas bonuses, Daisy. It's against corporate policy—"

"Mr. Johnson. I have an emergency. My roof is leaking." Daisy hated asking for money. Her pride lay bare on the floor in front of her. But she knew how to do it. It was how they'd survived all these years. She felt the color drain from her face. She had to see Mr. Johnson every day. It was stupid to bother him. "Never mind, Mr. Johnson. I apologize about the call. Enjoy your holiday. I can work this out myself."

"No, wait," said Mr. Johnson. "Don't hang up." He cleared his throat. "Leaky roof's no good. Can't do advances, it's against corporate, like I said. But I've got a son-in-law who's a roofer. I could send him over."

"Oh God, Mr. Johnson. You're saving my life by doing this. God bless you, sir."

"Now, now. I'm not doing anything special. He's family. This way you don't have to worry about paying me back. I don't want to hear another thanks for it. Anyone would have a family member help a person out. 'Specially a good, dependable worker like you."

She had fixed yet another nightmarish situation. Now, there was the back rent to consider. At least she had bought herself time. Walker would wait on the rent as long as the roof and mold were taken care of. With a groan, she flopped on the couch, wiping the droplets of sweat from her brow. One thing after another. Always uphill. But, she thought, it is what it is. No use blubbering about it.

Chapter Seventeen
GHOST STORIES

Patsy stepped outside for a cigarette—she'd quit a year ago; so much for that—and began walking. She inhaled the mild, salty air and set out for the little pink house down the driveway. Down the hill, away from her parent's sprawling home and manicured lawn, Cypress seemed different to Patsy. Maybe the homes less than a mile away had always been tiny, had always needed a paint job. Perhaps the roofs had been sagging since before Patsy was born. Perhaps she had forgotten about the cracks webbed through the sidewalks. Or maybe she had just never realized that the Bundy family was a world away from their neighbors. Not that the rest of town was dilapidated; it was just an ordinary world that Patsy had not been a part of as a child. Not till she moved away from her sheltered existence.

Patsy had worried it was too late for a visit, but Ruth swept her into a hug when she arrived at the door, though. "I thought you'd never get here," she said.

Tommy seemed so big on the yellow flowered couch. A lifetime of shrimping had made him broad-shouldered. His muscled body must have helped him get on the college football team. He was like a St. Bernard, cock-eared and sweet, unaware of his size. The three of them were crammed into the living room, like Alice after she ate the wafer, but then Patsy realized, we're just grown up, we have all grown up. It messed with her perception, being gone for so long, and then back to her childhood town, where she felt younger. Where she felt judged.

Tommy had the same gold-flecked eyes she remembered from childhood, from high school, from the days he had taken her side when no one else did.

Stop, she thought. Do not get sentimental. Do not let it happen.

"Do you love him?" Ruth asked, leaning forward in her seat, palms pressed against the sides of her face.

It took Patsy a moment to answer. "Pierre?"

"Of course, Pierre!" said Ruth. "Good lord, is there something you're not telling me?"

Tommy cleared his throat and gazed up at the ceiling.

"Well, do you want to discuss this now? Tommy probably doesn't want to talk about all that."

Ruth waved her hand. "He doesn't mind. Do you?"

Tommy shut his eyes. "I don't care. It's fine."

"I think I do. We've had our issues, but we've sorted them out. He got a job, for one thing," Patsy said.

"Oh, that's right!" said Ruth, slapping her knee. "The Southern cooking magazine. He mentioned that to your ma."

"Southern cooking?"

"Yeah. The magazine, *A Slice of Life*. Well, I guess your mother gave him some good material."

"Goddammit!" she yelled. She could not help but raise her voice. "He insisted we come here. Insisted. Said he needed to meet my parents." Patsy bit her cheek, got up, and paced the room.

"Well, I'm sure he did—"

"Nope, nope. He wanted to come out here to do research for that magazine. I'd bet a million bucks on it. For seven years, he hasn't mentioned going to Louisiana. And he didn't even say it was a *Southern* cooking magazine!"

"Yeah, I did hear him mention something about Cajun-style Christmas celebrations, but I didn't hear much after that," she said.

"You didn't need to." She bit the inside of her cheek. "I need to go, Ruth."

"Are you okay, Patsy?" She tucked a red curl behind her ear and put her arms on Patsy's shoulders. "I worry about you, sometimes."

"I just need some air, that's all."

"All right. Just don't bail for the airport before saying goodbye," Ruth said, with downturned lips.

Patsy had no intention of leaving town, not yet. "I'm not bailing. I'm just pissed off."

Ruth laughed. "Yeah. I suppose you're entitled to that."

Patsy held her heels in one hand and ran, her mind spinning. *How dare he? How dare he make me come all this way? Oh, I love you, let's start over, sweetie. Bullshit, all of it bullshit.*

She did not want to be in this town, with all its secrets and memories pouring back at her, oozing through the cool breeze that swept back her hair. She ran, in her stockings, to the place she knew most, the wetlands. A sliver of moonlight illuminated the otherwise dark path before her. Stars flickered beneath the silhouette of clouds scattered aimlessly across the sky.

Patsy was so angry she didn't notice the jagged bits of gravel piercing her flesh. Stockings in shreds, she slowed her pace and meandered down the dirt road. The familiar shadow on stilts lived inside her, breathed within her. It whispered the secrets of the Bayou. Secrets that Patsy would uncover, if only she listened.

Her tin shack. It was the same. She closed her eyes. Crickets and owls called to the wild. A blue heron squawked a song she knew by heart; she could even imitate its cry. Her feet sunk in the mossy earth. She wiggled her bare toes in the mud, its coolness soothing to her raw feet. She trudged her way to the house, and before folding herself inside, she looked out to the water, which moved in a quiet sort of way, like it had no one to impress. Patsy understood why she loved this one spot on the Bayou. It had nothing to prove, nothing to be but some water, flowing whichever way the earth sent it, whichever way the wind blew.

It just *was*.

And then, the reflection of the incandescent moon on the water cast a glimmer of light on the trunk of a bald Cypress tree to the left of the house. Patsy knelt and touched the tree. Ran her hand along its rough bark till she reached what she saw in the light, something gleaming and white.

She knelt closer to the ground, digging through the mud to get a closer look. A bone, half-felted in overgrown moss. It probably belonged to an animal. She ran her fingers down the length of it, which was hard and smooth. A piece of it gave under pressure, and she held her hand out into the moonlight once more, where a fine black powder lay in her palm. She touched the tree again, more ash. Her heart thumped a familiar beat, to the same rhythm the swamp had always had, to a crescendo rising from the belly of the earth. She knew it through and through, that this place could speak to her, that it would, like a person, if she only listened long enough.

Patsy dug around the tree, cool mud sticking between her fingers. A bra, caked in layers of mucky dirt, torn almost to shreds, was beside the tree. Dirty and weathered, it was still obvious that it had once been a lacy underwire garment of clothing

Patsy held the bone and the bra to her chest. The ghosts of Cypress did not need to appear in a gallop of horses or the sight of a woman dying, or a fire on the Bayou. She clutched both items and ran back to Ruth's.

•   •   •   •   •

Ruth thought everyone knew about the murder and the fire that night on the Bayou right before Patsy was born. She thought she had told Tommy the story of how she and Jeb paced the house with him as an infant, deciding whether to evacuate. It had not occurred to her that the children knew nothing of it until Parson's upcoming release hit national news twenty-five years later.

And certainly, she hadn't considered that Patsy's childhood visions had anything to do with the murder on the Bayou. Cypress had done its best to forget.

So, when Patsy showed up hours after she'd gone for a walk, clothing in tatters and feet bleeding, Ruth thought the worst. "Oh, dear God," she said. "Tommy! Call the police. Something has happened to Patsy!" Patsy's bizarre physical condition was shocking, but worse still, Ruth had never seen her shaken like this, with tears in her eyes, almost in a trance.

"No, dammit. Don't call the police. Nothing's happened to *me*." She produced a half-charred *bone* and half a bra, hands quivering. Ruth almost fell right over. "Look at this. Where could this have come from? I thought it was an animal bone, but it can't be."

"What the— Patsy, please. Sit down," said Ruth.

Tommy stood in the doorway, thumbs in his pockets, eyes fixed on the floor. Ruth had the odd sensation pulse through her about these two, remembering how close they had been as children, and how he looked up at her now. What were they not telling her?

"Holy shit," said Tommy. "Where could that have come from? It looks like it was burned. A fire, I'm sure...You think *the* fire? It probably is from an animal, though. That bra could've gotten there at any point."

"Tommy," said Ruth. She knew her son was a grown man, but she still didn't want to hear about it. She liked to pretend her son had never seen a woman's undergarments.

"I wonder if this is her bone," said Patsy. "Matilda Greene. You know, from *the* fire."

"How do you know it's not from your little flag burning adventure?" Ruth said dryly.

"Mama, stop." Tommy sounded weary of the whole situation. "That fire was contained to the flag. Which sunk in the water."

Ruth waved her hand dismissively. She had suffered through enough drama tonight, dealing with Edna. "Oh, honey. What do you want to do, go take it in for a forensic examination?"

"He should not be released," said Patsy.

"That's not a human bone, the bra could be from anywhere. It can't have anything to do with the murder," said Ruth.

"I swear I saw this happen. I swear I did. A woman with the lightest blonde hair, killed right there where our shack is."

Ruth did not mention that paranormal visions don't exactly hold up in court. "But there's nothing that can bring this woman back. It's devastating, I know. But what can you do? He's up for parole."

"You don't remember when they all said I was practicing witchcraft down there?"

"Well," said Ruth, "yes but, what's that got to do —"

"I *did* see things, Ruth."

"I know you did, honey, but you were a kid. A kid with a very active imagination. Not a witch, of course. A child. It never would have been a big deal at all, if people around here hadn't made it one. The whole situation would have worked itself out."

"I *saw* this woman murdered, and I wasn't born yet. He had a horse and a Confederate flag."

Ruth finally said, "No one is going to believe that, Patsy."

"I tell you, he killed her. And he had a Confederate flag."

"So that's why you burned your father's flag up?"

"No, that's how I figured out the Confederate flag was evil."

Ruth agreed with this, but whether Patsy *saw* this or *thought* she did was another issue. When Patsy decided on something, it was best not to argue with her. "God, Patsy," Ruth sighed. She needed a painkiller. "You may have seen pictures. They did Civil War reenactments all the time down there, back in the day. Maybe even when you were a kid."

"Tommy," she said, "you know I'm telling the truth."

"Let's not get into it," he muttered under his breath. "Not tonight."

"I know about the rope, too. The one around Jeb's neck, the night he died."

Ruth's tone sharpened, as she felt she'd been slapped with memories against her will. She could only handle so much. "What are you talking about? Tommy, why'd you go 'round talking about that?"

Tommy sat beside his mother on the couch and put his arm around her shoulder. "Because she knew about it, Mama. She had a vision of what happened to Daddy, and she's just tellin' you so you'll believe she had a vision of the murder, too."

He said this to Ruth with such a rational tone, looking at Patsy with his pretty eyes as if he knew what she said was God's truth. Her boy had always been so damn gullible.

"That was common knowledge," said Ruth.

"You said people didn't know about it, only Stanley," Tommy said.

"You both were *seven*. We didn't exactly talk 'facts'."

Ruth knew this boy from baby to a man, sharing private pain in a town where everyone lived the same lives, where theirs had been radically different. This would not be spoken, this would not be spoken of ever again, but Ruth would clear the fire that had burned inside Patsy for all these years.

She caught Patsy's eye. "I suppose there's a chance the bone belongs to the woman, as he did dump her body in the swamp."

Patsy nodded and held the bra and the bone closer. "He should be there for life."

"I agree with you, Patsy. Oh God, I'm tired." She rubbed her forehead, wanting this evening to be over.

"Why the hell would they free him?" said Tommy.

"Because," Ruth sighed. "Because she was a hooker. And back then—"

"If you were a hooker, you got what you deserved," he said. He pursed his lips as if he was going to cry. This whole evening had affected everyone. Patsy had a way of doing that, with her presence. Ruth had forgotten how intense she could be. She sat back in the couch, stretching her arms above her head, yawning.

"Do you think he took part in those reenactments?" said Patsy.

"Could have been, I suppose. They were all over here, at one time," said Ruth.

"But this man. He had a Confederate flag. He rode a horse. There were lots of horses."

"Patsy," said Ruth, who was as frazzled around the edges as the Confederate flag Patsy had set fire to years before. "I'm so tired, but I'll tell you this—he's a murderer. That's enough."

"Let's go bury this stuff," said Tommy. "It should be buried out there properly." He gazed at his mother, and she mouthed 'thank you' to him.

"No. We can go for a walk, but I'm still handing the bone to the police before I leave. They can sort out whether it belongs to an animal or not."

Ruth nodded, and Patsy and Tommy headed for the door. "Grab a pair of shoes, Patsy," she said, and closed her eyes. In the morning, she would go to work and dig up some information on the case. She got up for the shoes and a glass of water. She opened the cabinet beside the kitchen sink and searched for Tylenol. Her heart was in that place she hated so much, that place where it landed the night her husband left them. It was a dark kind of aloneness, a sorrow that thrived in solitude. Through the years, her grief had waned from sharp, painful waves to a controllable, yet permanent state that turned up on anniversaries and birthdays. She had come to accept it, but she was now rendered incapable of conversation. Tommy kissed his mother on the forehead, and he went with Patsy out into the night. This was the strangest Christmas ever.

•   •   •   •   •

"I have to leave him, Tommy," she said. "I cannot tolerate the bullshit." They sat on the little bridge, where they'd had so many conversations. Sitting here on the crooked slats of wood, they dangled their legs over the edge, just above the water. The moon shone in the quiet salty night. Like a pair of well-worn gloves in the back of the closet, they still fit, even though they had not sat together like this in years.

"Well," said Tommy cautiously, "perhaps it was a coincidence. The whole *Slice of Life* thing."

"It was no coincidence." This was irritating. She balled her hands into fists. "Besides, I thought you were on my side."

"I am on your side, Patsy. Geez. I just meant, it seems like a small thing. He wanted a job. To contribute to your finances. Maybe he was embarrassed to ask?"

"He was not embarrassed," she said, "and besides, it's complicated." Patsy thought about how many jobs Pierre had quit, how many pairs of expensive shoes he had purchased with his parents' money. Pierre had no desire to contribute financially. He had something to prove. Maybe he thought getting this job would appease Patsy for a while. Who knew what went on in the man's mind? "It's really not the magazine."

The truth was, she would love nothing more than for Pierre to act like an adult. She'd be ecstatic for him to take a job just about anywhere, if he kept it for more than a month. But Patsy knew this job would eventually go by the wayside, just like the others. Nothing would be good enough for Pierre.

"Ah, complicated. I know how that goes," he said. "I should have left Linda. Instead, I waited for her to do it. I'm a coward like that."

"You're just too nice. If you had even an ounce of mean in you, we wouldn't be friends," she said. "I've got enough mean for us both."

"Well," he said, "are you going to tell him now? That would make for a helluva plane ride home." He laughed.

"You're right," she said, thinking. "It can wait."

"What's it like in the big city?" he said. "I wanted to bail out of here when you did."

She wrinkled her nose. "You don't seem like the leavin' type, Tommy."

"What do ya mean by that?" he said. "I want to do something with my life besides shrimping. I've got no desire to die on a boat like my dad."

"Hard labor, too," she said. "But there's something about being out on the boat. I used to love just being out on the water with my pops."

Tommy nodded, swinging his legs. "That's the fun part."

"What would you have done, if you didn't stay here?"

"Let's see," he said, "I went to college with my *mother*. Let that shit sink in. I'm proud of her too, but while you were in Boston, hanging out with poets and going to art museums, I was playing football and going to college with my mom."

Patsy nearly cried, trying not to laugh, imagining Tommy sitting next to Ruth in a lecture hall. "Okay, that's actually hilarious."

"I know I want to teach kids. That's what my degree is—secondary ed. I'd teach high school English if I could finish my certification. I'm stuck here, for now."

"Because of your mom?"

"Hell yes, because of her! My whole life has been mapped out to accommodate the fact my dad died and left her a widow. You know how it goes— 'you're the man of the house now, son,'" he said, in a mocking tone.

"I don't think your mom feels like that anymore. That's why she got her education. Why she does everything for herself. I think you're getting that stuff from the rest of the people around here."

"You think so?" he said, twisting his face.

"I know so. Having lived elsewhere. There's a lot of backward ideas that permeate this place."

"There's a lot of kindness too, Patsy."

"True," she said, thinking. "That's what complicates things." She sat up and looked at him—part little boy in the sleeping bag beside her bed that awful night Jeb died, part grown man she'd only just met. In the glint of the moonlight, she caught the familiar dimple in the corner of his smile. She took a breath, the misty air coating her lungs. She turned her head towards him, that's all it took, as they lay inches away from each other. He ran his palm down her shoulder and smiled. "Remember that day you beat the shit out of that girl by the locker?"

"We ran down here, right to this very spot."

He leaned in and kissed her on the lips. She leaned into him, running her hands through his hair.

She laughed nervously. "I'm covered in mud."

"That's ok." He smiled, and kissed her again. This time, she hesitated a little.

"What?" he said. "If it's not right—"

"It isn't you, Tommy. It's not even just Cypress," she said. "Lots of things are complicated."

She brushed off her legs and pulled herself up. She needed a shower. Her clothes were caked in mud. Her chest felt hollow, like the tin shack, as good as abandoned. She took a deep, steady breath, and wiped her eyes.

"You headed back, then?" said Tommy. He leaned back on his elbows, staring at the water, away from her.

"Yeah," she said. "I'm headed back to Boston tomorrow. I've got a lot of shit to deal with."

"It was nice seeing you, Patsy." He sighed and lay back onto the bridge, taking a more detached tone. "I'm going to stay here a while. If you can make it back to your parents' house by yourself."

She could make the trip home blind-folded if she had to. "Yeah, I'll be around again soon. It's been too long." The ease she'd felt just minutes before had disappeared. She shifted on her heels in silence.

"You know," he called, as she walked away, "not everyone in Cypress is stagnant. Some of us have spent our lives working on changing the wrong here. Just 'cause I didn't run off doesn't mean I don't care."

She turned towards the gravel road, taking one last look at Tommy, as he lay under the moon with his eyes closed, before trudging away. There was nothing left here for her. Her parents and their patriarchal bullshit, and that damn flag that still flew over their plantation, hanging like an announcement that the war was still on. As this occurred to her, that familiar rage burned in her throat. The war with her family was still going strong.

"Yeah," she said. "Well, you try stickin' around to fight the assholes who let a witch hunt out on you at the age of six. You do that and let me know how it goes. All right?"

She thought about Tommy, about being with him. It stirred her heart in a hundred directions, and part of her wanted him every bit as he wanted her. It just was not healthy for her here. She wanted to go; she wanted to stay.

Someone wants to tell me something.

This rattled through her brain, on an unending loop, even as she was falling asleep that night.

Chapter Eighteen
MOTHERHOOD

The next morning Edna had the worst hangover she'd ever gotten from two glasses of champagne. Except she didn't feel sick, exactly. No, that wasn't it. Her soul weighed her down physically, trapped in a mind that refused to quiet.

Stanley had asked, right before Christmas, "Do you love her, Edna?"

Now, she lay in a pile of Egyptian cotton sheets, wrapped in the fluffiest down comforter money could buy, and wondered if he sensed something that she hadn't even admitted to herself. To say she didn't love her daughter was harsh; she did love her, as in, she felt love in her heart and pride in Patsy's accomplishments. Her heart jumped a little when Patsy achieved something amazing that she'd never dreamed of doing herself, like running off to Boston or talking back to her father like that. But she thought of this as a quiet cheer for women; Patsy had done what women in Cypress did not. Well, they did more and more, but not so defiantly as her child.

Her heart may have swelled a little at this, but most of the time, Patsy exhausted her. Edna did not like chaos, and Patsy was a literal ball of flames. Edna didn't feel safe when the neighbors talked about her, year after year, all because of this kid. And yes, this had affected her ability to bond with the girl. Obviously, she felt guilty. What kind of mother even *thinks* such vile thoughts about her own child? No wonder Patsy hated her.

Edna resented Stanley's role in this, too. Maybe she would have a relationship with Patsy if Stanley hadn't screwed it all up fighting with the girl all the time. It was hard to say, given that his stubbornness had run her out of town when she was just a teenager. Sure, Edna knew lots of mothers who got frustrated or even angry and took off for 'me time' at the beauty parlor.

This was a new thing amongst mothers Amanda's age. Self-care. "She's taking care of herself, Mom," Stan Jr. often said, when he brought the kids by for an afternoon. "Women are better moms when they take care of themselves first." Edna had nodded in agreement, and felt proud of her son, for being such a good husband and father, and hoped she had something to do with that.

And then the darkness enveloped her mind again, when she thought, "But what if we'd just stopped at Stan?"

Terrible, terrible thoughts for a mother to have. Patsy had always been so damn inconvenient, straight from the womb, whereas Stan touched their lives gently. He was portable, didn't cry much, she could put him in the car and go about her day. Patsy needed the afternoons planned around her nap schedule or life would be hell. Edna hated herself for thinking these things, yet her mind reeled with them that morning.

Maybe she just never got over Patsy's birth. How they'd both nearly died. Maybe it was easier to maintain a distance.

Edna had felt altogether miserable the last few days of her pregnancy. Granted, she had enough experience to know that the miracle of birth was preceded by the hell that God bestowed upon women, but this time her mind was as unrecognizable as her body. She had little right to be focused on how fat she was, or how the first time she'd escaped stretch marks, how this time she was branded for life. No, because every time she exercised her God-given right to passive aggressive complaining, or so much as thought about it, other, morbid visions swam through her brain like a loose alligator.

How much worse do you think it'd be if you were that woman's children (if she had them) How did it feel the last moments of her life? You're not bein' killed and dumped in the damn swamp, Edna. Shut the hell up...

And on it went. Back and again, for three days. "Whatcha thinking about, love?" her husband would ask, with soft, tender eyes. He planned his words with great care. She was a volcano, growling with lava. He did not want to disturb her.

"Nothing," she'd snap back, because she felt he was intruding on fears he was not allowed to step near. *Don't be such a bitch, Edna! It could be worse. Y'all could be dead, like that poor woman...And stop thinking about the fact there's a murderer loose around here. Poor woman didn't have a clue.*

It could have been someone she knew, Ruth had told her. It was usually someone you knew. This was before they knew much about Parson or the victim. When it was all a mass of confusion that seeped its way into Edna's brain.

A person could go crazy thinking like that. Especially with hormone-saturated blood pulsing like venom, as Edna had. She did not have the right to her annoyance at well-meaning comments like, "Haven't you had that baby yet?" The surge of irritation would begin to hit and then she'd grit her teeth till her jaw hurt, because after all, it could be worse. There was a murderer on the loose and a woman dead, and here she was, about to give birth, a happy event.

She had just finished mopping the floors and making some freezer meals for after the birth. She hoped it was nesting. She couldn't be sure of it, because she had not been particularly compelled to push a wet mop around or heat up the house with the oven. Rather, feeling too tired for chores, she felt guilty. *Suck it up. It could be worse. You could be dead or orphaned.*

It was disturbing. Her head ached from the confusion.

As she worked, she noticed that the light waves she'd felt in her uterus became more intense and predictable. Knowing she had plenty of time, she continued to mop in an almost trance-like state. Swish forward, swoop back, dip in the bucket, squeeze the mop. And again. There was a meditative feel to the swishing of the mop.

She radioed Stanley, as the waves inside her were bearable but intense, and the floors were very, very clean. By the time he and the midwife arrived at the house, everything had been polished and scrubbed. "Wow, the house is sure clean, honey," Stanley said, giving her an odd look—well, she couldn't quite tell, since her mind was still in the swooshing of the mop.

"Nesting," said Lynn, who had delivered her son as well. "It's the way mamas get ready for the babe's arrival is all." She gave Stanley a reassuring nod and he smiled. "Let's check and see how close we are."

Snapping on a rubber glove, Lynn said, "There now, lean back." Edna winced as Lynn slipped her fingers into Edna's vagina, the cold gel a shock. Lynn moved her hand around a bit, which hurt like hell, then announced, "Six centimeters! You're in active labor, dear."

Edna turned back to her mop. Swish. Swoop. Swish. Swoop.

"I think we should check you again," said Lynn, her voice soft and far away.

Edna ignored this. An hour passed before she set the mop against the wall, where it slipped down with a thud. Her uterus balled up so tight it swallowed her breath.

At the slow release in her belly, she padded down the shiny wood floors. She stopped every few minutes when a hard, painful contraction hit. She would lean on the wood-paneled wall, narrowing her eyes intently on a photograph of tendrils of pea shoots, the tips bright green and wispy. Her focal point reminded her of new life. She breathed the pain out from her belly, down through her feet, grounded like trees. This continued for four hours. She wanted it quiet. Each time Stanley or Lynn offered a word of encouragement, or attempted a whisper of light conversation, she put her finger to her mouth to shush them. Swaying her hips to the primal world of birth, she needed silence. Edna wanted solitude.

The pacing lessened. She groaned and leaned against the wall, hands splayed and holding her body upright.

She screamed, "Water! I need water." Scattered salty tears fell to the wood in droplets and Edna thought, "But I just cleaned the floors." Of course, she realized the mess was going to be far worse than a few tears and thought herself ridiculous.

Still, her floors...

Lynn held the straw to Edna's lips, and offered her sips. "There, dear. You must be close." Stanley peeked around the corner, but he hung back with his arms folded across his chest.

"I've got to lie down," said Edna. "Please." Her energy wore thin. The daylight had faded, leaving a soft glow through the skylight in the living area.

"Do you want to go to the bed?" Lynn asked, pursing her lips as if she suddenly realized this should have been accomplished earlier. Edna could not trudge the circular staircase to the bedroom. "Hmm," she said aloud.

"No, just—"

Edna felt another contraction and a sudden gush, which was to be expected at this stage. Except with the pop, she felt the umbilical cord, her baby's lifeline, bulge through her vagina. Caught in an ethereal state, she could not convey this to the others. "Something is wrong," she said, as the midwife offered encouraging words. Her baby would die, within minutes. Edna's mind whirled as if in a dream, from the pain, from the danger. "No, no...Lynn. THE CORD!"

Lynn sprang upright, as if she'd woken into a nightmare. The cord had prolapsed, fallen from her uterus and through the cervix when her water broke. It compressed with each contraction, cutting off the baby's oxygen supply. With each wave, Edna felt her baby's life slipping away. "On your hands and knees, now," Lynn said, and yelled at Stanley, "She needs a Caesarian-section or the baby will die."

They were five miles from the hospital.

Lynn shoved her hand up, all the way into Edna's uterus, holding a section of cervix open so the cord could continue to pulse. "God, I hope this works." She said this under her breath, but Edna knew it was dire, probably too late. This just could not end well. Her body was ripping, her hip bones shattering with every wave. Can a person sustain this for long? She wanted to die. She wanted to give up.

"Okay," Lynn said, eyes wild. "We have to lift her into the bed of the truck. In exactly this position. I cannot move."

Stanley's followed instruction, his own face cadaverous. He screamed for help, for anyone. No response, no time to call Jeb...the nearest neighbor a half-acre away.

Somehow, Edna would never know how, her husband lifted the two women into the truck bed, in the position Lynn wanted them in. Edna on her hands and knees, belly hanging down, and the midwife with her hand all the way inside of her. Blood and water poured everywhere. Edna felt like a cow being handled like this. It would never leave her, ever, this willingness to do anything to save her child, swirled with the pain and indignation of driving five long miles through town half-naked in the bed of a pick-up truck.

What happened next Edna could not tell you exactly. It was like flipping cards of incomplete sketches together to form a cartoon, except Edna did not get to see the finished production. She'd never know what parts she had remembered, or what had been told to her, yet each puzzle piece laced together like a horror movie that would never end.

Her hips above her head, doctors and nurses donned in surgical wear rushed her to the operating room. They ran fast, their shoes squeaking along the waxy floor, the wheels of the gurney whirling, the scent of Lysol hitting her nose. She was cold, so cold.

They yelled, "Hurry, hurry. The baby's heart rate is low...mother is bleeding out," and covered her face with a mask. She slipped under, into a darkness like murky swamp water filled with alligators and snakes.

Edna wrapped the comforter around herself and sunk into the crushing weight of her heavy soul.

$\bullet \quad \bullet \quad \bullet \quad \bullet \quad \bullet$

Patsy lay on the chaise lounge in her parent's backyard, arms splayed at her sides, the tepid air warm to her skin. Strange how you get used to a place, she thought. If not for the dark history of her hometown, she might have felt like she was on vacation from the icy cold. Lots of people did that in Boston—went somewhere warm for the holidays. Patsy had always balked when Pierre suggested they go to Hawaii or Mexico. I love the snow, she'd said. I never had white Christmases as a kid, she had said, let's stay home.

Patsy gulped her glass of orange juice and headed down the lush lawn with its honeysuckles flowing over the wooden fence toward the water. She peered over the balcony, where foamy waves lapped over the white sand of the Gulf. A salty breeze filled her nose.

A million summers she had spent running on that beach with her father, collecting rocks and seashells. She had swum in the pool in this very backyard, and of course, trudged through the neighborhood to the swamp. Those wild horses clicked through there, ran through her mind, because they had something to tell her.

She always knew she'd be back. And yet she understood she would not stay. Now, that muddled sense of sorrow she felt that night on the Bayou with Ruth, years before, had returned...

The French doors burst open at that moment, and Jr. and Amanda stepped outside, along with little Norene, who tumbled into the yard, chattering happily about her Christmas gifts. "I love my new bike, Mommy," she said. "It has a horn, and a basket, and—"

"All right, sweetheart," said Amanda, laughing. "Daddy will put it together later." She scooped the child up in a tender sort of way and whispered something in Norene's ear that made her giggle.

"Hey, sis," said Stan, "you all right out here?"

"Yeah, just about ready to get packing," she said, feeling a presence beyond her brother. She peered around the French door. "Is that Daddy?"

"It's me, Patsy," said Edna. Her voice cracked as she spoke.

"Oh, hi, Mama," she said, turning her attention toward Amanda and Norene once again. Amanda adjusted her daughter on her hip, and Norene lay her head on her mother's shoulder, little arms wrapped around her neck.

"I thought you left this morning," she said. She set her coffee cup on the glass table, sliding into the chair beside Patsy. With wet hair tucked behind her ears, a terry cloth robe hung from her thin frame. "But I'm glad you're outside."

Stan turned toward them, his shadow softening the sun's rays. "We came out to say our goodbyes too. Unless you're planning on staying." His eyes sparkled with hope, and Patsy quickly shook her head.

"All right then," he said, leaning down to embrace her. "I hope y'all have safe travels. Don't be such a stranger, Patsy."

"I'll be back more often. I promise," she said. She stood and wrapped her arms around his neck, still watching Amanda and Norene.

Amanda caught her eye and meandered towards her. "See you soon then, sweetie." She kissed Patsy on the cheek. The three of them stepped back into the house, leaving Patsy and Edna silent except for the light whisper of the water below.

"Having children seems like hard work," said Patsy.

"Don't I know it," said Mama, almost under her breath.

"Remember that awful night Jeb died?" said Patsy.

"Of course," said Mama. "A terrible, terrible thing."

"It was pouring outside," said Patsy. "I was supposed to be sleeping. But the rain dumping on the house. I thought about Daddy out on *The Patsy Mae*.

Remember that, Mama? It was the first time they took the new boat out."

"He was so proud of it," said Mama. "That brand-new red boat..."

"You came in and woke me up."

The truck had sat running in the driveway. Her father spoke in fits and starts. They drove to Ruth's to pick up Tommy. But what stuck so clearly in Patsy's mind, when her thoughts went back to that evening, was Mama carrying Tommy to the truck. Patsy had watched from the back seat, the engine running, rain pelting the roof like BB guns. Mama appeared in front of the headlamps, holding Tommy to her chest like an infant, as he clutched his sock monkey. She kissed his head and whispered something to him, before placing him beside Patsy in the back seat. "It'll be okay, Tommy," she had said, in a soothing tone.

Patsy's mother had never been so reassuring in her life. The way she held him, the way she stroked his hair.

They sat together on the terrace now, fifteen years later. Edna's eyes shone with tears, and Patsy realized that she would never understand this woman.

Patsy sighed, and said, "I guess I'd better get to packing then." Mama was clearly in no mood for conversation, and Patsy didn't have much to say to her, anyway.

Chapter Nineteen
MATILDA GREENE

Patsy traipsed down the stairs at the sound of the doorbell. She needed a break from packing. Ruth stood outside, peeking around the curtains in the kitchen, shifting on her feet. Patsy opened the door a crack.

"I'm glad it's you," said Ruth. "Come outside." Patsy followed her out to the yard, barefoot.

"Yeah, you don't wanna deal with Mama right now. I'm packing and heading back."

"Patsy," she said. "I should not do this. I know it. But I'm going to." Ruth placed a folded piece of yellow paper from a legal pad in Patsy's hand.

"What is it?"

"I'm a library scientist, and I get information. That's all." Ruth smiled, but clenched her hands. "Do not tell anyone where you got this. You hear me?"

Patsy unfolded the slip of paper. A name and address were scrawled across it.

"Who is this?"

"The mother of the victim. I don't approve of you goin' down there. But if this is what you need, here."

Patsy nodded. "Come with me, Ruth."

Ruth sighed. "Oh, all right, Patsy. You are exhausting, I'll tell you that." She rubbed her temples and closed her eyes.

"This one last favor. I promise."

"Dammit," said Ruth, appearing pale. "I would say no, but you'll fuck this up. Believe me."

"I wouldn't—"

"Just get in the car. I wanna get this over with and never think of it again," said Ruth.

Minutes later, Patsy gripped the steering wheel as they drove to the outskirts of town, past an old bar and away from the little community. "Where are we going?" said Patsy.

"Realville," said Ruth, grimacing. "Just so you know— shit is about to get real."

They reached the address, which Patsy thought must be wrong. An essence of despair hung over the tiny house, with its sagging roof and paint peeled almost to the bone of the structure. A Pontiac sat parked on the grass, so rusted you could not tell its original color. "It looks abandoned," said Patsy, then looked at the note again.

"No, someone lives there. A light is on in the kitchen. Her name is Daisy Greene. Her daughter was Matilda Greene," said Patsy, reading the note. The muscles of her neck clenched. "Should we do this?" Suddenly, she understood what an intrusion this was.

"No. But we're gonna," said Ruth. "I'll do the talking."

Patsy nodded, frightened.

"You know what, Patsy Mae?"

"No, but I'm sure you'll enlighten me." She sighed.

"The truth of it is that people left a dead woman's memory, her murder, all of it, buried under layers of earth." Ruth pointed her finger and stared at Patsy, a hardness in her eyes. "But a little girl with a big mouth and the nerve to burn a racist piece of trash of a flag had to be shut up."

Patsy looked straight ahead.

"Don't let them shut you up. Don't let them run you outta town with their stupid little stories." She waved her fingers through the air, tight-lipped. "Look at where this woman lives, all hidden away here. It's sad." Patsy pretended not to see Ruth cry. "They don't care to make shit up about her or her daughter's line of work 'cause she keeps quiet."

Patsy was still for a moment. Silence buzzed around them, echoed through the littered streets of the neighborhood. Patsy spoke first. "Come on, Ruth. Let's go in."

"Anyway. You let me do the talking," Ruth said, wiping her face.

They got out of the car and stepped over a hose strewn across the lawn. Weeds and brush sprouted so haphazardly that you couldn't quite tell where the lawn and sidewalk met. Ruth knocked on the dark green door. A brusque voice yelled from inside, "Get the door, Rosie!" Patsy wanted to run back to the car, but if she didn't speak to this woman, at least try, she couldn't rest.

I must know where this bone came from.

"Yes?" said a young woman. Sunlight sliced through the crack in the door, illuminating crystals of dust suspended in the room.

"Hello, I'm Patsy Bundy," she began, forgetting that the talking was Ruth's job. She felt like she'd trampled over the dead woman's gravestone. And what would she say? That they had stopped by to see if Matilda's entire body had been found? Because they might have found her bone? Oh God. Patsy stepped back. She wanted to sink into the ground and become part of the weeds.

"Bundy?" said the young woman, scrunching her pale face. She had stringy blonde hair that fell in pieces down her back. She was vaguely familiar to Patsy. "I think we went to high school together, though we weren't friends." She cackled, an odd smile creeping across her face.

"You went to Jackson?" asked Patsy. Ruth kicked her in the calf, glaring.

"Oh yes. Patsy Bundy, rich bitch from up the hill. Daughter of Stanley Bundy. Back from up north, are you? You're the witch, right?" The woman spoke venomously.

"I'm sorry," Patsy began. Coming here had been a mistake.

"Look," said Ruth, pushing Patsy out of the way, "We just came to offer our condolences—"

"'Bout what? That my mother's killer was freed?"

Mother?

"Oh, my God," Ruth whispered. "You must have been an infant. You poor thing."

It swirled in Patsy's mind, the impossibility of this. Matilda Greene had a child.

"What, you think she must have been a terrible person? Because she was a prostitute? That's what you all think, up on the hill in your mansions. You think you're different, but you're not." She hissed, so close to the crack of the screen door that saliva collected in the corners of her mouth.

"No, we don't...we just...we're sorry—"

"Sorry?" She laughed, glaring at them. "My grandma raised me, because my mother was killed by a son-of-a-bitch, just trying to take care of me after my father bailed. Fucking men. Don't trust 'em, Patsy. Even with your goddamn trust fund."

Patsy backed away, as Ruth said, "We apologize for interrupting your day."

As Ruth led her to the rental car, she said, "It's about time for you to understand that through all your wisdom, there are things you just *don't* understand."

Daisy listened to the exchange between her granddaughter and Patsy Bundy, and sighed, a deep pain rattling in her chest like a fit of pneumonia that had never gone away. Her skin a patchwork of deep wrinkles, and her hair that had been matted and gray for decades; she had long since lost that spark of rage Rosie had. It had been replaced with an unending sorrow, one that only a woman who had lost a child could understand. Fatigue penetrated the marrow of her bones, and she concerned herself only with keeping her head above water. She scrubbed those toilets at the Walmart in the city, prayed the car would make it there and back. Outside of this, she spent her days fixing financial crises. Rosie fixed dinner and cleaned up; she was a good girl, that one.

"It isn't the Bundy girl's fault, Rosie," she said. She gazed up at her granddaughter, who was easily four inches taller than her. Her cheekbones were chiseled, her smile pinched. The girl put so much energy into her anger that even the muscles in her face had wasted. Everything about Daisy, on the other hand, had gone placid and weathered. It is what it is, she thought often. No sense in wallowing.

"Easy for you to say," Rosie retorted, glowering with crossed arms. "No one has taken interest in Mama's death in years."

This was not at all easy for Daisy to say. Matilda was her child. But she asked softly, "Did anyone your age even know about her?"

Rosie tucked a piece of near-white hair behind her ear, sitting beside her grandmother on the couch that they'd found at the Salvation Army and scrubbed clean. Still, there were patches of dark brown covering the formerly beige fabric. Daisy did not like busy patterns, as a rule. Too complicated. Those flowered couches with vines tangled all over them gave Daisy a headache.

"If they did, they didn't say anything." She shrugged. Her grandmother knew that Rosie had been a reclusive child. She knew the whispers about Matilda's death had relegated to a hum rather soon after Parson was arrested, if only because people didn't want to believe such things as poverty and prostitution and murder existed in their world. Now, she was fishing for evidence that Rosie had been bullied. It seemed to her that Rosie had spent her school years sunken so far from the other students she'd melted in a sort of nonexistence. This saddened her, remembering her happy Matilda, who did not seem to notice how poor they were.

"You know your mother only did what she felt she had to."

"I know." She sighed. "We've gone over this before." Rosie dug her nails into the couch, and wrapped her arms around her knees, her own little escape. Daisy understood that it was best to leave her be.

Daisy's own husband had left when Matilda was just a baby. Just up and left in the middle of the night, for some woman he screwed on the side, leaving her with a six-month-old baby and little else. Daisy worked three housekeeping jobs, which worked out because she could bring Matilda, having no childcare options. At night, she studied books from the library. As Matilda grew, Daisy took on better-paying jobs— secretary work, things like that. They were poor, so poor at times that Top Ramen sustained them for the last day or two till payday. No one understands how expensive poverty is. You borrow money from a pawn shop or get a high-interest loan for folks with low income, and then you spend half your next check paying it back. Then you do it again, this time for just one more month, this last time. Until three weeks later and there's nothing left to hock.

So, Daisy and Matilda made it, stuck at the bottom of the hill. Each time they began climbing up, another doctor visit or car repair sent them sliding back down. Yet, they were happy, Daisy thought. Matilda wore clean clothes, and ate well, save for those in-between paydays where the cabinets were bare. The local foodbank held only canned beans and soup, gifted from the back of well-meaning folks' cupboards during the annual food drive.

Matilda graduated Jackson High and even had a chance to go to the junior college, before becoming pregnant. That would turn out to be the end of her.

Rosie came into the world uneventfully, born at home with a midwife attending. Soon, though, the newborn's breathing grew rattled, alarming both Matilda and Daisy. They had no choice but to scrape together change and a week's worth of grocery money to drive her to the hospital. The quick, labored breaths intensified in the car. The doctors thought for sure they'd lose her to a septic infection. However, little Rosie fought hard. Two weeks later, they were released with a hefty bill. And from there, it became apparent Rosie had asthma, as her wheezing continued. So, more doctors, more tests, more medication, and no health insurance. Public assistance didn't cover the one medication that really helped Rosie. The house reeked of fear, for the baby's life, and for how they would afford this.

Daisy did not tell Rosie any of this, because her asthma lessened as she grew. Thank God.

To keep up with the ever-rising stacks of bills and collection calls and the rent, both mother and daughter worked two or three jobs. It never satisfied the barrage of calls, and soon, Daisy knew Matilda was taking on untoward jobs. She didn't exactly approve of them, but she sighed in relief when the pharmacist agreed to release the next medication refill. First it was a bit of dancing at the nude bar deep in the next town. Then the men paid her, in stacks of bills, for a little more. Daisy didn't ask exactly what this entailed; she didn't want to know. Matilda would sit with all that money in front of her and just stare. Neither one them had never seen so much cash in their lives. And she'd made it in just an evening. It wasn't all *that* much money, as it hardly kept the bill collectors at bay and the doctors satisfied enough to continue treating Rosie, but, of course, this is a matter of one's perspective.

Matilda had those round, perky breasts of a breastfeeding mother, and her stomach had gone flat, probably from the minimal calorie intake of a half-starved woman. But it worked in her favor. Her hair flowed down her back, platinum like Rosie's, but thick and delicious to men. Placid blue eyes gave off just the right hint of innocence, but Daisy knew her daughter could be coy, too.

"Mama, I'll just finish out this one night, and then I'll be done with it," she had said, many times.

When you're so very poor, and your baby is sick, you'll do anything. Daisy understood this, though she'd often remark, "We're cursed in this family, by men. They leave. That's what they do. They up and leave."

Matilda went to work that last night, the night she met Parson, because they needed a refill for Rosie's steroid inhaler.

Daisy wished so deeply she'd stopped her daughter, hated to admit that she went along because it was the only way out. Yet, inside her lurked a feeling that she had prostituted her daughter, that she should have admonished her. Insisted they find another solution. There had to have been another way.

"The Bundy family is a bunch of rich assholes, that's all I mean," murmured Rosie.

"It's hard to like people who're born privileged, Rosie. But that family didn't murder your mother."

"No, but they're part of this town, part of this world that doesn't get it. They swept Mama's death away, because in their hearts, they thought she deserved it."

Daisy bit her lip till hot blood formed in her mouth. "I just want you to be happy, Rosie. 'Cause that's what your mama wanted."

"Stop tellin' me what Mama wanted. She's not here, and this is what we've got." She waved her hand across the room, which smelled dank and stale, like a cave without windows. The mold had been cleaned, supposedly. But the aroma lingered. Daisy poured additional bleach on it, though it was probably fruitless.

That night, years before, when flames engulfed the Bayou, a sort of dread fell over Daisy. The blackened sky and soot raining down swept a quiet awe over the whole town; people were in shock. But Daisy felt a deep and layered fear; somewhere inside, she knew that something very bad was happening. She pushed these thoughts away, but as time passed and her child hadn't come home, her chest tightened with anxiety. Where was her daughter? This thought undulated through her mind on a molecular level, billowed through her chest even darker than the clouds of smoke that whipped through town.

They found her body in the swamp, naked and strangled. Parson fled on foot, leaving his horse behind, and blotting out almost all of Daisy's soul. In the aftermath of finding and prosecuting him, she thought there'd be a satisfaction of sorts when his ass was thrown behind bars. But left to the quiet of daily existence, her daughter was still gone. Here she was, with her daughter's daughter, just trying to survive.

As they say, you do what you have to do. Daisy now watched as a glowering Rosie folded her legs to her chest on the old couch, off to the one side where the springs hadn't broken. She shut the curtains tight, knowing that the Bundy girl wouldn't be the last to show up at the little house. "Rosie," she said, kneeling beside her, "We best not answer the door, okay? They'll all be comin' by to ask our 'perspective'..."

Mother and granddaughter exchanged serious glances. They both knew no one cared about their 'perspective'. Sure, no one wanted the monster free. But in some corner of their minds, even in Patsy Bundy's mind, Matilda Greene had been a lesser victim. Whispers flowed through Cypress now, twenty-five years later. But in the 70s, people had forgotten about Matilda's murder so quick none of Rosie's schoolmates even knew about that night on the Bayou. How long would it take for that monster's release to become old news?

"If one of the Bundy women had been murdered, stolen from her mansion or somethin', you can bet no one in this town would ever forget," said Rosie.

Daisy nodded. "That's sure as shit."

"Instead, they're thinkin' she deserved it."

"Nah, Rosie. They just don't wanna believe it could happen to them. And that was 1970. I'd like to think times have changed."

Rosie snorted, and flipped on the TV.

This too, shall pass. Lord Jesus, let people simmer down quick this time, too, Daisy prayed. It troubled her that the Bundys were poking around in her family business. Especially because she suspected Patsy Bundy wanted more than gossip.

"Know what's weird?" said Patsy, rolling her window down a couple of inches. She lit a cigarette. "That no one mentioned she had a baby. Did you ever hear of a baby?"

Ruth sighed. "No, I didn't. Not even at the time. But that's no one's business."

"Of course," said Patsy, blowing a thin line of smoke to the open window. "It's just awful."

"Don't start meddling. You left the South 'cause you hated that, remember?"

"I'm not meddling. I'm trying to figure out if that was the same murder in my vision. Because he was vicious. He should not be free."

Ruth's eyes widened, and she said, "Patsy Mae, don't you dare go playin' cop."

"I'm not playing cop. I'm just disturbed by this. I can't go home yet. Can I stay at your place for a few days? I just want to find out more about this Parson dude before I leave."

"I guess. Your mama is already pissed at me." Ruth sighed. "And the rest of the world."

"That's why I'm not staying with them," she said. "Besides, Pierre's leaving today."

"How'd he take it?"

"Not well, exactly. But he didn't put up a fight. I've known we were done for a long time. I just didn't want to admit it. I put so much energy into him."

"You're doing the right thing. You're young. Never settle, Patsy. It was devastating to lose Jeb. But I can look back and say I had true love, and that makes the heartache worth it."

Patsy smiled. "I wish I remembered him better. I just have little flashes. Does Tommy remember him?"

"I don't think so, not really. Are your little flashes just of the night he was killed?" Her tone was laced with hesitation.

Patsy thought for a moment, and said, "Of course not. Just little moments of the two of you with my parents when Tommy and I would play. I bet it was weird."

"Not being part of a couple? Yeah," said Ruth.

Patsy took another drag of her cigarette and said, "Let's go to the library. Show me where you work."

At this, Ruth perked up. Once Ruth got her degree, she'd been promoted to head librarian at Cypress Library. "My promotion thrilled Tommy," she said, beaming.

"I bet he's proud," said Patsy.

"Besides that, you know how he loves books," she said.

"That's right, he does," said Patsy. "What else has he been up to?"

Ruth gave her a sideways glance, but Patsy drove on, casually positioning her hands on the steering wheel.

"His heart just broke when you left. I feel terrible, because I think he'd have followed you, but he was worried about me."

Tommy would have left Cypress for me? She drummed her fingers on the wheel. "I thought he loved it here."

"Oh, Patsy. You know he'd have done anything for you. I wish he'd go teach high school literature. He'd be great at it."

"Why doesn't he?"

"He thinks it'd be a betrayal to Stanley. Or Jeb. I've told him if he gets killed shrimpin' it'd be a betrayal to me. But he speaks his mind to me, that's the thing. He's afraid of your father," she said.

"He can be intimidating," said Patsy, smiling.

"Yeah. But nothing intimidates you, darlin'. Least of all, Stanley. The both of you are stubborn."

"Oh, Ruth. You aren't intimidated by much, either. I learned from the best." Patsy smirked and shifted in the driver's seat. This visit surprised her; deep, layered questions formed in her mind. She hesitated. "I'm not going back to that house. She hates me."

"She does not hate you, honey. Your mother has got her own issues, that's all. It has nothing to do with you, or her love for you."

"Eh, forget it. You don't understand."

"I kinda do. I've known her my whole life, and she treats everyone like that."

"All right, all right." She laughed. "Well, here we are. Show me what y'all got here, technology-wise."

The little blue library sat on Main Street as it always had, nestled between the post office and a row of businesses. Cheery flowers and manicured foliage surrounded it. The Cypress Library had always reminded Patsy of a quaint house, perfect for reading.

Patsy's mouth fell open when they entered the building. The children's area, just as large as the ones in Boston, was lined with computers. Books were stacked in high shelves, many more than Patsy remembered. "Wow, there are so many books," she marveled.

"I've had to beg the county for money, but yeah, we've upgraded everything. Kids come here from two towns over to get books the other libraries 'round here don't have or are always checked out."

"Amazing." Patsy twisted around, taking it all in.

"All right. What is it you want?"

"I want some information on Parson. Local papers at the time of the murder. Like, who is this man? What did he do for a living? Stuff like that."

"All I remember is that he lived in Fuller. I didn't listen to the rest of it. Your mother had a difficult time."

"Mama?" This confounded Patsy.

"Well, she was within days of giving birth to you, and then we all had to evacuate because of the fire—"

"Why is this the first I've heard of it?" Patsy said, incredulous.

"I told you, your mother was upset." Ruth looked at her with narrowed eyes.

"Oh, all right. I guess we'll be investigating him together, then."

"I've gotta get microfilm for this." She ran her fingers through her hair. "Internet records don't go back this far." Ruth strode toward the front desk.

"Frannie," said Ruth to another librarian, who was going through a stack of books. Her silver hair was pinned into a tight bun and her glasses slid off the bridge of her nose. She shifted her gaze to Ruth, who continued, "We'll be in the back a minute. I've got to go through some microfilm."

"That's a tedious job," said Frannie. She cleared her throat and continued thumbing through the pages of a large atlas. Patsy recognized her. She'd worked at the library since Patsy was little, which is to say, much longer than Ruth.

In the back, Ruth slid open a filing drawer marked 1970-1979, and sorted through the stacks of film lined up in the drawer. "At least it happened in 1970. I'd hate to work through to the bottom of these. Okay, here's several rolls from the local paper between December 1970 and February 1971. That gives you a nice range to start with."

"All right," said Patsy, balancing the numerous cylinders in her arms.

"You know how to use a reader for these?"

"Of course." Patsy gathered them up and brought them to the last reader remaining in the library.

"They're going by the wayside, but we don't have records of newspapers that old."

Patsy nodded, hands shaking, lifted the glass, and spooled the film under it. She flipped through the December paper quickly, maneuvering the buttons like a video game. She came upon the article posted that evening, which wasn't what she was looking for.

What she wanted was printed three days later, when Archibald Parson was arrested.

"Archibald Parson is implicated in the murder of Matilda Greene, an alleged prostitute from a nearby town. He panicked and set fire to the part of the Bayou located in Cypress, Louisiana."

Patsy seethed at this. Who cares about her vocation? He killed her.

She continued reading. "Parson lives in the nearby town of Fuller with his wife and daughter, who have left the state to an undisclosed location. His wife was unaware of the murder and says her husband expressed sadness the night of the fire. He had told her he was working with his horses when he witnessed the smoke. He owns hundreds of horses and works the shows. He also offers riding lessons..."

Patsy's throat cracked as she yelled, "Ruth! C'mere. Look at this!"

Ruth's corduroy pants swished back and forth as she approached. She leaned on the desk, reading over Patsy's shoulder, murmuring to herself. "Sweet Jesus. Well, there's your horses."

"Do you think the wife— Jenny Parson, it says— came back to town?" said Patsy, narrowing her eyes on the screen. "I mean, what would have become of these horses if she'd left for good?"

"I wonder if that's mentioned in the police records," said Ruth.

"How the hell do we get police records?"

"I've been friends with the sheriff since high school, Patsy Mae. Small towns have their benefits." She fished her keys from her purse and headed toward the front desk. "Frannie, you're in charge. I've got a quick errand to run," she said. "Come on, now. Just this last thing, and we're done."

"Well, I suppose," called Frannie as they hurried out the door.

Patsy did not trust cops, but she remembered Sheriff Landon as a kind man who collected toys for tots during the holiday season, and that he hadn't given her too much shit about the flag burning incident.

When they arrived at the police station, he emerged from behind his large desk, littered with stacks of paperwork, with a genuine smile, and hugged

Ruth tight. "How're you doin' Ruth?" he said.

"I'm well, Frank. And how's Betty?"

"Still the same. Diabetes is tough, you know." Frank stroked his short beard, gazing out the window. His soft belly hung slightly over his belt. He folded his tanned arms over his chest.

"I'm sorry, Frank. Send her our well-wishes." Ruth patted his shoulder gently. "You remember Patsy, right?"

"Of course! Patsy Mae! We used to call you the Samantha Stevens of Cypress. Said you'd put this town on the map." He chuckled.

"Well, Cypress is on the map again, Sheriff," said Patsy.

"I'm afraid that's why we're here," said Ruth, lowering her voice. "The Parson man."

"No one here's happy about it either, ladies."

"I get that. Served his time, all that bullshit. It's just, Patsy found this bone, down by the Bayou. We wanted to see if it belonged to Matilda Greene."

"Good Lord. I highly doubt that," he said, shaking his head. "I guess. Anything for you. I mean, I could hand it to forensics for y'all." Sheriff Landon smiled lightly towards Ruth. "Even if it was…what can we do 'bout it now?"

"It's probably an animal bone. I've been telling Patsy this. But just to be sure." She lowered her voice to a whisper. "It doesn't belong to someone else. Someone other than Matilda Greene."

The sheriff laughed. "Oh, no way, Ruth. Not a chance in hell."

"I'm sure you're right. And one more thing. Do you know what happened to Parson's wife? His horses?"

Sheriff Landon rolled his eyes. "Good God. Who gives a shit? All right. I'll grab the file. But I swear, this is between us."

He unlocked a back room and left for a long time. "He's the one who came over with the news of Jeb's death," she said. "He'll help us."

Patsy's stomach twisted.

"All right, ladies," said Sheriff Landon as he strode through the door, interrupting the silence. "This is what I've got. They had an infant together, no more than six months old. She divorced him and moved to California, where her parents live, after his conviction. Beyond that, who knows? It was twenty-five years ago."

"And the horses? His business?" said Patsy.

"Sold," he said. "I know the guy that bought 'em. It was an easy sale. Those horses are moneymakers. At least they were back in the day."

"Thanks, Frank. That's all we need. Where do we drop off this bone?" She stifled a laugh.

In the car, Patsy said, "So, you don't think it's remotely strange that he had a baby, and so did the victim? And Tommy and I actually went to high school with Matilda's *daughter*?"

"It's Cypress. It's a small world."

"I guess." Still, an essence ran through Patsy. Something was not right. She could *feel* it. "I'll get going back to Boston tomorrow, okay? I'll get my plane tickets in order by then. I've got dinner with Elodie and Leo tonight, and then I'm leaving. I feel terrible for putting you through all this for nothing."

Ruth pursed her lips. "Patsy, I'd do anything for you. Are you sure 'bout going back?"

"I'm sure. I don't think there's any more I can do," she said. "I need to get home anyway. Make sure Pierre moves out."

"Patsy," said Ruth, and gave her a sideways glance. "Never mind." She shook her head. "All right, don't be a stranger."

Patsy couldn't get Matilda Greene or her family out of her mind. The billows of smoke from the Bayou had snuffed out any rational thought processes she had left.

●　　●　　●　　●　　●

She intended to drive straight to Elodie's house; she knew she was about to make a huge mistake. But the rental car seemed to drive itself back down the deep gravel road. It winded through the streets like it had been programmed to do so. I'm possessed, she thought. Fucking possessed. She maneuvered the wheel with her palm like a crystal ball.

Even as night fell, she drove toward Daisy Greene's house, this gravitational pull sending her up the driveway, kicking up dust as she parked. As she walked to the door, a light flickered on inside the darkened house. She hoped she hadn't scared them, but she needed to talk to Daisy, just one more time.

The door creaked open, and Daisy's body shadowed the light from the house. She opened the screen. "You're back."

"I need to talk with you, please."

"Come in," she said, widening the screen door. It breathed open.

Daisy had let her in. Patsy let go of her breath.

Patsy nodded and slipped inside, eyes adjusting to the light. The living room smelled of stale smoke; the rust-colored couch sagged. "I'm sorry to bother you, ma'am. But we've got to talk."

"Sit," said Daisy. "Rosie is at work, so I can only talk a few minutes."

Patsy slid onto the couch, arranging her body on the unbroken spring. "That was her." She pointed at a photo of a stunning young blonde woman. Her mind filled with puffs of smoke, and the woman's scream echoed in her mind. She was going crazy, that had to be it. She turned from the photo.

"Lemme ask you something, Patsy Mae. What is it about you? Does my daughter have something to do with your witchcraft down in that tin shack? Rosie told me all the stories."

"I'm no witch."

"Then what is it?"

"I have visions. Maybe you could say I see ghosts—"

"Did she talk to you?" Daisy said this with the kind of desperation the bereaved have for contact with the dead.

"No, no. It's not like that," Patsy said quickly, not wanting to lead this poor woman on in the wrong way.

"I saw the murder, saw the fire. I've had these visions since I was very young, of people who've died, usually down at my tin shack."

"So why?" said Daisy. A trance-like feeling swept through the room.

"Because I'm scared. Your granddaughter is my age. His daughter— Parson's, I mean— is also our age. Matilda died the week before I was born."

"I don't understand," said Daisy.

'I don't, either. But I'm gonna, before they set him free. All these babies; your daughter, his, even me, because I feel like that's why I see her. Because she died right as I was born. She wants me to find out what happened."

"You're creepin' me out, girl. Why're you telling me this?"

"I think Matilda may not be the only one. I know you feel it too. Why else have y'all been holed up here since? The cops shoved this under the rug quick as they could."

"Girl, I don't know what you're trying to say, but I think it's best you leave now. Rosie will be home soon," she said, standing.

"All right." Patsy sighed. "I just don't know what it is, ma'am, but I'm nervous."

"Patsy, he's a killer and he's being released. You ought to be nervous. But not 'cause of some strange powers you think you've got."

Daisy had clearly had enough. It was time to leave. "I'm sorry, again, Daisy. For your loss, for intruding."

Patsy ran back to the car, breathless from her own stupidity. Again, she missed the highway entrance. A melancholy sort of homesickness sat heavy in her heart, seeping right through her hands into the steering wheel. She considered how she'd left things at eighteen, how filled with animosity she'd been. It occurred to her that now, at twenty-five, a proper goodbye was in order. The strange, complicated mess of family swirled in her brain, and she wondered, what do you do when your father's a bigot, and yet, he raised you? He loved her, even though he was wrong. And damn, was he ever wrong. She thought about this as she made the drive to Elodie's house.

She'd stop and say goodbye after dinner. Pierre had been right about one thing— she didn't have to start a shitstorm. She lived in Boston, after all. Evening fell, with purple and orange shimmering along the water.

Chapter Twenty-Two
FRIENDS AND FAMILY

Elodie Johnson poured two glasses of tea and put one before Patsy. "More sugar?" she asked, pouring a heaping tablespoon in her own glass.

"No thanks," said Patsy. The tea was already so sweet it felt thick on Patsy's tongue. She'd gotten used to black coffee in Boston. Unsweetened, with an occasional inch of milk. She did not care for change, and lately she had been immersed in nothing else.

"Want coffee instead?" she asked, walking toward the kitchen.

"If it's not too much trouble," said Patsy.

"So, where've you been all this time? Up in Boston with a handsome French man! I'm jealous." Elodie laughed, and the sound of her voice made Patsy want to close her eyes and take it in. Her light southern accent anchored Patsy to the floor. The goodness in her voice smoothed the hellish experience she'd just had at Daisy Greene's house, even if she'd created it for herself. Patsy loved this simple exchange, sharing a drink with a friend. She had so few genuine friendships with women her own age, it was nice to sit and just breathe. Her life was a whirlwind of intense waves of emotion she tried to squelch. She wondered what it would be like to be a grownup, to be relaxed and comfortable in your skin. To be calm.

"Yeah, I'm afraid that's done, Elodie. I don't think it was even the party or *Slice of Life* cooking magazine—"

Elodie burst into a chuckle.

"What?" Patsy said, annoyed. "You remind me of how y'all laughed at me down at the Bayou. Me and my 'visions'."

"Oh, stop," Elodie said. "All I'm sayin' is it's pretty damn obvious you wouldn't leave a man over something stupid like that. Especially one that looks like him." She twirled the braid in her fingers with a smile.

"True," Patsy agreed.

"Want something stronger in that coffee?" said Elodie with a grin. She pulled a bottle of whiskey out of a laundry basket in the closet.

"Hell yeah. Is keeping liquor hidden around the house a requirement for parenthood?" she asked, waving her hand.

"Pretty much." She plunked down beside Patsy on the couch and folded her legs. "So, what's up, girl? You know something about this murder. I can feel it."

"You never cared about any of that before," Patsy said.

"I never knew," she replied. The light cheer between them faded. The crack in Elodie's soft voice penetrated the room. Elodie's questioning eyes and how the flesh of her lower lip curled as she began to cry; it all overwhelmed Patsy. She was not accustomed to feeling overwhelmed. Elodie squeezed her hand, and she felt embarrassed by her own vulnerability and the state of her fingernails, bitten to the quick.

"I didn't, either," Patsy admitted, because this was true. "My visions weren't as clear as all this. Elodie, can you believe this? Can you believe a woman died and the whole town knew it?"

"Yes," she replied. "I certainly can."

She stood. "Look. You're going home, and we're all gonna have a nice, calm dinner before you get on that plane, Patsy. I expect they'll shuffle in soon."

"All right. I'll try hard not to exhaust y'all."

Elodie put a firm hand on Patsy's shoulder. "You're exhausting yourself, honey. It ain't me I'm worried about. I hate to say it, because I'd love for you to stay here forever and marry Tommy—"

"Tommy? What?" Patsy laughed.

"Oh, girl, don't play stupid with me. But that's not where I'm going with this. Point is, it's not healthy for you here." Elodie shook her head and peeked out the window. "Oh, they're here! Let's just have fun, okay? No negativity. I'm serious, too. John took the kids so we could hang out tonight." Elodie was failing at her signature eternal optimism; she could not hide the sheen in her eyes.

Leo entered the dining room carrying several boxes of pizza, and Tommy shuffled behind him with Coke and beer. Her neck loosened at his smile. She felt the urge to run her fingers down his arm. He set the drinks next to the pizza and flopped on the couch beside her. "Hungry?"

"No, but I should probably eat, regardless of that."

Leo told them of his adventures at law school, glowing. "Well, you know what a different world it is, Patsy," he said. "But I still love it here. Cypress is my home."

"Apparently, there's more crime here than we knew," said Patsy. "You could be a defense lawyer, or work for the district attorney." She smirked, and they all laughed with a tinge of nervousness.

Patsy didn't think Ruth would tell Tommy about their visit to Daisy

Greene's house, and she did not intend to, either. It felt as though she'd trampled into an unknown world where she did not belong. Still, she searched Tommy's face for clues. "We can't do anything about it, Patsy," he said, in a firm tone. He did not want her to mention the bone. An intuition flowed between them; anything they knew about the murder beyond what had been released would not be spoken of tonight. She leaned back and sank deep in the couch.

"How's your visit so far, Leo?" said Tommy.

"Dad's a pain. Always talking on the shrimp business."

"Right when Mama can argue that he should buy his own boat," said Elodie.

Leo scoffed, and Patsy remarked, "She's always finished your sentences. Y'all are twins. She can't help it."

"*Fraternal* twins. Which means genetically we are the exact same as regular siblings. There is no way she can read my mind. She just interjects her opinion all the time—"

"Uh-huh," said Elodie, waving her hand.

Leo made sure everyone knew he and Elodie were not made entirely of the same genetic material whenever she irritated him.

"Leo, Daddy could leave that damn business if he wanted to. That's a fact. We can think what we like, but he and Stanley love each other, in spite of it all."

"What the hell?" said Leo.

"It's because of that night on the Bayou," she said. "The night Jeb died—" Elodie caught Tommy's eye and stopped. "Anyway, they were there together. He feels as if the two of them are the last men standing. Or somethin' like that."

"He's stupid. I'm sorry, Patsy, but your father is an asshole," said Leo, as he took a gulp of his drink. The pungent shadow clouding the reunion had nothing to do with her father. It came from the mention of Jeb.

Patsy drew a cold breath through her teeth, and patted Tommy's hand. The group fell silent. Too many feelings here, thought Patsy. She considered leaving, hitting the road. This place with its ghosts...

Instead, she blurted, "Do y'all remember a girl named Rosie Greene from high school?"

At first, the group appeared relieved at the change of topic, but then Leo's eyes went dark. "You mean the blonde girl? Dirt poor?"

"That's the one," said Patsy. She fell into his space, the Leo bubble she remembered from childhood. His personality could be enervating because it was much like her own, willful and opinionated. If Leo's face clouded over, if he saw what she did, even for a moment, it made it feel more real.

"I've seen her. She used to hang out on that tree stump by the hideout. Always crying," he said.

"That's the girl we saw the day of your mama's party!" said Tommy.

The four huddled on the couch, a haunting sadness hanging in the air, thick as molasses. It felt like when they were children, folded inside the tin shack, rain pattering on the roof.

Leo cleared his throat and said, almost in a whisper, "She stayed after class a lot, talking with Mrs. Hanson. I stayed and did homework there often, because math wasn't so much my strong suit, and I wanted to go to law school. Anyway, I got a weird vibe from her. Kinda creepy. Something. One afternoon I followed her home. She lived in this old, falling down house. Slipped right inside like she had something to hide."

"So what?" said Patsy. "Lots of poor kids went to Jackson."

"Yeah, but there was something different about this girl, Patsy." He said this, thinking. "I feel terrible about this. But I freaked out and ran away. She opened the screen door and yelled at me for spying. I thought, if anyone's crazy, it's that girl."

Elodie said, "I remember her. She hid by the lockers alone. Didn't have a single friend. Why are you asking this, Patsy?"

Patsy's cheeks burned. She hadn't remembered that afternoon at the Bayou, either. "Never mind. I ran into her earlier today and hadn't remembered her. She knew my name, is all."

Tommy stood wordlessly, and meandered to the cabinet, where he produced a bottle of liquor. "This is all too weird. Let's play cards and drink and pretend to be normal."

They nodded in agreement. Normal. An abstract concept the four of them had an unquenchable thirst for.

• • • • •

Patsy rapped on the thick, wood door. The tap of her mother's footsteps grew louder. Patsy held her breath, waiting. The clicking heels sent a swell of anxiety through her chest. She had the urge to scream, "Mother, just open the goddamn door!"

The screen wheezed open, and Mama stood across from her with colored cheeks. It was hard to say if she'd been working around the house or if Patsy had upset her by coming.

"Patsy," said Mama, biting her lip. "Did you forget something?"

"No, I came to say goodbye, Mama. And I'm sorry for fighting with Daddy and ruining your party."

Edna sighed, and pulled Patsy close. She smelled like Ivory soap and Lemon Pledge, reminding Patsy of her mother's embrace when she was small enough to bury her face in her dress at the waist. A light layer of dew had collected at her mother's temples. "Cleaning?" she said.

"Just tidying up," said Edna, straightening her dress.

"Well, I need to catch my flight soon. Is Daddy around?" She peered inside.

"I don't know, Patsy. I'm exhausted. This whole thing has me bone-tired. It's not you, exactly. The whole neighborhood fightin'. The murderer being set free in my neighborhood here soon."

"Why didn't this ever come up? Tommy didn't know. I didn't know. Hell, Leo hadn't a clue."

"I suppose nobody wanted to talk about such a horrible thing," she said. "Look, just come in and sit at the table. Come see your father. Poor man's so upset because of y'all, Patsy. You know despite his flaws— and Lord knows the man is flawed— he loves you."

Patsy followed her mother through the unblemished house. The lights were dim; the television played in the study. She followed the sound and waited in the doorway. Daddy leaned back in his orange chair, reclined with his slippered feet up. He stared at the TV.

"Daddy," she began.

He looked up from his show, startled. "Oh, you're back. Pierre left a while ago. You two fightin'?" He pushed the foot rest down and stood. He gazed at the floor, hands in his pockets.

"It's a long story."

Stanley nodded. "Look, I'm sorry about what a mess this turned out to be. It's the last thing I wanted."

"What did you want, Daddy?" Patsy looked at her father in earnest. He rubbed his eyes. She wondered if her mother made him whole.

"I wanted us to be a family again."

"What about your family? I never hear about your parents, your brother."

"My father worked the mines in Appalachia till I was eight, maybe nine. He mined for coal and drank. He left, and my mother brought us here, where your grandma lived. And then she died. I'm not sure what else you want to know. None of it matters anymore." He turned back to his television show.

"What does matter?" she said.

"I don't know. I just don't know anymore. I'm just so goddamned tired and everything has to be hard. And I'm sick of it."

Patsy stood, tight-lipped. "Seems you've had seven easy years, with me being gone and all."

"Good Lord, you've got no idea, none at all. I hope you don't experience this shit with your own kids."

"If I have kids, I won't sell 'em out to the neighbors, Dad," she said. Heat ran through her. She didn't take to being spoken to this way. "This is why I left. Right here. This."

Edna walked in, and leaned against the wall, arms squared against her body. This infuriated Patsy. She could not say why, even. Just that her mother standing with a smirk on her face like she'd won another gold crown at a beauty pageant made her think: she's won, she's won again.

"I'll go now," she said. She held her breath. Don't show her she's upset you. Don't let her upset you.

"If you think that's best," she said, and smoothed her pretty skirt.

"If I think that's best? Oh, Mother, you can be such a *bitch*!"

"Get out of my house." Edna spoke quietly, unaffected.

"Daddy," she said, keeping her gaze steady toward her mother's eyes. "Is this what you want?"

Already standing, he said softly, "Edna. Patsy. Don't do this. This isn't right."

Patsy had already slammed the door.

She needed to get out of Cypress. This place brought out the worst in her. She ran for the car, and drove off, hitting the gas hard and gripping the steering wheel. *Stay present, goddammit. Stop floatin' away with the ghosts of the Bayou and go the fuck home.*

Chapter Twenty-Three
THE BONE

Patsy brushed the snow off her coat and tossed her keys on the granite countertop. The place was clean at least, considering that Pierre had left her with little but the king-sized bed she now slept in alone. The apartment felt so quiet.

He'd vacuumed on his way out. How kind of him.

It must have been the poetry, Patsy sighed, glancing around the empty apartment.

She flipped through the mail, nothing interesting, a few bills (was he still paying half?!) and some Christmas cards she hadn't gotten while out of town. And...a little orange slip from the post office. A package waited for her in the apartment manager's office. The return address was scrawled in barely legible writing, but she didn't have to read it to know it where it came from.

She yawned. The week in Cypress and the breakup had her in a state of exhaustion. She had not been eating well. Patsy told herself she'd have dinner that night, even though she was alone. She didn't have weight to lose. Stress killed her appetite.

Patsy decided to get the package. She had nothing to lose by peeking at whatever had been sent, she reasoned.

The apartment manager dug through the cabinet beneath the mahogany counter and produced the crumpled Mylar envelope. "Yeah, here it is, Patsy. Late Christmas gift? The snow has slowed the mail for sure."

Patsy nodded and sat in the lobby. She took a breath and tore into the plastic. Under several sheets of red tissue paper was a heavy book, embossed in gold. Inside was a photo album, with pages filled with snapshots she'd taken during her childhood— of Tommy, of the tin shack, her house, every gorgeous Cypress sunset on the wetlands. She thought, this must be where I learned to photograph.

Tommy hanging from his legs off the branch of wide gnarled cypress tree with an upside-down grin, his t-shirt up, little boy belly exposed. She'd taken that one with an old Polaroid.

The tin shack with just the right tinge of light hitting the water as the sunset flooded the trees. Daddy and Gilmore, smiling from the *Patsy Mae*, holding up red and yellow buckets of shrimp in their sweat-drenched shirts...

A card flittered from the package, landing softly on the red carpet. Patsy knelt and picked it up, fingering the soft ivory paper.

Dear Patsy,

I thought you said you photographed still-life...These photos are so full of soul, they're almost breathing...

Love, Tommy

Depressing, she thought. Living in Cypress would drive her insane. She wrapped the gold and red book carefully in tissue paper and put it back in the box. Touching the card with her fingertips one last time, she slid it into its envelope, and sat on the floor of her barren apartment. The phone rang. She ignored it.

As she lingered, thinking about what to do with the rest of her life, the phone squalled again. Goddamnit, she muttered, but picked it up to stop the interminable ringing.

"I don't want to talk right now, Pierre," she said.

"Hello?" said a woman whose voice she did not recognize.

"Yes?"

"I need to speak with Patsy Bundy," said the woman. Her authoritative tone irritated Patsy.

"Why? Do I owe someone money?"

"This is Jennie Parson."

Patsy could not produce a single word.

"Hello? Patsy?"

"Um, yes. Yes, that's me..."

"I'm Archie's wife and he's bein' released soon. I know you're aware of this."

"Yes," she said, twirling the phone cord, "What do you want? I thought you were in California—"

"Not anymore, darling. I'm not that stupid, and neither is my daughter. And I'm gonna strongly suggest you stay the hell out of this. You have no idea what he's capable of—"

"Oh, I think I do," said Patsy, eyes bulging at the stupidity of this woman.

"Listen here. He's gonna be out in the wild in ten days. You better not go back to that town. Not ever again. And you gotta stop stirring shit up. He'll ruin your life and make it look like your fault. Believe me, please. He did it to me, he'll do it to you."

"What the hell does that mean?"

"That man beat the shit out of me for years. Fucked other women and said it was 'cause I was fat and pregnant. I tried to get out. No one cared till he killed someone—"

"Is that why you're on the run?"

Jennie laughed. "No, we've been out of there for years. You know he's capable of stuff behind bars, don't ya?"

Patsy's hands went cold and numb. She whispered, "Like what?"

Silence.

"What? Jennie, you've got to tell me…"

"I can't. Because I don't know, exactly. I've got proof of nothing. But he was out all night, lots of nights. I know there's more. And so do you."

Patsy hung up the phone, shaking.

•   •   •   •

Tommy chucked his dog-eared copy of *The Catcher in The Rye* against the wall with a thud. Holden Caulfield is a pompous little prick, he thought, indignant. He wrapped the thick blue comforter around him, buried his head in the pillow, and tried to sleep. He'd stayed at his mother's the previous night; he was officially pathetic in every way.

The morning sun trickled in the window through the wide slats in the blinds. He thrived on little sleep, maybe because he'd worked early mornings since he was a teenager. This irritated him now. His internal alarm clock blared. He got out of bed, yawning, and stretched his arms high, rolling his tight neck in circles. Seeing Patsy had been a disaster. That palpable sweetness welling inside, followed by the bitter reality— she was a leaver. He could not trust a leaver. He'd thought of her as a warrior, that fearless girl he'd always known. But she disappeared when she was afraid, and it had taken him seven years to understand it. With this thought, he felt vaguely worried for her. Why had she left so fast, with hardly a goodbye? She'd left for college in a flurry of rage, but this felt different.

He whacked *To Kill a Mockingbird* against the wall next. Maybe, with her back to Boston, this pain would subside back to its usual nostalgia that hung around him wherever he went. It was more pleasant than this aching.

He realized something, though, with her visit. He did not have his father's passion for the sea, or the boat, and it sent a shiver through him that Stanley expected that he should. His father had died on *The Patsy Mae!*

He tried, because of Stanley, because he'd always said, "You've got your father's talent, boy. He'd be so proud of you!" He'd felt it might be insulting to Jeb that he'd do anything *but* become a shrimper, though he kept this feeling close to his heart. He wasn't sure if he wanted to spend his life on the boat or he just thought he did because it was what he'd been groomed for; it was like two kinds of metal welded together till you couldn't tell where one ended and the other began.

Sometimes, he'd envision himself taking up his father's body while they were out shrimping, to force himself to love being out on the boat. He'd feel the water lacquer him with its thin layer of salt; he'd try to absorb that invigorating sensation of bringing in the shrimp. He imagined his father inhale the beauty in that, except the next vision that crossed his mind was his father being yanked in the ocean by that rope. He wondered how long he'd been dragged for, and if it hurt to drown. All kinds of morbid things.

There was no way around it. Tommy enjoyed rolling up the full nets of shrimp because it meant it was almost time to go home.

Patsy and her life in Boston did make him consider other possibilities for his life, tore open that place he kept his imaginary love of the sea and spilled the truth out everywhere.

He slipped a sweatshirt over his head and ran his hand through his messy hair before heading to the computer. He flicked it on and waited for it to boot up, drumming his fingers on the desk as the modem rang AOL. There had to be a teaching position somewhere, anywhere, in the country. He clicked open several positions, frustrated at the pay, but acknowledged he was chasing a dream and not a dollar sign. His new cell phone rang, bulky and expensive, but a Christmas gift from his mother. He almost ignored it, but assumed it had to *be* his mother, testing it out. "Hello, Mother," he sighed, "call back on the landline. This thing costs fifty cents a minute and burns my ear in the process." He searched for the button that turned the phone off.

"No, Tommy! Wait!" said a male voice.

"Who's this?" he replied, confused.

"It's Sheriff Landon."

"Is it an emergency?" Tommy's heart palpated. "Is something wrong with my mom?"

"No, son, no it's nothing like that. I just need to talk to your mother, and the home phone is busy."

"Oh, right. I'm on the Internet. Hang on a second."

"I have no idea why the Internet has to take over your damn phone line, but sorry to scare you, son."

Tommy ventured into the living room, where Ruth watched The Price is Right. "Higher!" she yelled, shaking her head. "Why don't these people know how much a damn washing machine costs?"

"Oh, wait! She is home. Sorry, I thought she'd gone to work," he said.

"The Sheriff's on your new gadget," said Tommy. He tossed the phone on her lap, where it landed with a thud. "Sorry," he said, and padded across the carpet in his socks, lingering in the hall.

"Really?" she said. "It wasn't Matilda's bone, then? Different DNA? What do you think it means? Good Lord, another woman was killed on the Bayou."

What the fuck? That bone she found…

<h1 style="text-align:center">Chapter Twenty-Four
HEADACHE</h1>

Tommy bit back tears as he gripped the steering wheel, heading to the dock. Work needed to be done; life needed to be attended to. It was best to get back to normal, though Patsy's whirlwind spirit had excited him, and now that she had gone, his life had gone back to cardboard. He rolled down the window an inch or two, the whizz of the truck motor like a lullaby, the smell of earth and salt calming. Still, he picked his cuticle nervously. Blood dripped down his hand. Dammit! He held the wheel with his knees as he searched for something to stop the bleeding. A bunch of crumpled napkins from some fast food joint had been shoved in the center console. He ripped the napkin in half, applying pressure to his thumb.

The last place he wanted to be was on the boat with Stanley, yet he'd promised, and he was a man to keep his word. He rolled the window all the way down and tried not to yawn. Stanley and Edna had run Patsy out of town once again, and he had lost her, all over again. He turned his thoughts from her to them and considered the moments of exhaustion the Bundy family had caused, when he had his own problems.

He was deeply troubled by Stanley's flaunting of that damn flag. Shame flooded his body, remembering how Gilmore and Leo and Maggie had stomped out the door hardly acknowledged by anyone. And Leo would be heading back to Yale soon.

He didn't want to go out on the boat. He needed the money, that was for sure. He ruminated about that bone. His childhood hideout, so steeped in memories, contained fragments of a woman's soul. Maybe two women.

Tommy rarely thought about the afterlife. Everyone assumed his father was in heaven and that he should be satisfied with that. He and Mama exchanged indignant glances whenever someone made this comment. "You'll see your daddy again someday, Tommy." Or, "Ruth, you know he's in a better place."

Tommy knew that his father's place was with them, his family. Just as the murdered women belonged with theirs. Worse yet, Cypress had stolen their memories, boxed them up, and shoved them away. Tommy bit his cheek until the copper taste of blood filled his mouth. He'd get the work done and get home.

•   •   •

Stanley's head felt like a fishing knife had filleted it in two. The gentle rocking of the boat in the marina was anything but comforting. Each swell brought vomit up in his throat, then back again. Stupid migraines. Always from stress, the stress of her leaving, the stress of her hating him, stress because she'd never understand him or attempt to. She always thought the worst of him; he was a racist, sexist pig. Goddamn it, they were different. But he *loved* her. Stop thinking, he told himself. You're gonna make yourself throw up, and the crew will be here any moment.

His face was prickly since he'd been in too much pain to shave before getting in the truck that morning. He rummaged through the drawers of the little bathroom, searching for a razor with one hand, holding his head with the other. A bottle of Tylenol was in the first aid kit. He swallowed several pills with a gulp of water, and lay back on the bed, hanging his legs off the edge, the cool pillow pressed against his face. He groaned. Shaving would have to wait till the Tylenol kicked in.

The stomp of boots entering the boat made it slosh around even more. Stanley knew it was Gilmore or Stan, but he grumbled under his breath anyway. He shoved another pillow back over his head, covering his ears tightly, to tune the clopping noise out.

"Hey," said Tommy. "Got a headache?"

"Sweet Jesus, yes."

"What, did ya drink a bit much last night?" Tommy avoided Stanley's eyes. He seemed distracted, but maybe it was just Stanley's headache.

"Nope. Stress gives me headaches. Migraines, according to the doc. I really need to get my pills from home."

"I'm sorry. Are we goin' out today?" Tommy shifted his feet, and Stanley cringed.

"I guess we can give it a shot. It feels like the Gulf is dryin' up. Takes twice as long to pull in the same catch." Stanley removed the pillow from his eyes, still holding it tight over the rest of his head. "You were at the party, right?"

"I was. I wanted to see Patsy, since it's been forever."

"Well, why didn't you come up and talk?"

"You two were arguing. You know damn well why I didn't interrupt that shit." Tommy laughed, but with an unmistakable nervousness.

"Damn, can you keep it down?" God, any movement or noise pierced his skull. He needed complete silence and no one to move, but how do you tell a person to sit the fuck still and be quiet? He groaned again. "Tom, I can't go out on the water today. I just can't. But lemme ask you something. What's going on with my daughter? She and her mother fighting nonstop. And then of course, Parson."

Tommy hesitated, shifting his feet again. Dammit, Stanley was going to go insane. He hated when people did that to begin with, and now each click back and forth was torture.

"Well, if I'm being honest, Stanley...I guess it is because of Parson—"

"Is it because you love her?" Stanley felt his face flush that he'd blurted the question out.

"Well, not exactly."

"Tommy, just tell her. You're meant to be with my daughter, and maybe—" This just rolled off his tongue, as if the searing agony of his head caused words to just tumble from his mouth uncensored.

"You think she'd stay in Louisiana because of me?" said Tommy, hesitating. He took a deep breath and said, "I can't do that—"

"I know." He sighed.

Tommy said, "I don't think it's you, anyway."

"What do you mean by that? We both know she hates the flag. Thinks I'm racist."

"Stanley, please—"

"Oh, all right. I understand your position." His head was killing him. By now he was worried. Fighting with Tommy was stupid, he realized now. Talking with Tommy about this, even! That's how bad his headache was.

"You shouldn't fight with Patsy 'bout this, Stanley. If I were you—"

"Tommy, stop it. You know nothing about this!"

"All right. Forget I mentioned it. Are you even okay?"

"I cannot take this boat out today. I need to go home. The doctor said I could go in to get extra meds to break a migraine. I think I need to head over." His heart fluttered. He could almost hear it thumping outside his chest.

"Okay, Stanley. I hope you feel better...you do look bad..."

"Tommy," he said, grasping his hand. "Thanks for bein' straight with me. We go way back, right? Till you were a baby."

"'Course we do," said Tommy. He headed out to the deck, not acting much like the boy who went way back, judging how quickly he departed. Stanley held his head tighter.

"Wait, Tom!" he yelled, hoping he was in earshot.

"Yeah?"

"Come back down. I need a favor."

Tommy appeared in the door of the cabin, filling the small space with his tall frame. "What's wrong?" Now his brow furrowed. "You look whiter than usual."

"I'm sorry, buddy. I shouldn't have said anything. I'm only mad at my daughter."

"No need to be sorry. Dude, you look awful." Tommy's face twisted in concern.

"Help me up to the truck, please. I need to get some meds from the doctor. This migraine is just killer. I can't imagine driving myself home."

He hesitated. "You sure you don't wanna just head to the emergency room? They can get you the meds faster that way. You might need an IV."

"An IV? Oh God, the thought of that makes me nauseous. Just take me home to Edna, and she'll bring you back to your truck. It won't take long, I promise."

"It isn't getting back to the damn truck I'm worried about, Stanley."

Stanley tried to stand up, at first very dizzy, a swooshing feeling running through the left side of his body. "Tommy, is the boat secure? It feels like the ropes might be loose." He felt like he was speaking underwater, his voice hollow and echoing around in his head like a rack of pool balls struck by a cue stick, banging into each other.

"No, it's secure. It's not the boat. Stand on your other foot, Stanley!" Tommy's voice rose, but he was far away.

He tried to settle his body straight, but he couldn't move his left side. Fear ripped through his bones, as he tried to anchor his left leg on the ground, and instead, toppled over onto his shoulder. The boat shook from side to side with a hollow thump from the impact of Stanley's body.

"You're stuttering, man!" said Tommy. "I've got to radio for help. Something's goin' on here. Just hold on, someone will be here in a minute." Tommy grasped his hand tightly. "I'll have someone here in a minute. Please. Hold on."

He lay his head against the light blue carpet, listening to the sounds rushing in and out of his consciousness. Blue and red lights whirled in his vision, vibrant one moment, then fading away like the end of a film. Sirens sounded and Tommy continued speaking, but Stanley could not make out what he was saying. The boat spun through his mind like a carousel, and Tommy just moved his lips, kneeling beside him, forming soundless words. He felt he was in another world, maybe trapped between two worlds. He was numb, melting right through the boat, into the salt water, sinking in the Bayou. The sun was nowhere to be found. There was a swirl of colors and lights and the sweet smell of his wife. "Edna," he called, to no one.

Someone lifted him up, the sound of monotonous voices creeping upon each other like a snake in the marsh, getting closer. The stretcher clicked into place and they were off, rushing from the boat, and one, two, three, the paramedics lifted him up onto the dock. They raced toward the ambulance. At least that's what Stanley thought, with his brain shifting in a million directions, wondering if this was Death. Or if he'd taken some drug. It was hard to say.

"Edna!" he called into the darkness of the ambulance. Then click! He floated above the stretcher.

"Move your fingers, sir. Can you move your fingers?"

Stanley wiggled his right fingers, back and forth.

"Move the other side, sir. Can you try that for me?"

The numbness started to subside. He moved his left fingers slightly, though not with the same vigor as the other side. It took effort, concentration. He pulled his fingers back and forth, engaging his muscles.

"What's wrong with me?" he said, panic rising from his belly.

"We don't know yet, sir. What's your telephone number, can you tell us that?"

Stanley knew they were testing him. Tommy knew full well what his phone number was. "Ask Tommy. He'll tell you it, and you can get my wife. Get Edna. Please." He heard within his own voice, that he sounded drunk. "What's wrong with my voice?"

"Let's just stay calm, sir. We're going to the hospital. The doctors will figure it out."

Stanley drifted in and out of an odd sort of sleep, dreaming about his children scampering about as toddlers, screeching so loud throughout the house that even in the dream he was yelling. "Quiet down! I can't hear myself think!" He must have said that often, he thought, when he'd wake, hearing his own voice ringing in his ears. Maybe he'd given himself this headache.

"Quiet down! Stop pacing like that"

"I can't hear myself think! Stop stomping, dammit I cannot stand that sound."

"Goddamn it, BE QUIET!"

He remembered these things and the time he spanked Stan Jr. for being disrespectful and regretted it not a moment later...But in the dream, they were sticking Play-Doh together in all the different colors, and the reds and the blues and the greens were pieced together in mismatched lumps. He yelled at the boy in a small lump. He held his daughter high on his shoulders on a warm night as she laughed and reached high in the sky for lightning bugs, squealing, "I got one, Daddy," and opening her palms to try again. And then Stan, bouncing on his lap in a game of patty cake. These were bigger lumps, collected in the messy ball of family.

Stanley imagined his daughter, darting down the Bayou to set his flag ablaze, leaving it to sink in the swamp. It all ran through his mind, a montage of different moments. In the dream Edna told him that it couldn't have all gone perfectly, raising children was just hard. She should know, having been home with them all those long hours he was out catching shrimp.

He woke in a hospital room to the rhythmic beep of the heart monitor and the blood pressure cuff squeezing his arm. He was alive. His left arm. He must've gotten feeling back.

The door flew open, and Edna rushed beside him. "I'm here, sweetie, I'm here..."

Stanley gazed into her worried eyes, her hair tucked back in hastily as if she'd just woken up, too. He would be okay, as long as his wife was here.

Part Three

Edna stood as straight as possible, attempting to ignore the disinfectant smell and the stark hospital walls, the unfamiliar sight of her husband lying on the bed, pale and hooked to an IV. She shifted her gaze to the television mounted high on the wall and breathed through her mouth. Stanley would be okay, she thought. She knew this with every part of herself. How could he not be? She swallowed hard, poured water from the pink plastic container into a cup, and brought the straw to his lips. "Here you go, honey. Have a sip of water." Her voice trailed off, and she pretended she was a nurse or a candy striper, anyone but the wife of a man who had arrived here by ambulance.

This is not my husband. This is not my life. Stanley is on the boat, hauling in a ton of shrimp. He's never been sick! This is another man.

She breathed in and out, repeated the mantra in her mind. It started to work; she felt stronger. They could handle this. It was a migraine, or that inner-ear thing some people got—what was it called? Tinnitus? One of the ladies at the club had gotten very sick from tinnitus. It was a fixable problem.

Except when he tried to drink, water dribbled down his mouth, saturating his hospital gown. He smelled of rubbing alcohol and sweat, and the left side of his face twisted up like a corkscrew. "Edna, thank God you're here. I had a dream..."

His words slurred on top of the pronounced stutter. Her hand shook as she slid the cup away. "It's okay, honey, you don't have to talk. Please don't talk. The doctor will be in soon."

This is another man.

"Is Patsy coming back?"

That stutter.

"Please, Stanley, let's just hear from the doctor..."

Edna squeezed his shoulder and quickly let go. She did not want to make anything worse. The air conditioning blew frigid air into the room. Pulling her sweater tight, she placed a thin hospital blanket over Stanley.

"It's weird. I can hardly feel that," he said.

"You will soon, I promise."

"I'm okay. It's just weird, is all."

"Be quiet, Stanley," she said, her voice firmer now. Maybe too firm. She slumped in the chair beside him and ran her fingers through her messy hair. This was incomprehensible; she didn't know how to act. The wait for this doctor seemed endless. There had been nurses with blood pressure cuffs, and "How are you feeling, Mr. Bundy" and "Can I make you more comfortable, Mrs. Bundy?"

"Yes. Get the doctor. Please."

Then there was the quick and authoritative rap on the door, followed by the doctor in his white coat and spectacles hanging on the edge of his nose. *Finally.*

"I'm Dr. Genova," he said, and shook Edna's hand. His hand was freezing. Edna wondered if it was a sign of something terrible; a doctor with a lifeless handshake. Maybe his hands went cold when he had to deliver terrible news. *No, don't think like that...*

"What's wrong with him?" she said. She hoped he'd have the answer to fix this mess. "You see him stuttering like that?"

"Mrs. Bundy, please. Let's just have a seat and calm down—"

"Oh, sweet Jesus, don't tell me to calm down. Say anything but that."

"All right, then," he said, pushing the glasses up. He set his clipboard on the table beside them. "Come with me."

She followed him in a haze. The halogen lights lit up the hallway, and she felt exposed somehow. She trailed behind him, as he led her into an office. "Sit down, Mrs. Bundy."

Here it comes.

He slid behind the plain desk made of plywood. The floors in his office were the same green waxy squares as everywhere else.

We can afford better, we can afford anything.

"It's fairly obvious your husband has had a stroke. That much we know."

"Is it— can he get better?"

"That depends. The same? Probably not. But the unaffected side of the brain sometimes, with physical therapy, compensates for some of the damaged—"

"Oh, good. Well, that's good news."

The doctor sighed. "Not exactly. That's the best-case scenario. We don't know—"

"What? You don't know what?" Her voice rose. "What exactly could happen?"

"We need to examine the CT scans to find out the cause. I'm sorry, but we'll have news after the neurologist takes a look—"

"When will that be?"

"We're working on it, because if he's got a blockage, we need to get him in surgery. Do you understand, Mrs. Bundy?"

"I think so," she said carefully, straightening her skirt, hands trembling. She clenched her fists at her sides. "I am going back to my husband then, until someone tells me what's going on, what to do." Her voice shook, and she made her way to the corridor, alone.

"Mrs. Bundy," he called after her. "We'll be down in about fifteen minutes."

She waved her arm to indicate she'd heard, and continued walking, saltwater building in her eyes as her heels clicked against the floor. The walls closed in on her, in this confined, awful space. Edna remembered the night of Patsy's birth. She could feel it now, rushing through the bright hall to the operating room, on her hands and knees, hips in the air with the doctor's hand in her uterus, pain so hip-shattering she didn't have time to be embarrassed. They'd almost lost Patsy, that night. Her daughter should not have survived. She clenched her jaw, thinking of how that memory never quite settled, and that her feelings were not normal, not maternal. A normal mother would have been grateful; she had been apathetic.

She slid down the avocado-colored wall outside Stanley's room. Edna wanted to leave in this moment; her chest felt like a deluge of water had collected in it, it ached from the pressure. She perched on her toes, waiting, though she wanted to run. Again, she was not a normal wife; she was the one who had cheated, the one who had not loved enough. And yet she was so bitter she wanted to yell at him for stuttering. She didn't want to hear her steady-voiced husband slur his words.

"Mom!"

Edna gazed up from the floor and at her son. "Stan."

"I missed Tommy's call earlier. I'm sorry. What's going on? He said something was wrong with Dad."

"We'll find out soon, the doctor says," she said. She did not want to speak to her son, but to absorb this alone.

"Mama?"

"Stan, don't. I don't want to talk. You can see him, if you like." She waved towards the door.

"Mama, what can I do for you?" His voice was raspy and far, far away.

"Call Ruth." She blurted this out, surprised at herself, but as she mulled over these words, somehow it felt right. "Yes," she said. "I want Ruth."

Stan knelt beside her and put his hands around her shoulders. She remembered his tiny hands encircling her neck, when she held the coveted title of boo-boo healer. Now, they both knew there was no such thing as magic. He lifted her chin towards his, and said, "Daddy will be fine, Mama. He's always been strong. He'll pull through this. Okay?"

Edna curled her lips into the best smile she could. "Let's go in his room and wait for the doctor. I just needed to collect myself."

"Is that him?" said Stan, motioning toward Dr. Genova, who headed towards them.

Here it comes. I wish it could be this morning.

Dr. Genova slid to her eye-level and said, "We have some results." He wore a neutral expression. Stan held his mother's hand as they went back to the doctor's little office. Inside were two other doctors, neither wearing white coats like Dr. Genova, but button-down shirts rolled up at the sleeves. It felt crowded here, now.

The first doctor extended his hand, though Edna found the thought of introductions unfathomable. She flicked his hand away. "Just tell me what's going on."

"Okay," he said. "I'm a neurologist here at the hospital, and Dr. Smith is the oncologist from the clinic—"

"Oncologist? I thought he had a stroke," said Stan.

"What's happening? Stan?" said Edna. Cold settled in her belly.

"Please, just sit. I can't talk like this." said Dr. Smith. Edna realized that she and her son had encroached the doctor so far into the corner of the office, he had no breathing room.

"Sit, Stan," she said.

Dr. Smith took a slow, measured breath. Edna picked at her nail, watching him. "We saw something on your husband's brain."

Stan opened his mouth to speak, to spew questions at the man, Edna could tell, but she held her hand up to silence him, as if he was a little boy interrupting an important conversation.

The doctor cleared his throat. "The mass, along with the increase in white blood cells on his labs—I am almost certain it is malignant. We need several more tests to confirm this, an MRI, for example."

"Can you remove it?" said Stan.

"It isn't operable. We would do chemo and radiation to prolong his life," he said softly.

"What are you saying?" said Edna, eyes wide. Stan began to cry.

"It looks like a glioblastoma. Here, take a look," he said, clipping the image to a lit screen. "Do you see the mass that looks like fingers coming out from it?"

She nodded, swallowing hard.

"It's a very aggressive cancer, because it's not contained into one mass. It's sort of spread out, and since it's so large, we can't just remove it."

"Chemo can shrink it? Cure him?" said Stan. Edna had an urge to wipe his nose.

"No, like I said, it can prolong his life, we hope."

"How long does he have?" said Edna. She couldn't feel her hands.

"With treatment, maybe a year? Without, weeks. We want to transport him to Shreveport, where they have more options." His voice trailed into her life, she thought. He's thanking God it isn't his own.

Edna stood, and the world spun. The floor rose toward her face, her heels slipped from beneath her and she pummeled sideways to the ground. Her new reality spread from the CAT scan clipped to the wall; it slid under her skin, into her molecules, metastasized throughout her entire body. It moved like its own cancer, from her husband and right through her.

• • • • •

Stanley lay in the hospital bed, stark and chilly, surrounded by doctors as his wife held his hand. She looked like she'd been crying; he knew the news could not be good. He turned to his side, and said, "Maybe it's not so bad. Maybe it will get better. Do you hear my voice? I'm not stuttering as much."

"We expect some variation in symptoms," said the doctor.

"You said with physical and occupational therapy, I could improve."

Dr. Genova— he thought that was his name— furrowed his brow and gazed toward the floor.

"Did the tests show I need surgery? You said with a stroke I could need surgery." Now Edna's tears dribbled down her sweater. "Edna, I'll have the surgery. It'll be fine."

The doctor sat in the chair on the other side of Edna, his good side. "We found something else on the CAT scan, Mr. Bundy. A tumor."

"What are you saying?" he said, his voice shaking.

"I'm saying—"

"Cancer," said Stanley.

No one spoke. Edna put her head in her lap, and swept her knees into her arms, rocking. Voices blasted through the hospital loudspeaker, someone was dying, as people did in this place, and Stanley sighed, "How long do I have?"

"With treatment, about a year."

"And without?

"Less."

"Mr. Bundy, there is a chance, if we transfer you to Shreveport, maybe eighteen months. They have stronger medicines, clinical trials—"

"No," said Stanley, and with this he was firm. "I do not want to go to Shreveport for a bunch of meds. For what? Six months of pain?" He knew he had begun slurring his words again. He sounded foolish, he thought. Still, he turned to Edna and said, "Come sit with me. I just want you to sit with me...Sit with me and stay a while."

She got into the bed beside him, and the doctors slipped out. She laid her head on his chest, like she'd done so many times, since they were teenagers, for God's sake. Since they were kids. He thought, this is unfathomable, that she will be alone. He was not afraid of death, but he did not want to leave her to navigate life all alone. "Edna, promise me something," he said. "Dammit, I know my words are slurred, but I mean this. I mean it so, so much."

"Yes, baby," she whispered. "Maybe the doctors are wrong. There are always miracles. Chemo, the chemo could work."

"Listen to me," he said, narrowing his eyes so they would not mist over. "If there is not a miracle, promise that you will let me die a man."

"Okay," she said, nodding.

"You know what I mean?"

She nodded again, and he knew she understood. When you're married to a person thirty years, you know their thoughts without words. There were no words right now, anyway, other than, "Don't leave me, Edna."

He knew she would not, if she could take it, but he wasn't sure she could handle this. "I think we should go to Shreveport, get the best of care."

He sighed. "Of course you do. But one year. I'd rather be at home for one year, than in a strange hospital for eighteen months."

They lay on the bed together, wordlessly, as he imagined his wife without him. He touched her cable knit sweater, wrapped it tight around her body as she shivered and convulsed with tears. He tried to hold her pain, as she was the one being left. He'd always thought she'd be the one to leave, after some fight or need for freedom. And here she sobbed over his ugly green hospital gown that wasn't even tied around his ass. His thoughts went deeper still, into what he would experience next.

"Have you ever wondered what dying feels like, honey?"

She just sobbed harder. "What a terrible question right now, Stanley."

"Sorry," he mumbled. What other time would he ask this question? What other time does one consider the process of death as desperately as he was now? But he said, "You're right. Maybe there will be a miracle and I won't have to think about it."

She sat up, rubbed the snot and tears in her bare hands, and wiped them on her sweater. "I'll be back with Stan." She stood, smoothed her dress and pushed her hair back and said, "I love you, honey."

Outside the door, he heard her screaming. He covered his ears with the scratchy hospital pillow.

Stanley's bones dug into the porch swing, despite several pillows propped underneath him and behind his back. His body ached these days, and he struggled with perpetual nausea. Today, he felt loose and sleepy, which was a relief from violent illness, so he let his limbs hang and his mind wander. He listened to the lawn mower rev up and whirl across the lawn, the scent of fresh cut grass wafting through the yard. The sprinklers made that ratcheting sound of early summer, and the neighbors murmured as they worked. Gilmore mowed, while Mitzy from down the hill helped Edna pluck the tiny weeds that sprouted up in her petunias. It was annoying, she said, how they kept growing back. Stanley wanted Edna to hire a gardener, as his shrinking pride deflated further, being stuck in that chair, watching the neighbors do his work, but she insisted it was best to let them help, because if they didn't feel useful, they'd be inclined to talk. Because that's how it was on the Bayou. People prayed. They brought casseroles made with copious cream-of-something soup; they baked cookies he couldn't stomach. Whatever. He did admit to loving the place. He was born in Cypress; he'd die here, too.

He closed his heavy eyes as the sun warmed his face. Of course, not two seconds after he drifted to sleep, a sudden noise bristled up the porch steps. He couldn't identify it, not quite, but only one individual had the nerve to stomp across his lawn with that kind of authority. He opened his eyes wearily to find his suspicions correct. Ruth Marks hovered over him, blocking his sunshine, her hair a ball of orange-red frizz she claimed was from the humidity, and wearing pink shorts and neon flip-flops.

"When are ya gonna let this go, Stanley?" she said, pointing to his beloved flag, which flapped gently in the afternoon breeze.

"Why, hello to you too, Ruth. I believe we've had this discussion before, I don't know how many times," he said.

She snorted and put her hands on her hips. Here she goes again with that bossiness, he thought, sighing. "Fine. I've got one point to make, and then I'll go back to my own damn house."

"So, make it then."

"Is it more important to be right— which is another subject entirely— or to see your child? She's coming, you know. And you're the damn parent. Be mature enough to let this go."

He considered this, as she fumed down the steps. Ruth Marks, always finding her way into people's business, especially when it involved Patsy. "Don't ruin it all by bringing up the damn Confederate flag, Stanley."

His hands shook. "Edna! Edna!" he yelled.

Edna rushed across the lawn so fast she tripped over a sprinkler head and tumbled onto the grass. She pulled herself up, brushed off her capris, which looked like they'd been scribbled with green and brown ink, and ran up the stairs. "Stanley," she said, panting. "What is it?"

He cringed. "Look at your pants. Will that come off in the wash?"

"Never mind that! What happened?"

"Nothing." He squinted at his wife. "Be careful, running across the yard like that."

"Why are you hollering at me like that? You scared me!"

Stanley rolled his eyes. "Not everything is some big emergency, honey."

"When your husband has cancer, yes, it is." She smoothed her pants, scratching at one of the grass stains with her fingernail. "What is it, then?"

"Why didn't you tell me Patsy was comin' home?" he said, unable to contain the excitement in his voice. "She really wants to see me."

"I didn't know," she said. "Did she call?"

"Ruth just ran up here and announced it," he said.

"Hmm. Where did Ruth take off to? She could have at least said hi, given that she's so energetic this morning."

"Oh, come on Edna. You were way over there weeding. I doubt she even saw you. I just wanna see Patsy. I don't care about the rest of it." He waved his hand. "It doesn't matter whether Patsy called Ruth, or whatever. I ain't got time for the bullshit. Life is not a popularity contest."

"I suppose you would know, with this newfound grace in your heart." She gazed up at his flag. "Well. I hope she really shows up. I don't want her to disappoint you. Anyway, I've got work to finish up."

"Ruth's pissed at me, not you," he said.

"Call me if you need anything urgent, honey. You scared the hell out of me."

Stanley sighed as his wife stomped down the steps, competing with Ruth for most annoying noise of the afternoon.

Patsy was coming home. The most delighted feeling surged through his body for the first time in a month.

•   •   •   •   •

Ruth had convinced her to board the plane. She hadn't wanted to come at all. One, Sheriff Landon's news had delayed Parson's release by six weeks. There wasn't a thing she could do but wait. Ruth used the DNA discovery to bait her into coming to town, but Patsy didn't tell her about her conversation with Jennie Parson.

When her mother called, Patsy was certain she was exaggerating the situation to manipulate her after the Christmas Eve fiasco. Or perhaps that's just what she wanted to believe. She thought, this is Daddy. He'll recover, any day now. But then, in the same swish of racing thoughts, she'd see him sickly and yellow, on his deathbed, calling for her.

Ruth said, "You'd better be sure this is what you want, Patsy. 'Cause I can tell you this: you'll never regret saying goodbye. You might regret the alternative."

And Patsy had said, "He's not going to die, Ruth."

"If he does, and you regret the choice not to come down here, that's on you, honey. Because you gotta live with that. Not him."

"He's not going to die." She had said this with a forceful tone.

"If he does, do you wanna live with this? You've got your whole life to fight the Confederate flag. You've got a short time to make peace with your father."

"I'm not coming," she retorted, bile rising in her throat.

"Let. This. Go."

"I cannot go shrinking back there. I am not timid, like my mother."

Ruth sighed and said, "No, that isn't it at all. You cannot *stand* to see him weak."

"I'm not my mother. I won't go in there, Ruth."

"Your mother isn't timid. Holy shit, you don't know her all that well, do you?"

"I won't support—"

"Your mother is weak. Do you wanna be weak, like she is? Do you want to see her fall and die with him? 'Cause you are strong, and she is not."

"I can't do this! Fuck you!"

"It isn't support. It's love. You know you love him. And he sure as hell loves you, even if he's foolish."

"Fuck off! Just hang up, Ruth," she said, and she'd held her face in her hands, crying so hard she choked on her words.

"You are not timid, Patsy. You're alive. Everyone has to be vulnerable, sometime."

"I don't want to come!"

"I'm sorry," she'd said, her voice softening. "This is what you do. This is how you make it."

Patsy hung up and reserved the plane tickets. Archibald Parson was scheduled to be released in fourteen days, but she pushed this aside. There wasn't anything she could do about it, or her father's illness, which made the trip pointless and depressing.

Patsy listened to Ruth, though. She wouldn't admit it, but she trusted her. Neither Ruth nor Tommy had never betrayed her, while the disconnect from her own family spread wider than the Mississippi River.

•   •   •   •   •

She couldn't believe she'd landed back in Cypress, after she had sworn she'd never, ever return. Then again, no one saw this coming. Slouched in the seat of the rental car, Patsy hid from the neighbors. This is paranoid, she told herself. No one can see you here. Still, Cypress was the same nosy, little Southern town. Folks watched out for strange cars, especially those containing witches. She pursed her lips and scowled. *I don't want to do this. Goddamnit, I don't have a choice...*

The anger that seeped through every molecule of her body that night at the party still boiled beneath her skin, to such an intensity that it did not dissipate until she saw him. And then, it was impossible not to feel a child-like tenderness for the man who raised her. Who loved her.

Part of her wanted to be here when Parson was released, to watch the secrets of the Bayou unfold, though she'd never admit to this. So, she made her way up the familiar path, two steps up, a wind to the left, a bend to the right, the same four cracks in the sidewalk. As a girl, she'd trace her way to the door like a melody. Now, she traveled towards the creaky screen door uneasily, tip-toeing, as if the earth was riddled with land-mines.

She lifted the clay potted geranium plant on the steps and retrieved the key from beneath it, wiping the dark soil off. "Mama!" she called, turning the key in the lock. She pushed the heavy wood door open. She didn't want to frighten her mother with its screech. "Mama, are you here?"

Her mother yelled, "Come in, Patsy. I'll be down in a minute!" She scanned the foyer and stepped in the kitchen. It sparkled, like always, with cast iron pans hanging over the stove-top. It smelled like lemon Pledge and Windex. She ventured into the living room, where the furniture shone, and the carpet had been freshly vacuumed, with lines of light indentations in stripes, as usual. Patsy took slow breaths, imagining Daddy in a wheelchair, the slurred words turned unintelligible. Maybe he couldn't speak. Maybe he was in a coma. Had she boarded the plane a month ago, she could have heard her father one more time.

"Mama, where are you?" she yelled again. Waiting here alone was interminable.

"I'll be RIGHT THERE, Patsy!"

"Oh, my God, hurry up." She muttered this under her breath. Don't fight with her, she told herself repeatedly, which was a mountainous goal.

Edna appeared at the top of the circular staircase, her light green dress and hair swept in a bun. This gave Patsy hope. Edna hadn't lost her mind yet, still the epitome of conventional attractiveness. Patsy sighed. "Mommy," she said, taking off her shoes. She remembered to set them in the closet. "Where is he?"

"We're in the bedroom downstairs now," said Edna. She led Patsy to the former playroom, once stuffed with toys and games organized in little totes. Now, a hospital bed filled most of the space, with a small fold-out cot beside it. Daddy lay sleeping, his chest moving up and down with rhythmic little snores catching each breath. A pole with an IV stood in the corner. "A nurse gives him his chemo here," she said.

"How's that working?" asked Patsy.

"He's having another MRI next week. So far, the tumor has remained the same size." Her eyes misted over. "That's a miracle, in itself."

"Do they think it could shrink—"

"Not likely, honey. I don't think that way anymore." She shifted her arms against her body as if she was cold.

"So that's it? It's hopeless? We just wait for the end?"

"I just mean," said Mama, clearing her throat, "I mean every day is a gift. It isn't hopeless if we get one more day."

"There's no chance of a cure?" Patsy was incredulous. There had to be *something.*

Edna shook her head and sat beside Daddy. "I sleep on the cot most nights. But we watch TV together on the bed." She folded a light blanket and set it on the cot. "How long are you staying?"

"I don't have definite plans. I thought I'd try taking some pictures here."

Mama turned her lips up slightly, almost to a smile. "I sure could use the help."

"Mama."

Edna put her hand up. "Patsy, this is hell for all of us. We just have different ways of dealing with it is all."

"I'm sorry for not coming sooner," she said.

"You're here now. That's all that matters. He's gonna be so happy. I almost want to wake him up, "she said, now with a wide smile. Daddy continued gently snoring and she added, "Almost."

"Got any tea?" said Patsy. She squeezed her mother's cold hands. Edna waved her toward the kitchen.

"Sure do. I bet Ruth saw y'all pull up, too. How much you wanna bet she comes banging on the door in a minute?"

Edna set out glasses of tea and slices of pound cake. Not a second after she sat, Ruth pounded on the door. Edna didn't bother to stand. "Come in, Ruth."

"Why, hello, Patsy!" Ruth said in mock surprise.

"Oh, don't act like you didn't know she was here," said Edna. "You knew before we did."

Ruth ignored this and served herself a glass of tea and a thick slice of lemon pound cake. She took a bite and said, "Mmm. Thanks. And you're welcome. For calling your daughter and all." She wiped her mouth with a red and white checked napkin.

"Make yourself right at home." Patsy hugged Ruth tight, tears welling in her eyes.

"How is he?" Ruth asked.

"Sleeping. It's good; he's not in pain. Although I read on the Internet they get sleepy near the end."

"The Internet doesn't know jack shit. I just got AOL and I haven't even figured out how to work the damn thing."

"Anyway, we've got the MRI tomorrow," said Edna.

"I'm surprised the ladies from the club aren't over," said Ruth.

"Yeah, well, they've got their own lives. They're a big help, though. I'm not sure what will happen with the business. Stan Jr. has taken the boat out a few times, but he doesn't seem too interested."

Ruth placed her large hand on Edna's shoulder. "What about Gilmore?" She took another bite of cake.

"What about him?" said Edna.

"Have him take over," said Ruth.

"I don't know. It's been in the family a hundred years."

"I don't mean 'take over'. I mean he could manage it, like any other business. Y'all have ownership, and he hires a crew."

Edna leaned back in her seat, thinking. "You know, that just might work. I'll mention that to your father, Patsy."

"It's okay, Mama. Let's not worry 'bout that yet." *Let's not act like he's already dead.*

"Even if he gets better, Patsy, he'll still never be fit for shrimpin' again," said Mama, reading her mind, "Of course, we're praying for a miracle. Don't go thinking I've got him dead and buried."

"No one's fit for shrimpin' much past our age anyway, in my opinion. I sure wish Jeb had stopped...oh, never mind." Ruth gathered the dishes and rinsed each one methodically, loading them in rows in the dishwasher.

"I'm sorry about the boating talk," said Edna.

Patsy glared at her mother.

"Look, I'm sorry! I'm in the middle of my own goddamn tragedy to think straight!" said Edna.

"Edna. It's nothing you've *done*. I lost my husband to the sea and I hate thinking about it. Even Tommy will keep going out if you want him to. I've never liked it—"

"But what? I endanger Stan because I've allowed him to go out on the boat all these years. Jesus Christ, accidents happen!"

Ruth ran her fingers through her hair. "You know what I think?"

Mama clearly did not care what Ruth—or anyone else, for that matter— thought, as she sighed in that incredulous way she did.

"The honest to God truth is—"

"Ruth, I don't give a shit."

Patsy sipped her tea, waiting. Mama had no interest in the truth, whatever that might be.

"I've always wanted to be just like you."

"Coulda fooled me," said Edna, and stirred another lump of sugar in her tea, the spoon clinking against the glass.

"I followed you around high school like you were God's gift. And after that, I played along with you and the Ladies' Club members, shallow as they may be, and I never quite understood you. But now, I've figured it out."

"Ruth, not now," said Patsy, sensing a fight brewing.

"No, wait. I'm gonna say my piece here," she said, pointing a finger at Mama.

"Oh, Lord, please, enlighten me."

Ruth leaned on her elbows, close to Edna, and whispered, "You're insecure. Always have been."

"This is hardly appropriate."

"No, no. It's true. We've spent our lives tip-toeing 'round you, but the reality is, you need everyone to act just so, because heaven forbid anyone rock your secure little world."

Patsy considered this. She leaned back, listening. Mama blinked and bit her lower lip hard. She patted her mother's arm, because Ruth was right. Patsy's chest went heavy as the truth grew thicker than the slices of pound cake and compliments about nothing that Edna had served up her entire life.

"You'd better get used to it, honey. At some point, you're gonna need to suck it up. Stanley won't be here to save you forever," she said. Edna leaned over the sink crying, as Ruth held her. It was strange, watching her mother unfold into a person, rather than Cypress's raven-haired Town Debutante. Patsy stepped back from the two women, shaking.

Patsy considered this, she agreed that Charming Mama blushed and bit
her lower lip before she started her motor's engine. Perhaps Ruth was right.
Patsy's heart grew heavy as she again revisited that the slices of pound
cake and compliments about nothing (that Edna had served up but really
you'd better get used to it, honey). At some point, you're gonna need to
learn to—Stanley would...she...she...she...she...Edna leaped
over the sink crying, as Ruth, held... ...turning Mama into her mother,
turning a person, killed than Cyrille's... raven-haired Roux. Debutante.

Chapter Twenty-Seven
NORMAL

"C'mon, Tommy! When I get to three, we lift him over," she yelled into the
wind. Tommy smiled, but she knew those wide eyes. He was scared shitless.
"Dude, we got this! Okay, now...one, two, three!" Patsy and Tommy heaved
Stanley's wheelchair onto the dock. She had aimed to be enthusiastic about
this trip, but they encountered a minor predicament before they'd even
boarded the boat.

She had arranged a wheelchair ramp for the boat, but forgot they'd also
need to get him from the gravel road onto the dock itself. The wheels to his
chair weren't exactly off-road friendly. Tommy said, "I've got it!"

Now Patsy, open to anything at this point, and a tinge desperate, sighed
with relief.

Thank God. We've put so much effort in this fishing trip for him.

Tommy said, "We'll lift him up half a foot onto the deck by hand, and then
hope to God he doesn't fall out while we push him down the dock."

"Oh, sweet Jesus, Tommy."

"You got a better idea?"

Patsy didn't. With Daddy safely on the dock, Patsy gave the chair an
enthusiastic shove, hoping to gain a bit of momentum, and the three of them
flew down the dock, wheels clanking against the uneven wooden panels, the
aroma of salt water invigorating to their noses. Stanley yelled, "All aboard!" as
Tommy pushed him onto *The Patsy Mae*. Then he leaned forward, palms on
his thighs, to catch his breath.

"So, are you happy, Dad?"

"I love it," said Stanley. "You remembered fishing gear, right?"

"Of course. Except this may be a lazier style fishing trip than you're
accustomed to, Daddy."

"Exactly. We're going fishing. With poles, not giant nets. We're going to
enjoy the sun and eat sandwiches," said Tommy.

"I know," said Stanley, grumbling. "Put bait on a hook, toss it in the water,
and reel in a fish. Or just sit there waiting."

Tommy dug through the cooler of slimy bait, put a worm on Stanley's hook, and threw out the line. Stanley held the pole, while Patsy carefully watched his grip.

She went through the sandwiches, cookies, fruit and Ensure she'd brought. Stanley peered into it and demanded a beer. Patsy reminded him that his extensive list of medications did not mix with alcohol. However, when he grew sullen and quiet, she said, "All right, Dad. We'll stop on the way and get a six-pack."

The tumor had grown. Patsy suspected this, even before the results of the MRI came back, because of the two nights he'd cried in pain as she hooked up his morphine. Mama didn't want to admit it and had a myriad of reasons why he could not get his words right. Sure enough, the finger-like mass had spread through his brain like a thick spider web, all the way down to the base of his spine. "Let him have all the beer he wants," Tommy whispered, leaning over from the back seat of the truck.

"Can't we get regular Coors?" said Patsy, popping open a can of Coors Light that her father insisted upon. "It has more calories." Even as she said this, it felt like swimming in another reality. Who *says* that? Sick people and their families floundering in a new and fucked up world, one where you take this detour and that, and end up wherever you end up, because you never expected to be on this terrible journey.

Stanley replied, "I like the taste of Coors Light better."

She bought Coors Light and Ensure, not knowing what else to do. He had the stomach of a newborn, but he insisted on beer.

"Patsy," said Tommy. Her eyes misted over as she handed her father the can. "Let's just make this fun for him, okay?"

She bit her lip. She hated being out on the boat, two or three miles from land and fifteen from a doctor. But, as Tommy had told her, there were no more rules. She buried her head in Tommy's chest and cried.

Patsy pulled away at the sound of her father screaming. His yell cut through the Gulf like a knife, and she rushed to the mast of the boat, thinking what a mistake this had been. "I caught one!" he said.

"Sweet Jesus, you scared me," said Tommy. "Dammit, you did catch something. Something heavy." He grasped the pole, which lurched toward the water, as he reeled it in. "It's gonna break this thing!" It swished back and forth, still flapping as it hit the deck.

The blue-finned fish had to have been a foot and a half long. "It's a catfish," said Patsy.

"A beauty. Here, let me get it into the other cooler," he said, after the fish stopped moving. His voice undulated through the wind as he disappeared into the cabin, leaving Patsy and Stanley alone together. The boat lingered, engine off, in the middle of God-knows-where, the sun melting their faces over the serene sea. It neared mid-day, and the heat grew thicker, the familiar blanket of steam settling over the Gulf. Far away clouds dotted the sky, and a dreamy trance draped over them. Daddy took her hand. "This is fun, Patsy," he said in a raspy voice.

"Wait a minute, Dad. I want to get some pictures." She ran down to the cabin to retrieve her camera. It was magic hour, that time between dusk and nightfall when the sun is warmest, when the colors slide together and make the loveliest pictures. Wind in her hair, she shot photos of the catfish and the water, and Tommy, and eventually Daddy. He sat in his wheelchair, pencil thin, in the same awkward vulnerability as cranes standing on still water. He fell asleep, his bald head tucked between the corner of his wheelchair and his pillow. He reminded her of a child dozing, lovely and quiet.

Tommy stepped back on the deck. "Havin' fun?" he said.

She dried her tears. "I'm not sure you'd call it fun, exactly."

He put his arms around her, and said, "This is awful to watch. But it'll be okay, you know. Eventually."

"Not only do I get to watch my father die, but I get the pleasure of riding 'round the Gulf with his Confederate flag flyin' in the wind, and my name on the side of the damn thing." She shook her head.

"Can't pick your family," he said.

"Easy for you to say." She really did love Ruth.

"You're stubborn as hell, Patsy. Let's go *do* something about racism and this refusal to concede the Civil War around here. The old man isn't gonna change."

"Beyond him, there's this issue of an unidentified dead woman showin' up at our hangout."

"That's just astounding. How many people have gotten killed down there? We're lucky to be alive."

"I think there's more to it than that. I just don't know what. Not yet."

"Let the cops figure it out. You've got enough shit to worry about. Don't create more."

"I'm doing the best I can. Definitely can't mention it to my mama. She's worried about Parson's release, Daddy, all of it."

"Patsy," he said, sighing.

Tommy's gold-flecked eyes shone in the sun, and she almost asked him to pose for a photograph. But she got wrapped up in his beauty, and the heaviness of the moment, and leaned close to him. His breath smelled of Tic-

Tacs and felt warm against her cheek.

"I'm annoying, I know," she said.

"Nah, you're interesting. I'd spend my whole life watchin' your kind of passion..." he said, but as soon as the words slipped out, he turned his face.

Whole life?

"Were you in love with Linda?" she asked.

"I met her after you bailed. I thought I was."

"I *bailed*? I didn't know we were a thing, Tommy. I'd have needed that information for leavin' for college to qualify as *bailing*." She found this trait men had irritating, how they thought you should consider them in all your decisions.

"I've loved you since I was seven," he said, and shrugged like she should have known this, and acted on this information. Heat spread in her cheeks, and not the kind he was hoping for.

"Did you love Pierre?" he said.

"I don't know anymore. I'm not sure love is what I'm after, anyway," she said.

"Well, what are you after?"

She gazed out at the ocean, and at her dying father. "Peace," she said. "Life is complicated enough to worry 'bout anything else."

•   •   •   •

Edna cradled the pay phone by ear, waiting for him to answer. It had been years since she'd met him at Cypress Market. She'd been appalled by his phone call, which was ostensibly to check on Stanley, but she couldn't get him out of her head. She pushed aside the memories of how she'd browse Cypress Market for an hour, buy a basket of ripe plums and a loaf of artisan bread, and follow him back to the Bundy house, all while her virile husband worked long hours on the boat to provide for her. Her cheeks flushed with shame at the thought of it.

But then she called him back, fully aware she had lost her mind at this point, of course, because Stanley had vomited on her three times the evening before, and she'd screamed in the shower till her voice was gone.

"You want to meet now?" he said, sounding dubious at this. It was hard to say, given how screwed up her thinking was.

"I thought it'd be nice to catch up," she said.

"You've still got that husky voice I find so sexy," he said.

"Meet me at Cypress Market then?"

"Uhhh, well..." he said.

"What, you don't want to?" She tried to be coy. How desperate she'd become, begging a man to accept her invitation for sex.

"You broke off our affair due to your commitment to marriage, is all." The line went silent.

She understood this looked terrible, even to a man who committed adultery shamelessly.

And she had indeed ended the affair due to her marriage, because she knew that Stanley was the man who'd truly love her, and she ought to put more effort in. "I have missed you," she said.

"I bet Stanley isn't able to—"

"Well." Edna felt as if her eyes might pop out of her head.

"I know you have a voracious appetite."

"Shut up, Mitch. Just meet me at one." He could think what he liked, as men do. His lovemaking skills were less than impressive. But he'd wanted her in the past, and now she needed a diversion, and didn't know who else to call.

Anyway. She paced Cypress Market and squeezed fruit for their freshness, piling her basket with more than she intended to purchase. *Make sure he rents a hotel room with a mini fridge. Cut pineapple goes bad in this heat. Edna, you've gone mad.*

She tossed a jar of artichokes in olive oil tied with a pretty red ribbon into her basket and got in line. They couldn't have their rendezvous at her place anymore, so she'd follow him out of town. If anyone asked, she would say Stanley had doctors out that way, which wasn't a lie. He just refused to go there. She mapped the scenario in her mind, half-knowing no one would question her, but enjoying this idea that someone could. Then she thought of her sick husband and felt nauseated herself, the way these ideas fired around in her head.

Susan rang up her groceries, and she smoothed her skirt. "Hello, Susan," she said.

"Why, hello, Mrs. Bundy. How are you?" she replied and placed the artichokes in a paper bag softly. There was a slight, yet palpable hesitation to her tone, an emphasis on the 'are'. Edna had developed the keen ability to gauge whether she was the subject of town gossip by the natural variation in the inflection of a person's voice. A store checker was supposed to be brisk. Susan had not sounded brisk, and Edna's radar went off. It was a necessary talent living in a small town, albeit one that Edna hadn't used lately, being at home with Stanley.

"I'm just fine, Susan. Obviously, things are difficult, but..." her voice trailed off, which she did not intend. Edna saw Mitch's Mercedes pull up in the parking lot. He'd bought a new one since the last time they'd seen one another. Blue, same model.

"But," prompted Susan, "what?"

Do not tell her anything. "How are you?'

Oh, shut the fuck up, Susan.

"But I'm in a bit of a rush. Have a good day, now," she said, handing over a wad of cash.

"Mrs. Bundy, your change…"

"Keep it," she said, wheeling the cart toward the exit. She loaded her trunk, and just like before, paid no attention to Mitch's Mercedes. She started her car and followed him toward the main road, three cars ahead, but something in her deflated when she understood that no one paid attention to what Edna Bundy did in her spare time. They wanted the details of Stanley's illness, sure. But she was no longer the wife of Cypress's biggest shrimper, no longer beautiful, no longer much of anything special. Just an old woman, waiting for her husband to die in an acrid-smelling room.

She turned on her blinker and drove towards the highway, over the large bridge that led to the city. Downtown used to overwhelm her, a blur of people and buildings and fast cars. Hotels lined every inch of the water, with malls and endless cement. She and Stanley had enjoyed many trips over the years since the children left home, but it always felt good to get back to Cypress where she could breathe again. The city had an essence of business, something Edna had never liked, but now appreciated. The brisk atmosphere held no secrets; it moved too fast. A person could get lost here, sucked away from life and given a do-over on the whole thing just by traipsing down the street, wandering into a shop or a casino. She'd never see these people again.

In the city, no one knew her name or that she'd been Miss Louisiana in 1968. The hotel shimmered with a grand chandelier and boasted three restaurants right on the first floor. She experimented with different identities, thinking about what kind of woman would saunter into the little boutique with expensive women's clothing. Maybe a woman from New York, with a career or a young, healthy spouse. You could make up anything you wanted here. Be anyone you wanted.

When she arrived at the check-in desk and asked for Mitch, the clerk said, "Oh yes, Mrs. Smith. Your husband is up in 402. Here are the keys." Then, she gave Edna a little envelope with two plastic key cards and an invitation for brunch in the morning. Edna would not be here for breakfast, obviously, but she imagined herself eating a Danish and coffee from the continental breakfast on Mitch's arm. The way Mrs. Smith rolled off the hotel attendant's tongue made her feel hopeful. Yes, her marriage to Stanley was ending. But, unlike Ruth, she'd make herself someone else's wife. She pretended she was indeed Mrs. Smith, meeting her husband during his lunch hour. She cleared her throat, stood straight, and knocked on Mitch's door.

He welcomed her inside, still wearing the pressed blue suit, this time with a mauve tie. Maybe she should ask him what his business job consisted of, if they were to marry someday.

"I like the tie on you. Very professional." Maybe she didn't need to end up alone.

Mitch kissed her, and she had to tune out the slobbering noise he made. She'd forgotten about that. He pushed her onto the bed, hands everywhere. Okay, she could tolerate this. She'd done this before. He panted in a way that irritated her, but the sex was quick. "Did you get divorced?" she asked, looking deep into his eyes, and ignoring the way he lay there sweating, with the fuzzy belly of a middle-aged man that had never been hers, and therefore made her feel gross. He wasn't Stanley, and he wasn't even attractive. He was a slobbery old man.

"No, I ended up staying. For the kids. You were right, Edna," he said.

"Aren't they grown up now?"

"Yes, but...Edna, I'm still confused. Why are you here?"

"I don't know, Mitch." She sighed. "Why are you here, after all these years, if things are okay at home?"

"My wife and I have incompatible sex drives. We always have. So, we developed an understanding."

"What do you mean? You just sleep with other people, and she doesn't mind?" This surprised her.

"Not exactly."

"I don't get it then," said Edna, furrowing her brow.

"She knows. But she loves me and we're happy in other ways—"

"She puts up with you fucking other women?" said Edna. "But she's monogamous to you." Edna grew very confused, and at this moment felt dirty. She was the worst kind of 'other woman'.

She gathered her clothes and went in the bathroom. "I've got to go, Mitch. This was just a big mistake."

How disgusting she was, trying to replace Stanley before he'd even died. While he suffered at home. She'd thought for a moment (and oh, this embarrassed her now!) that she could find someone to fill the spot he'd taken since she was just a teenager.

That *feeling*. She understood that he'd be gone soon, that she would never see him again on this earth, and yet it was unfathomable. It sliced her open and left her insides raw for all to see. She couldn't escape this even in the city. Because she couldn't escape herself.

Stay away from me now...don't look at me like this.

Chapter Twenty-Eight
SECRETS

The thought of enmeshing herself in the second murder on the Bayou conflicted Ruth, considering that Patsy had been consumed by it most of her young life. But, given the Bundy's family turmoil, she figured someone needed to do it, and she didn't think the Sheriff knew shit from Shinola when it came to criminal investigations. One major crime in the past twenty-five years. The man needed help. Patsy and Tommy had gone fishing with Stanley, and Edna disappeared somewhere, too. She had a little time before anyone poked around looking for her.

She didn't possess police training, but she was a library scientist, a detective at shuffling through endless piles of research. The question was very simple, yet the Sheriff rendered it complicated. "Well, I don't know who else's bone this could be, dammit. We need a living person to compare the DNA to."

Yes, he really said that. She had sighed, and said, "Who else has been reported *missing*?"

"I'm not stupid, Ruth," he said, sounding bored. "No one 'round here has been reported missing that didn't turn up eventually."

"Alive?"

"Not always alive. But never murdered," he said, and Ruth shuddered.

Anyway. He was "investigating" when she dug through dozens of old microfilm, looking for even the tiniest bit of evidence that a woman had gone missing. Going through the old paper felt like dredging the swamp itself. She even pictured herself there, in the middle of the mossy water surrounded by snakes and alligators.

Patsy discovered a bone by chance, and Ruth hoped she'd get lucky too. But after hours of clicking through dozens of newspapers, the print blurring together like one big swoosh of gray was hypnotic. She ran her hands through her hair and laid her head on the desk. Dammit, this was tedious as hell. She moved the button to one last frame. *I'm just goin' through these so fast I'll miss something...if there's anything here at all...*

She turned the reel, thinking she'd wind it up and try again later. Patsy and Tommy would be back any time. But a headline in small print in the lower left corner of the paper caught her eye… "Worried Parents Search for Runaway Daughter", 1969. Wait a minute. She scanned the article.

"An eighteen-year-old girl left home with an older man she'd met at the bar she danced at. The parents are concerned about the girl, insisting there must be foul play involved in her disappearance. The police believe she is a runaway."

Ruth did one quick search; finding the address was easy. She got in the car and headed to Janie and Robert Dickinson's house. Her heart thumped as she peeled out of the library parking lot. This wasn't what she had in mind, registering that first semester at LSU. She hoped to God she didn't end up making an investigatory trip to the nudie bar. The Ladies' Club members would love that one. She parked on the street in the middle-class Cypress neighborhood, at a house much like her own, not knowing what to say to these people. She took a deep breath and knocked on the door.

"Can I help you?"

"Hello, ma'am. I'm looking for Lainey Dickinson. I was hoping you could help."

"I'm afraid I can't. We haven't seen or heard from Lainey in years. What is this about?" Janie Dickinson was about Ruth's age, with striking red hair and wide green eyes. Ruth sensed a tinge of hope with her irritation.

"Ma'am, I'm looking for Lainey because I've got a question about a murder that took place here, many years ago…1970."

"Murder? Like I said, we haven't seen her in years. And before 1970, even. So, if Lainey's gotten herself into trouble—"

"No, it's not that, Mrs. Dickinson. Is that right?"

"Janie. You can call me Janie." She sighed and wiped her palms on the front of her dress. She studied Ruth closely and narrowed her eyes. "You can come in, though I have a feeling I'm not gonna like this conversation."

Ruth nodded, and said, "It's just a hunch. I need to talk to you. For a friend."

Janie Dickinson led Ruth to the couch and offered her tea. Ruth's mouth felt like sandpaper, but she shook her head no. The two women sat across from each other in the kitchen. "Did she tell you where she was going?"

The woman's eyes had gone from wide and beautiful to placid and pleading, and between them surged a maternal instinct they both knew. "She was dating a man. Much older. Too old."

Ruth gazed at the floor, and said, "She met him at work?"

"I'm sure that's so. We didn't talk much about the bar. She was too young to be workin' there! But with the baby and all—"

"Baby?" Ruth's eyebrows shot up.

"Yeah, my granddaughter. At least we've got Jennie. I just, he had to have coerced her, done somethin' with her. You're a mother, right?"

"Yes," Ruth murmured.

"I know my daughter would not leave her baby."

"Of course not."

"Well, the police acted like, a girl works at a nudie bar, then she's not a good mother. Or a good daughter. End of story."

"Dear Lord."

Janie Dickinson crossed her arms at the shoulders and rocked softly, back and forth. "She was a brilliant rider."

"You mean horses?" Ruth's stomach reeled and she thought she might vomit. "She rode horses." She whispered this to herself, knowing she had uncovered the secret to the Bayou. She hated this.

"Yes, she's won all kinds of awards, my daughter." Tears welled in her eyes, and she stood. "Sure you don't want tea? I can't sit still, thinkin' bout her like this."

"Yeah, I'll take some," she said. Janie paced the kitchen. The woman had been waiting for her daughter to come home for twenty-seven years and would find out in this moment that all hope was gone. Ruth felt that her presence had erased something in the woman, she wanted desperately to get up and leave. But she knew that other women would also die if Parson was freed, and time whooshed by them like the horses in Patsy's visions.

"Janie," she said, and took the mother into her arms, where they held each other up as they wept. Her love and loss unearthed, they stood like this for a time. They sat at the kitchen table, dazed, and waited for Jim to arrive. "I'm sorry it took this long to get someone to listen to you," she said. Ruth's heart ached because she understood motherhood, and what it is to be a woman, and that violence is many-layered and well-concealed, and therefore, acceptable.

•   •   •   •   •

Patsy flopped onto her childhood bed, her skin hot and lacquered with a thin coat of salt, with that warm tired feeling you get after a day on the boat or a beach circulating through her blood. She needed to rinse the film from her hair, but her eyes were so heavy that she sprawled out on the cool duvet and tried not to fall asleep. *I'll get up in a minute.* The ceiling fan whirled, and she sunk into the mattress. Life spiraled in new directions, ways she had not conjured: her father would be gone, and a murderer would be free.

Matilda Greene wafted through her mind with such clarity she thought for a moment it was real. Patsy envisioned her daughter Rosie, and tried to remember her from school, but she could not. The stringy-haired girl was a less-manicured version of her ruby-red-lipped mother; the one in Patsy's visions. Her eyes flittered shut and the whirl of the fan intensified, lulling her into a deep sleep where the horses roamed as they often did. But her weariness from the long day left her vulnerable and cut off her usual control of them. The clip of their hooves rolled faster, and when Patsy's eyes flew open, the fan above her spun so wildly she thought it might crash down from the ceiling. But then the clop turned to a gallop and she stood at the window, fascinated. They had found her here, at home.

The dank scent of wet ash hit Patsy before the billows of smoke had a chance to darken the room. She felt herself diffuse into the atmosphere as if she belonged to the fire. In the distance, the sound of Parson's voice shattered the haze. His tone pierced the melodic beat of the horses' hooves clicking against the gravel, and drove right through the vagueness of the night, and she could see this scene play out, leaning against the window frame on her elbows, palms pressed upon her cheeks, like when she was a little girl.

"C'mon, now! Get a move on!" His turquoise belt buckle shone in the light of the fire.

"But you said—"

"I *said*, come on," he said, pulling her arm.

"You said we would be together. That I was your best rider."

"You're nothin' but a whore. Us, together?" A deep cackle emanated from his gut, causing his weathered skin to pit deeply.

"You said you loved me!"

"You're just a baby, with a baby. Offerin' up your body to men. Why the hell would *anyone* love you?"

"I don't offer up my body to no one. I'm a dancer, and I get paid as such. Don't go bringing up my daughter," she said. "What's my child got to do—"

Parson kicked her hard in the stomach, and she hit the ground. She coughed, let out an animal-like scream, her scarlet red hair bright against the backdrop of night. "You ain't got a right to a child, Lainey. It just ain't right. Your parents don't deserve what you've put 'em through, either."

"What are you talking about?" she said.

"This," he said in a guttural voice, grasping her neck tight. Patsy turned away, and the figures dissipated, along with the smoke. She slumped to the ground, glowering at the man, and hoping to God Parson didn't get out of jail.

Who was Lainey? The afternoon sun poured in, and Patsy rushed for the shower, turning the water on high. She rinsed the salt from her skin, but she'd never rid her mind of Lainey Dickinson's face.

Chapter Twenty-Nine
IN SICKNESS AND IN HEALTH

Stanley sat with the walker in front of the bed, willing his atrophied legs to carry him. He stood, with significant effort, and wobbled back and forth before stabilizing his footing. Tiny beads of sweat leaked from his pores, but he was determined. Some force of intuition told him he must move; he needed to prove to himself that his body had a little left in it before he spoke with Gilmore. His sharpness faded more each day, and he needed to work out his affairs before his brain muddled completely. He pushed the walker, unsteady, as he rolled over the thick carpet, and he made it out of the bedroom. He intended to get to the wood flooring, which was about ten feet from the plush carpeted area. He wheeled the length of it until the soreness in his legs hit, like he'd been running for hours. Leaning over the walker, he was breathless and humiliated, but still Stanley. He would achieve his goal.

Stanley had made it over the carpet, legs shaking and weak, the rubber base of the walker teetering back and forth. His heart fluttered, skipping a beat here and there. He slid forward, leaning hard on the walker, dragging one leg behind to rest, then using the other to propel himself forward another few inches. He forgot that the carpet sunk, with the hardwood six inches above. Shit, he thought, as he halted at the base of the step, afraid to lose his footing. But he righted himself and considered how he'd maneuver the walker up and onto the smooth flooring. Leaning forward, he thought, just go for it. There's nothing to lose. He lifted the walker with a bump, groaning, and catapulted onto the step without falling. He leaned over the walker, heaving, till he caught his breath. Then he began again, sliding uneasily along the wood floor. He thought he'd pass out, overwhelmed by the headache and fatigue. He gained velocity, too much, and the walker took off without him. His legs buckled and crumpled to the wood floor.

He lay in a heap, crying.

"Edna!" he yelled, choking from the indignity of the situation.

"Honey!" she said, her eyes wide with disbelief. "What happened?" She bolted downstairs. Stanley could not stand the way her face twisted.

"Turn around. Don't look at me like this...please."

"It's okay, Stanley. It's okay." Her voice broke as she slumped onto the floor beside him. She held his body to hers, and he felt his bones touch her. This embarrassed him. "Are you hurt? Let's get you back in bed."

"Don't look at me like this, Edna."

"I'm not. I promise," she said this, but her voice shook, and Stanley wished she would leave.

She lifted him into bed and disappeared around the corner. He felt that she couldn't handle him anymore. The shame that flooded his body hurt more than cancer.

Still, his determination had not waned.

"Honey," he said, "can you help me into regular clothes?"

"That won't be comfortable. Got a hot date?" Her attempt at a joke made him feel worse, as her voice wavered.

"Yeah," he said, drawing a deep breath. "Gil's visiting, and I can't look like this."

"Okay, sweetheart," she said, almost whispering. "I'll pick out something from upstairs." She turned to leave, and Stanley's heart beat with guilt.

"Baby, I'm so fucking sorry."

"For what?" She smoothed her skirt from across the room.

"For leaving," he said.

"Oh my God," she said, "I have loved you so much."

"Please stop. Anything but this," he said.

She held him gently, like an infant, and stroked his bald head. The years melted together like hot wax. "Lie down now, and I'll get the clothes." She straightened her dress, smoothed her hair. She ran for the stairs and wiped her face with bare hands. Then, the bedroom door slammed shut, and her screams echoed through the big house. There had been dancing and childbirth and babies. Patsy and her witchcraft down at the Bayou. He chuckled at this now and wished he could go back to the time when she was his biggest problem. It was a life well-lived, and he loved his wife. There wasn't much more a man could ask for, except time.

Edna returned with sweats and a t-shirt. He dangled his legs from the side of the bed, and she scrunched up the pant leg and slipped it over his right foot. He tried to help, tried to maneuver his foot, but his muscles jerked the other direction. "Help me out a little, Stanley!" Her voice wavered with frustration and he gritted his teeth. Why should his wife should dress him like a child? Finally, with both pant legs up his thighs, he stood to pull them over his hips.

"One, two, three!" she said. She almost had the pants up when he slipped, flopped forward, and tangled up in them. His eyes filled with tears, because he was stuck in this position and his wife had to fix it. She lifted him and said, "Let's try this again." This time, in one swift move, she lifted him up and arranged his pants. He flopped back on the bed, dressed. Thick beads of sweat formed on her face, and she arranged him in bed, quivering.

"Thank you," he said.

She took a slow breath. "Are you okay for a few minutes? I need some air."

"Of course."

"Gilmore's here! I need to go. I just need a break," she said, and slammed the door. He sunk in bed as Gilmore entered the bedroom.

"Hey, Stanley. Edna okay?"

"I don't know. I just don't know, Gil."

"How are you doin' man?" he said, avoiding Stanley's eyes.

"Not great, they say. But I've got a favor to ask you."

Gilmore sighed. "What, man? Anything."

"I want you to take over the business. Full ownership. Shrimpin' is your life, just as it was mine. Stan Jr. just doesn't have the same passion. I know you can take it and make it what it used to be."

"I need to talk this over with Maggie, of course," he said.

"I thought you'd be happy."

Gilmore shifted his feet. "I am happy. It's quite the gesture. I just don't get— why me?"

"Hey, man. Sit down a minute, okay?"

Gilmore took a seat in the corner of the room.

"No, I mean, sit at the edge of the bed. I've had quite the mornin' and I can't talk too loud."

Gilmore sat beside Stanley, gazing out the window.

"I know I look terrible. No use pretendin'. And I know I have not been a perfect man. But this boat is rightly yours. You're the last original member of *The Patsy Mae* team. It's been you, me and Jeb, and I've been foolish in a lot of ways."

"I don't know. Maggie says—"

"Look, I know you gotta talk to your wife. And I am apologizing, too. You understand me?" Stanley patted Gil's arm, never having had a way with words.

"I think so."

"Let me know as soon as possible, Gil. I need sleep."

Gilmore bit his lower lip. "Don't hurt yourself, Stanley."

•　　•　　•　　•　　•

Edna stood in Ruth's kitchen, sobbing. Ruth thought it was over, that Stanley had passed. "No God, it's not that. Not yet," she said, choking on her tears. She ran her hands through her gray-streaked hair. The light lines sketched in her skin had deepened. Edna looked like shit. Ruth took a glass from the cabinet and filled it with water.

"I cannot do this, Ruth. I just can't. Maybe he needs to be in the hospital. I had to dress him today, and it was awful. He fell."

"Oh God, honey! Did he hurt himself?"

"No, but he was humiliated! His wife dressing him, and then tumbling over like a toddler. I just can't—"

"Sit," she said, and held the cup to Edna's lips. "Take a drink."

"I don't know what to do with this feeling! I don't know what to do! It's the worst part."

Ruth held Edna's hands. "What you can do, is drink some water."

Edna took a sip from the cup and continued sobbing. "Don't you have something to say, dammit? What do I do? I need something to *do*."

"There's nothing you can do."

Edna hesitated, twirling a strand of hair around her finger. "There's something I need to tell you. Something awful."

"What?" said Ruth. What could be worse?

"It's something I've done. Something terrible."

"What?" she whispered. She hoped Edna wasn't harming herself, or poisoning Stanley. She'd heard of these things happening. It was on *Oprah* all the time.

"I slept with someone else. A man I used to know from Shreveport." Edna gazed at the floor, tears gathering in the corners of her eyes.

"That's it?" Ruth pictured a second wedding for Edna. It felt plausible.

"Yes! I'm havin' an affair while my husband is dying and you aren't shocked, appalled, something?"

"Not particularly," she said, popping a cookie in her mouth. "Want one?"

"No, I do not want a cookie!"

"You really should eat more. You're getting too thin."

"What the hell, Ruth?"

"You mean about this man in Shreveport? He's just a warm body." She shrugged and said, "You sure you don't want a cookie? I could make you a sandwich."

Edna took a tiny bite of cookie.

"I think it's good. You and Stanley haven't been...active. You need a diversion."

"That's not the worst of it, Ruth."

"Then what?"

"I think I was tryin' to replace him."

"Edna, that is normal. That is *grief*. The hard part is when you discover you can't just up and replace a man you've been married to for decades. That's a bitch. Havin' sex with someone else isn't some terrible thing."

"This isn't fair, Ruth. It's not fucking fair. I have not been a perfect wife. And my friends!"

"I'm your friend!"

"'Course you are. You're my best friend. The only one who has stuck by me when things are rough."

Ruth pursed her lips.

"I know I wasn't there for you when I should have been," said Edna. "Why do they scatter? Why did I?"

"Cause y'all are weak."

"I don't think that's it—"

"Oh yes, yes, it is. I thought y'all just left me, which wasn't hard to believe, given high school." She cleared her throat. "Anyway, people are weak as hell until they're forced to be otherwise. They'll shirk away, glad it's not them."

"Yeah. Here's your casserole and your fucking peach pie," said Edna.

Ruth knelt on the floor and pointed to a crack on the fake brick floor. "You see that?"

Edna squinted. "It's just old linoleum. What's this have to do with anything?"

"No, see all the little cracks?"

Edna sighed. "I suppose."

"I'm serious. I'm gonna show you something. Think of it as therapy." Ruth opened the cupboard and took out a stack of plates. She picked one up off the top and threw it like a Frisbee. It flew through the air and shattered. That one was for Lainey Dickinson.

Edna jumped, wide-eyed. "What the hell is wrong with you, Ruth Marks?" The shock in her eyes sent Ruth into peals of uncontrollable laughter. She felt like they were teenagers again, except Edna didn't look put together in the slightest. Ruth tossed another plate, sliding on the broken glass in her slippers, this one for Matilda Greene, and one more, in case there were others.

"You got shoes on, right?" said Ruth.

Edna nodded, incredulous. Ruth chortled loudly. "Here, take one."

She held the Corning Ware plate in her thin hands. Ruth didn't think she had it in her. "Come on, now. Throw that baby with all your might. Don't worry 'bout the floors or walls. I've broken stacks of them in here."

Edna sunk into a pitcher's stance and flung a plate. They watched it break into a few large pieces.

"Nope. Harder. Throw it like you mean it. Don't hesitate like that."

Edna wound that plate so far behind her Ruth thought she was gonna slip in the glass. She hurled it, screaming, "Motherfucking cancer! I hate you!"

Ruth gave her another. "Here, give it another go. This time, harder!"

Edna smashed it onto the linoleum and jumped on it, screaming. "I hate you, Susie-Mae Baker! Take your casserole and shove it up your big white ass!"

Ruth calmly passed plate after plate to Edna, followed by a few bowls, before Edna slumped over, breathless. "I'm done. That was insane. You're crazy, Ruth."

"Feel better?"

"A little. Where'd you get that idea, Oprah?"

"Oh no, honey. Oprah doesn't condone violence. I made it up all on my own." She smiled wide, proud of herself. "Except you gotta replace those plates, sweetie. My job doesn't pay *that* well."

Edna nodded, looking dazed. "Okay, then."

"Here. Have some more water. Tommy!" she yelled up the stairs.

"Yeah Mom? Everything all right?" Tommy peeked around the bend of the staircase.

"It's fine, sweetie. I need you to clean up the kitchen, okay? Edna and I are goin' out to buy dishes. And wear shoes. I dropped a dish in here."

A heap of sparkling glass lay on the kitchen floor, big chunks strewn everywhere. Ruth had stopped buying the ones with little shards years before. They cost more and were far more difficult to clean up. You didn't want to end up in the emergency room with a shard of glass in your foot.

"Did you do something with your hair?" said Edna. "It's all shiny and a different color."

"I thought you'd never notice! Sally at the beauty parlor put some shit in it."

Edna laughed. "Well, I wish I knew what she used, because I need some of it."

Ruth drew in a deep breath and gasped. "That's *exactly* what you need!"

"Geez, thanks."

"No, I'm serious. Let's go to the beauty parlor. Maybe get your toes done, too. You need a break honey, or you're gonna go insane. Get in the car."

Chapter Thirty

WHEN IT MEANS SOMETHING

Tommy swept the piles of broken dishes into a trash bag, crunching over shattered glass with his boots as he worked. Three garbage bags filled to the very top, and cupboards empty except for a lone bowl that must have been missed, and several plastic cups from McDonald's. He went over the floor with a broom once more and poured a few capfuls of Lysol into the sink to mop any remaining splinters. His life had taken such a colossal detour from normal that when his mother announced she was leaving, he'd simply surveyed the kitchen, assessed the damage, and gotten to work. Nothing shocked him.

He popped the cap off a bottle of beer and sat on the one chair remaining in the kitchen, the smell of Lysol and sweat permeating the room. He got up and opened a window, listening to the sound of crickets and inhaling the salty smell from outside. Taking a long, cold drink of beer, he leaned back in the chair, and rolled his head, trying to soften the tight muscles in his neck.

Tommy wasn't the sort of man to whom relaxing came easy. He felt best when he kept moving. He didn't mind cleaning the giant mess of broken glass, and knowing his mother as he did, he just shrugged and got on with it. He'd spent more time at her place than at his own since Stanley's diagnosis. And since Patsy's arrival.

He'd known her since birth. She could be such a pain in the ass, but he loved her. Somewhere between their toddler days when she threw toys at his head and laughed as he cried, and grade school when they became the best of friends, he had noticed her strawberry curls, the way they lay against her face. She crossed Mr. Bundy like no one in the world did, and Tommy loved it. Damn it, she crossed everyone, he supposed.

He could not sit still. He meandered into the backyard, the spigot spraying the grass with its usual hizz. Tommy delighted in familiarity these days. Two slightly rusted aluminum lawn chairs sat on the patio. A lonely BBQ was unused and dusty in one corner. His mother would sit out here after Dad died, her quiet tears frightening him. Mama had seemed unbreakable to him, and perhaps she was. Or maybe she hid this facet of herself from him. The small yard held all their family secrets, kept them from ballooning out and through the neighborhood. At least this is what he envisioned. The neighbors' whispers of pity never seemed to bother his mother. They sure embarrassed him.

He wiped down the counters, squeezed out the mop, and plunged it into fresh water to give it another once over. Just as he finished up, Patsy knocked on the door. He knew it was her, because of the certain way she rapped on the wood beside the screen door. He wished she'd leave him alone. When he saw her, that molecular buzz returned, and it had begun to make him angry.

"Yeah?"

"Oh, hey. I was looking for your mom."

Why the hell was his mother all chummy with Patsy? He'd wondered this for years.

"She's not here…left with your mom."

Patsy looked around at the floor and the one chair in the kitchen, squinting at the three trash bags filled with glass.

"I'm just cleaning. Come sit in the living room," he said.

She shrugged and trailed behind him. They sat beside each other on the flowered couch, and she said, "Gilmore isn't taking the business."

"I don't blame him," said Tommy, taking a swig of his beer.

"Me either. Stan Jr. doesn't want it either, really."

"Patsy, I don't want to run a shrimping business the rest of my life, if that's what you're gettin' at."

"I don't want you to either," she said. "And I know your ma sure doesn't."

"Then what?" he said, massaging his neck.

"There's good news, if you can believe that," she said. "We're shutting down the Bundy shrimp boat."

"Wow," he said. "Got no one to take it? How's Stanley handling this?"

"He's happy," she said. "Because Gilmore is starting his own shrimping business. He and Maggie bought a boat and everything."

"He deserves it," said Tommy, shaking his head with a smile. "For putting up with your father all these years."

"Damn straight. Maggie would never let him take over that boat. I hate that my name is on it, for shit's sake."

He smirked. "I guess you can't change your family."

Her eyes glistened, and she gazed at him like a grand idea was forming in her head. "Do you wanna stay here in Cypress forever?"

"Hell no." He laughed.

"I can't wait to get out of here. I don't know if Boston is the place for me anymore, but it sure as hell isn't here."

"I want to teach kids *The Catcher in The Rye* at that developmental stage where it means something," he said.

"I thought *The Catcher in The Rye* was a classic," she said.

"Yeah, apparently at a certain age its profoundness wanes. There's a developmental sweet spot for it," he said.

Patsy laughed. "You can teach literature anywhere, right?"

"From the research I've done, yes. Pay is not a huge consideration. High school literature teachers are underpaid everywhere."

"Perhaps monetarily," she said.

"Yeah, well. They'd rather fund science. I can't *prove* that a book is good. All I know is the feeling words give me."

She hesitated, for just a moment, and slid closer to him on the couch. He remembered a million afternoons in the tin house, Patsy's eyes alive with a story she had to tell, be it real or imagined. Or the night his father died, how Edna skittered away, crying in the corner, while Patsy lay right beside him.

She turned, eyes familiar and loving and sweet. He felt her breath against him; they were so close, a wave of tenderness weaved between them, and in the lost lovely rhythm he wanted to dance. He went to the kitchen and turned on the radio he'd been listening to while he cleaned.

"Floor's dry," he said. She smiled. They laced their fingers together, moving in slow motion, and he knew that the smell of Pine Sol would always remind him of this moment.

He twirled her 'round the old peeling linoleum, and laughed, thinking how romantic, maybe this would be the only moment like this in his life, where he'd dance with this woman he loved so much, had loved since he was seven. Even if it was on crappy linoleum flooring with patched walls and wallpaper that had been glued back together in parts that had torn, it was worth every moment.

Then he thought of his mother, who'd raised him here, in this house, all alone, and he swallowed hard, and tried to concentrate on the smell of Ivory soap on Patsy's skin as the radio played Cat Stevens.

They continued to dance, and she kissed him softly. His eyes flittered shut.

She started crying; he'd never seen her sob like that. He held her body close, and imagined her pain flowing into him, so he could take up some of it for her, like sweeping a floor covered in mounds of another person's broken glass. "I love you," she said, and his insides popped, although he wondered if it was possible to play it cool with Patsy, after all these years. He knew her like tying his shoes, even in the dark. He would leave Cypress for her, he'd have done it all along.

"I love you too, Patsy. I have loved you all of my life." He took her hand, cold and shaky. "I would leave Cypress for you. I will go anywhere for you. Why didn't you just ask me?"

"I don't care where we go, as long as we're by the water, and away from the South," she said. She leaned towards him, and kissed him, moving onto his lap. She ran her hands through his hair and began undoing his belt buckle. He grasped her hands and moved them to his cheeks. Her fingers touched his flesh as he'd wanted them to, for so long. Her eyes caught his in the brightness they'd always had, but she was so pale, so exhausted. She'd been through so much. He understood this, though he'd been confused by her so many times in his life. She loved him. His heart swelled. This was enough.

"Not now," he said. "You're so tired, Patsy. Here, lie on the couch." He brought her a glass of water and covered her with a blanket. He lay beside her, and she fell asleep, her head buried in his chest. He watched her breath rise and fall, knees drawn up beside him, and stroked her hair.

Chapter Thirty-One
JUSTICE

Daisy slumped on the couch, covering her eyes as she thought. Matilda's murderer would be free by next week. The curtains were drawn; she'd kept Rosie's identity hidden. All she could do was hope it remained so. Images of the sky lit with roaring gold that night blistered her brain and made her chest ache. Her loss was a living creature inside of her that burned in surges throughout the years, always there, but sometimes smoldering in the background. Now, she heard a car pulling up the drive, and got up from the quietness. She peeked around the dark curtain, breathless. A black and white police cruiser sat out front, all shiny and removed from the cavern where she and Rosie hid. A kind of rage built in her, but she was determined to be calm. She did not want to hear about him. About that man. She longed to fling the door open and scream, yet she wiped her mind blank as possible, waiting.

"Mrs. Greene?" said the Sheriff, wiping his feet on the mat as if she'd invited him there. She smirked and inched the rusty hinged screen door open. It whined loudly. The Sheriff was not welcome. Her hands shook as she held them firm against the door.

"Yes, sir?" she said in a laconic tone. Go away, she thought. She would not cry. This conversation would be quick.

"Look, we've got some news 'bout Archibald Parson. Can I come in?" He peered into the dark living area.

"Why? I really don't have time—"

"He's not gettin' out, ma'am. We've got new information," he said, with downcast eyes.

Daisy's eyes widened. "Well, I guess I'd be willing to hear this, then."

"I'm Sheriff Landon," he began.

"I know who y'all are. Just get on with it." She sunk into the couch and swept her finger under a damp eye.

"Well, there's been more evidence found," he said, clearing his throat. "Genetic evidence that we were not able to identify so many years ago. From other missing women."

There were others? Daisy's throat burned.

"What do you mean by this? Did you not search for them at the time, at the very least?" Her voice was husky and dry.

"There were four other young women, ma'am. They had appeared to be runaways. But the swamp by the Bayou— where Matilda was—"

"Just stop it," she said, shoving her anger down. "What will happen to this son of a bitch?"

"He's been charged with four first-degree murders. I can safely say that he will never be a free man."

"Why didn't you search for these women, years ago?"

"We did, ma'am. Like I said, it was concluded that they were runaways."

"Yeah, I know all that," she said. "Their lives didn't matter much to y'all." She crossed her arms, glowering. "He'd have never been caught, if he hadn't set the town on fire, and y'all know that."

"We just wanted you to know." He said this softly. Daisy thought she heard a tinge of regret was in his voice.

She cleared her throat. "Do their mothers know?" Now she looked at him directly.

"Yes," he said, and turned away from her face as if it burned.

Daisy absorbed his words, let them sink into her bones. "You know she had a daughter, right? My granddaughter?"

"Yes, ma'am. I believe we saw that in the files."

"She went to school here in Cypress. Jackson High. But no one knew who she was, till recently."

"There's no reason she'd need to be identified. He's being charged with other crimes."

"Are you sayin' you don't need anything from me?" she said, confused.

"I came to let you know that you can open your blinds. Go out in public. The man is never gettin' out of prison. The son of a bitch can never—"

"I see," she said.

"I've just got one question. Why didn't you file a civil suit? Damages— you could have gotten money. Hell, you still could. There is no statute of limitations on murder. We could help you with an attorney."

"It was because of Rosie. I didn't want her a part of this. Didn't want her to be treated differently if people knew." Her voice trailed off for a moment. "Though I suppose it's a consideration now." She envisioned Rosie going to college. Living the life of a woman in her twenties. Rosie deserved that.

She stood and walked towards the hall, yelling her granddaughter's name. She clenched her jaw tight, thinking she should be very strong. Do not cry, woman. Don't cry in front of this girl. Turning around the dark bend, she nearly tripped over Rosie. "Dammit! What the hell are you doin'? I nearly toppled right over you!" And then Daisy breathed the situation in, that her granddaughter had been perched in the hall, listening.

"I'm sorry, Grandma," she said in her usual tone, which was not sorry at all.

"Spare me the attitude, please," Daisy said, sighing. "I know you're angry. You've got the right to be—"

"I sure as hell do, Mamaw," she said, sinking to the floor and pulling her knees to her chest. "They didn't care years ago. They didn't care when I hid, friendless around Jackson High, just so no one would stir shit up 'bout Mama."

"Rosie," said Daisy firmly. "These men have found another woman. Parson's not getting out. Do you understand what this means?" She looked at her granddaughter intently. "Do you?"

"Someone else died?" Rosie whispered, and pulled herself to her feet. She pushed a blonde chunk of hair behind her ear and followed her grandmother to the living room. She sat, listening, across from Sheriff Landon. They huddled together, absorbing this reality through one another. Another mother had lost a child. Maybe a child had lost a mother. A moment of familiar nausea hit Daisy in the gut, as she remembered the last time Sheriff Landon arrived at the house, his presence filling every crevice of her home.

And yet, a sort of joy ran between them. Daisy felt her daughter's ashes sink gently into the lush, mossy wetlands, her being escape into tranquility, and she heard Matilda whisper, "You are free."

Chapter Thirty-Two
THE BAYOU

Patsy and Edna huddled on the damp grass, with Ruth sitting on the painted stone in the garden, legs crossed at the ankle. An unreal calm settled between them, the essence of a numb sorrow, an introduction to the grief that would knock them breathless soon—but not yet. Life has a way of easing you into such pain, otherwise no one would survive tragedy. Patsy understood this through the haze of this moment that felt impossible to live through. Most of all, Patsy worried for Mama. Could her mother handle life without Daddy?

Ruth handed them each a tissue, and absorbed emotion for them, like the wetlands sucked in the rain. Patsy hadn't known another person who could do this. Everyone should have a Ruth, she thought.

"We're not leaving right away, Mama."

"We?" said Mama.

"Tommy and I," said Patsy.

Ruth did not appear surprised, only said, "Oh, I hope you end up stayin' here." She gazed wistfully at the petunias.

"What am I gonna do?" Edna dabbed her eyes with the tissue. "I just don't know how to do this."

"You will. First, y'all are gonna go in there," said Ruth. She crossed her legs again, sighing.

"My God, I don't want to," said Edna. "I can't stand seeing him like this."

"You can. You said you would," said Ruth. "Till death do you part. In sickness and in health..." her voice trailed off.

Patsy's head hurt from crying. Ruth fished another tissue from her purse. Patsy dug a cigarette from the pack of Marlboros in her front pocket and lit it.

"I wish you wouldn't smoke," said Mama, shaking her head.

"Sorry, I'm under extraordinary circumstances. I'll quit again."

"Well, ash the thing away from my damn flowers." Edna waved the smoke out of her vicinity.

"You gotta go in," said Ruth, squeezing each of their shoulders. "Say your goodbyes."

Edna gazed across the wide lawn. "I can't."

Patsy envisioned the heart monitor beeping slower and softer until it just stopped, a quiet gesture of saying goodbye, for her father. He could not have gone out without fighting; he just didn't operate like that. But his suffering was hard to take for the rest of them.

"Mama," said Patsy, "I'm sorry. I know I was not an easy child."

Edna pursed her lips. "That's just not true, Patsy. It isn't. I cared about stuff that wasn't important at all. I don't know how to change that now. Don't know if I ever can."

Patsy nodded. She could never understand Mama. Not really. "We're very different people."

Ruth had moved to another rock in the garden, strands of red hair curled up in a mound, glistening in the sun. She examined a blade of grass.

Mama's tears tumbled down her face and onto her white cardigan, mixed with black mascara. She gazed over at Ruth and murmured, "What is up with that woman's hair?"

"Her hair is fucking beautiful," said Patsy, gazing straight into Mama's eyes. "Beautiful."

"You're right," she said, and sighed, "It always has been. I just want us to be okay. I don't want to die with regrets."

"Mama. You and I are fine…Go see Daddy now." She patted her mother's soft sweater, though there was a hint of unfamiliarity to the gesture. Like how you might comfort a stranger. Patsy accepted that this was how it was. Her mother's love for her had unfurled in so many layers, each indistinguishable from the next. And that might have to do. Sometimes you just make do with what you've got and hope for the best. Peace. That's what Patsy wanted more than anything else.

Mama sat, staring.

"What are you thinking about?" said Patsy.

"Shopping," she said.

Patsy wrinkled her face. "What?"

"I was thinking," she said, clearing her throat. She wiped her eyes on her sweater, ignoring the black splotches of makeup. "I was thinking that I'd like to take my daughter shopping someday. We've never done that, you and I."

"Okay," she said. "I do shop now, Mama." Patsy scrunched her face, confused. "In Boston, there are lots and lots of places to shop."

"I guess I don't even know you, not as a grown woman," said Mama.

"Mama, you should go see him." Patsy insisted.

"I hate this."

"Come on now," said Ruth, rising from the rock and wiping her pants off. "Let's go." She led Mama to the house, whispering something in her ear.

Stanley needed to make things right with his family. A powerful impetus had struck him with the diagnosis, but he hadn't been sure what to say until he understood there might not be time to say anything, after the seizure. The home health nurse had turned the sheets, and given him his medication, when he asked her if she would shave his face.

She lathered the shaving cream, rubbing it into his skin, and ran the razor up in a straight line, around the angles of his face in swift little movements. She rinsed the razor off in a pink hospital basin of warm water, and combed his hair, too. He'd never been more grateful for a shave. "You've done this before," he said, and she smiled.

Edna sat beside him, as she did every day, holding his hand and making conversation. Apparently, Tommy and Patsy really had fallen in love, as she'd always said they would. Edna and Ruth had rekindled their friendship. He was relieved. He knew she did not think he was listening, or perhaps his brain wasn't operating well enough to understand, but he heard.

Tommy and Patsy. He'd loved that boy since birth.

Ruth always knew just what to do. She would be there to protect Edna when he could not.

He could see, though blurry, his wife beside him; her face the same as when they'd gotten married. He knew that people changed over time, got wrinkles as they aged, that their hair grayed, but Edna's familiarity was such that he saw none of these things. They'd whirled through time together so slowly, the changes were imperceptible to him, though the suddenness about how he'd become an old man made him feel like he'd slapped Edna, injured her in a way he never had, hadn't intended, and couldn't fix. "You men don't understand," he remembered her saying. "You just wanna fix things, when all we're trying to do is vent."

He wished he could fix this for her.

"I love you, honey," he began, with a labored breath.

"Please, Stanley. I know—I know all this. You'll tire yourself out."

"No," he said, lifting his hand. "Really, I want to talk...I want to tell you that this marriage, this life, has been everything I could have dreamed of."

"Stanley, please."

"I want you to know that I'm sorry."

"For what?" He heard her voice sort of hollow, like a whisper from a vortex far away.

"For this." His eyes watered, nose dripping down his smooth chin. "Please get Patsy."

Edna kissed him and wiped his nose, and he felt her presence, the smell of her perfume and Ivory soap that he knew her by, disappear.

"Daddy?" she said. She must have turned the corner. His sight may have dimmed, his hearing grown fuzzy, but always, always Patsy was there, the smell of strawberries in the curl of her hair.

"Patsy? Is that you?" he said, like waking from a dream.

"It's me, Daddy."

He took her hand and asked her to sit. "Just sit here with me and stay awhile. I need to make sure you and I are okay," he said, taking a shallow breath, the kind that hurts so much you must sip it slowly through your teeth.

"It's fine, Daddy. We're fine. I love you." She laid her head on his chest, and all over again, she was an infant, curled on his chest, her little fingers wrapped around his.

Thoughts of her swirled through his mind, hot and tender as the Louisiana nights when he rocked her, singing "Hush Little Baby" and "Twinkle Twinkle", when he played pat a cake to make her laugh, and when he threw her up in the sky in her favorite blue overalls, while she squealed, screaming, "Again! Again, Daddy." Summers, where the neighborhood children dashed through the giant Bundy yard, and he ran right after them, barefoot, blades of wet grass touching his feet. The smell of cut grass and barbecued steaks and children's laughter had given him one more childhood, a do-over for all the times he didn't have money for the ice-cream truck as a boy, for all the nights his own father didn't came home.

"Patsy," he said, "I may have been gone a lot, but I always came home."

"I— of course you did. You were a good father, you were."

"We disagree on almost everything," he said. "And I pushed too far."

"Daddy, you're tired."

"Tell me all about Tommy," he said. He leaned the hospital bed back. He would drink his youngest child's words till deep in the night.

"He's the one. He's always been the one," she said, her voice touched with sadness.

Stanley had known this all along, but he didn't say so, just laughed inside.

"Just so you know, we're not heading back to Boston or anything, not right away. We're gonna stay here with Mama, to make sure she's okay."

He nodded, growing weary, but wanting to hear what she had to say, like he'd turned into one of Edna's friends eager for gossip.

"That's good, baby. I know you hate it here, but I'm so worried for her."

"She'll be okay," she said. "We will stay until we're sure of it. I promise you."

With that, he closed his eyes, imagining himself on *The Patsy Mae*, the sound of the storm roaring through the ocean that night. That night on the Bayou, when Jeb was swallowed by the ocean; the image that haunted him for twenty years, of Jeb's foot slipping on the deck, of his body catapulting into the water. Instead, the wind swept him into a wave, the maelstrom saturated with light, as he crouched inside of it, watching the wildness from a quiet corner. The clouds floated across the sky and the boat slid over the horizon, bright pink and orange spreading out like an angel. The sun crossed over the moon, except Jeb had not fallen. Jeb sat beside him, with wet hair and droplets of water splattered across his young face. He said, "Where ya been all this time, bud?" and they sat amongst thousands and thousands of shrimp, so many that the entire deck was swarming with them. And they laughed, water slopping over the side of the boat, as the sun diffused into the warm, earthy night.

One Month Later

She trudged through the wetlands, feet sinking with each step, taking pictures as she moved. A red-headed woodpecker, with its glorious contrast of color glided across the mossy water, lunging for an insect, and landed upon a hundred-foot-tall oak tree, wrapping its talons around the thinnest branch. She got about twenty shots of the bird on its journey, and, clicking back through her photos, was satisfied. Patsy folded her body into the tin shack, which seemed shrunken, the red paint faded and peeled. It was hard to know if it had ever been as large as she once believed. Stanley had built it strong, and it still stood steady on its beams beside the wide-based cypress oaks. She brushed off one of the folding chairs and sat, watching the swamp through the window, her eyes narrowing in at the water, steamy from the humid summer day. Except today, she heard the rush of the ocean, rather than the still freshwater where alligators swam. She peered closer, envisioning that a gator or some other wild creature had disturbed the sitting water. Patsy watched, waiting.

Her line of sight blurred, hazy and mysterious as always, and she braced herself, waiting for the sound of horses galloping. The hanging leaves of the cypress trees rustled in a strong wind, but there was no clopping noise. The disturbance settled, and Patsy's fear dissipated; her hands relaxed, and a wispy version of Daddy appeared like a gust of smoke. The thick, muscular body of his youth had returned and he stood, watching her. Yet, his eyes had softened, and there was nothing challenging about his demeanor. He leaned forward, smiling, settled into the sky like he'd stay there forever.

"I thought you died," she said.

He did not respond, only smiled. His concession seeped through his body, and he slipped away, diffusing like smoke in the wind.

She did not feel frightened or surprised.

He just *was*, and she'd expected him here.

Lots of stuff happened on the Bayou. It was filled with a kind of delicious beauty only home and childhood can have—in that place where memory and imagination intertwine so deeply you cannot tell one from the other—and yet Patsy knew the evil that had also happened there.

Parson murdered five women near the tin shack between 1965 and 1970, when he was caught because he panicked and set half the town on fire, on the night before Patsy was born. She'd never know why these women haunted her so, why they chose this small child to tell their stories to, but she understood that part of the divide between her and Edna arose from these events late in her mother's pregnancy.

The continuum of reality and imagination is wide, and hard to decipher where one ends and another begins. The Ku Klux Klan was an integral part of the South, of everywhere, really. Women had been murdered on the Bayou, one of them engulfed in flames. A boy's father had drowned on a stormy night, not far from that hideout. Yet the hideout held refuge for a little girl and the boy she loved. Strange how Patsy's senses had focused in on death, yet she had no such vision that she and Tommy would fall in love.

But Tommy always knew. So did Ruth. She supposed they had a different kind of intuitiveness. Maybe, after Jeb's death, they needed love to continue.

The tin shack on the Bayou held mystery and truth all at once. Patsy had always known this, deep within herself, in the skein wound with the thread of a child's mind, with all its different colors mixed like a rainbow.

She stood, brushed her pants off, and whispered goodbye. Tommy would be around searching for her soon, and she had wanted this moment alone. She turned and trudged back to the little gravel road up the hill. She fixed her eye through the lens of the camera, taking a final shot of the little tin shack on the Bayou.

Note from the Author

Word-of-mouth is crucial for any author to succeed. If you enjoyed the book, please leave a review online—anywhere you are able. Even if it's just a sentence or two. It would make all the difference and would be very much appreciated.

Thanks!
Melissa

About the Author

Melissa Woods is a mother of six, and an author of literary fiction and suspense. She loves to explore humans and all their complexities, especially when it comes to moral ambiguity. When not writing, reading, or chasing tiny humans, she can be found running on the track. Her writing has appeared in *Coffin Bell Journal* and *Memoir Magazine*. Her latest novel, *The Weaver*, is slated for release in 2019. She was awarded The Stephen R. Kustra scholarship in creative writing for her short story, *The Irishwoman*.

Thank you so much for reading one of our **Women's Fiction** novels.

If you enjoyed the experience, please check out our recommended title for your next great read!

The Apple of My Eye by Mary Ellen Bramwell

"A mature love story with an intense plot. This book has something important to say." –William O. Shakespeare, Professor of English, Brigham Young University

View other Black Rose Writing titles at <u>www.blackrosewriting.com/books</u> and use promo code **PRINT** to receive a **20% discount** when purchasing.